Velda

Other books by Ron Miller

THE DREAM MACHINES
SPACE ART
THE HISTORY OF ROCKETS
THE HISTORY OF SCIENCE FICTION
THE SUN
MERCURY & PLUTO
THE EARTH & MOON
MARS
VENUS
JUPITER
SATURN
URANUS & NEPTUNE
ASTEROIDS, COMETS & METEORS
EXTRASOLAR PLANETS
THE ELEMENTS
SPECIAL EFFECTS IN THE MOVIES
BRADAMANT: THE IRON TEMPEST
THE BRONWYN TETRALOGY:
PALACES & PRISONS
SILK & STEEL
HEARTS & ARMOR
MERMAIDS & METEORS

With Frederick C. Durant III:
WORLDS BEYOND
THE ART OF CHESLEY BONESTELL

With Pamela Sargent:
FIREBRANDS

With William K. Hartmann:
THE GRAND TOUR
THE HISTORY OF EARTH
CYCLES OF FIRE
IN THE STREAM OF STARS

Velda

by RON MILLER

Timberwolf Press/Audio, Allen, Texas
www.timberwolfpress.com

Acknowledgements: The author would like to extend his gratitude to the anonymous chronicler of the mysterious case of Anna Spürman and *Her Other Self.*

Timberwolf Press, Inc.
202 N. Allen St., Suite A
Allen, Texas 75013 USA

Visit our Web site at **http://www. TimberWolfPress.com**

Printed in the United States of America
10 9 8 7 6 5 4 3 2 1

ISBN: 1-58752-126-1

This book is dedicated to Patricia Scelfo:
the very image of Velda Bellinghausen.

CHAPTER One

I GET OFF THE BUS IN PLANKTON KEY, FLORIDA AND IT'S LIKE STEPPING in front of a glassblower's furnace. The dank tropical heat hits me in the face like a blow from a wet army blanket. It's as easy to breathe as a blanket, too, each mouthful like a bite of dry wool. The air tastes like dust and my eyes water from a glare that seems to penetrate even the shadows. My body is instantly wet with perspiration which the oversaturated air refuses to accept so instead of cooling me like nature intended it just covers me with a salty, sticky coating. Droplets of sweat trickle from under my armpits, tickling like little insects, and I can feel a salty delta forming as sweat funnels between my breasts. Welcome to the Florida Keys, I tell myself, and a new record for instant misery. My thirty-dollar white silk blouse clings to me like wet tissue. I could have saved my money, I figure, and used a fifty-cent box of damp Kleenex to the same effect.

There's a punk-looking guy sitting on a bench just outside the door to the station. He must be waiting for God Himself to get off the bus since I can see no other reason to sit outside in this heat. He's trying to look cool in his cheap seersucker suit, but he's no better an actor than he is a dresser, which isn't much. He's sweating like a cheap hot dog, which he more than a little resembles. He's peering over the top of his limp racing sheet, scanning the platform like a weasel looking for a baby bird to drop out of its nest. He spots me and does a perfect Jimmy Finlayson double take. I do tend to stand out in a crowd.

I'd laugh if I could breathe, but I'm making a beeline for the station door, which bears a sign reading AIR CONDITIONED INSIDE in blue letters with little icicles hanging from them. It draws me like the North Pole attracted Peary. Weasel, though, unfolds himself from the bench like five feet of carpenter's rule and intercepts me four paces from the door. He's a skinny little runt who barely reaches my collar bone. His limp straw hat has a wide brown stain around the band and his suit looks damp enough to wring like a sponge, which is as dreadful thought as I've ever had. He has a voice like someone with a really bad sinus infection.

"Hey! New in town, huh? How 'bout I show ya 'round?"

I look at him with exactly the same fascination that an esteemed and learned PhD in tropical entomology would regard a housefly.

"I've *been* around."

I push by him—he squelches a little like a wet dishcloth—and finally get into the refrigerated station. The air inside is so frosty I think for a moment that my more fragile bits may snap off with the sudden change in temperature and my coating of itchy sweat suddenly congeals into a clammy slime. There's not much inside other than a couple of old benches with limp, bored people draped on them and a ticket counter. I go up to the old man behind the cage and ask, "Any place to get a cold drink around here?"

This doesn't seem to me to require a whole lot of thought, but obviously it's been a long time since anyone's asked him for more information than the time of the next bus and the old man is a little taken aback by the responsibility. He mulls the question for a while, savoring the moment, as he massages his gums with his tongue. I glance over my shoulder and there's Weasel, looking through the window at me. He turns away so quickly he bumps into a fat woman carrying a kid and she lays into him like he'd just tried to mug her or something. Meanwhile, the old man's telling me there's a fine bar just across the highway from the station, which I wouldn't have thought to have been such a hard thing to have remembered but then I'm not an old man stuck behind a ticket counter in a podunk bus station.

I can see the bar shimmering in the heat like a mirage on the other side of about forty feet of nearly liquid asphalt. It looks as far away as Timbuktu. I can just imagine someone someday finding my bleached bones scattered across the median line. I take a deep breath before leaving the station. It's like swimming through molten glass, but I make it. The tavern isn't air conditioned, but the inside is as dark and cool and dank as a cave, even if it does smell like stale beer and cigarettes. The place is practically empty which is OK by me. I swing myself onto a stool at the bar and toss my suitcase and jacket over the seat next to me. I set my purse on the bar in front of me a little more carefully because I don't want the automatic to make too loud a bump, pull a handkerchief from it and mop my face. The bartender has been eyeballing ever since I came through the door. I don't suppose I look much like a local.

"Get you something, lady?"

"Yeah. I need the coldest beer you've got and some directions."

"The first is easy," he says, rustling a bottle out of a chest of ice. A Pabst Blue Ribbon, too. Oh boy! The sound alone sends a welcome chill down my spine. I savor it, vertebra by vertebra.

"The second depends."

He pops the cap off and sets the bottle in front of me along with a tall glass. I surprise the hell out of him and pick up the bottle. I guess I'll never make a Southern lady. The beer goes down like a skier on a slope of fresh powder. I set it down half-empty.

"Depends?"

"Depends on where you want to go."

"Yeah. Well, you know where the Paughner place is?"

"The what?"

"Paughner," I repeated, "P-a-u-g-h . . ."

"Oh! The Paughner place!" He pronounced it "Poffner". I'd been saying "Pockner", like I'd been taught. But then, I'd been raised genteel.

"Yeah, that's it. You know where it is?" He's turned his back to me but I can see him staring at me in the mirror and I don't much like the expression on his face. Maybe it's just the dirty glass.

"Maybe. You got a minute I'll call a buddy and get directions for you."

"Thanks, You got any place I can clean up a little? The heat out there's really something. I must look a mess."

"Sure, lady," he replies with a gallantly skeptical smile "Through there, in the back. Only one door. Can't miss it."

"Keep an eye on my bag for me?"

"Sure." He tries to make it sound like he'd die to protect that bag, which would be just fine by me. I know what I got in the suitcase, I don't know him from Adam.

The room in the back is a stuffy little restroom with no ventilation, no evidence of regular cleaning and, awful to see, no seat on the toilet. Fortunately I'd taken care of that business on the bus, thank Hygeia. The only light comes from a single bare flyspecked 30-watt bulb dangling from a frayed cord and a cracked pane of frosted glass. I switch the light off and the room actually seems to get brighter. There's a green-stained sink and a cracked mirror, though I have to stoop a little to use either. It's nice being tall but sometimes it's, well, a pain in the neck. I turn on the faucet and let the water run to get cold. While it's trickling I look in the glass. Yup, the bartender was being gallant, all right. I look godawful. I look like I'd just spent a day and a half on a plane and a bus, can you believe it. My black hair is plastered to my head like wet licorice. Fortunately, it's exactly for times like this that I keep it cut in a simple pageboy. It's hopelessly out of style but all I have to do is give it a shake and maybe a couple of brush strokes if I think of it and it's as good as new.

I peel my blouse off, being careful to not let it touch anything in the room, and hang it from the hook on the back of the door. My shoulders are so naturally broad and level I have to cut the pads out of all my blouses and jackets, otherwise I'd look like a character from *Things to Come*. I unhook my brassiere and hang it from the doorknob. The sink's full of cool water and I splash it on my face. I soak a paper towel and use it to swab out my armpits and the undersides of my breasts. Still damp, I lean on the sink and look closely into the mirror. Mirror, mirror, on the wall, huh? Well, I better not ask questions I might not want to hear the answers to. There's only one man I've ever known who went goofy over my looks and, well, that's a story I'd just as soon not get into right now.

The pale lean face looking back at me is a lot more like something out of *Vogue* than *Rogue*—not exactly man bait. Suzy Parker instead of Jane Mansfield, if you get my drift. Okay, so maybe it's not the face of man bait—but is it the face of a man killer?

The hell with it.

I get back into my bra and blouse, both of which are now cold and clammy. I consider abandoning the former altogether, which feels like a big leech snuggled against my chest, but I don't quite yet want to put too great a strain on Southern sensibilities.

When I get back to the bar, the bartender has another beer waiting for me along with a scrap of paper with some directions scrawled on it in thick pencil.

"It's on the house, lady. Don't get too many tourists in Plankton this early in the season."

"Thanks. I imagine you're right, but I'm not really a tourist." I tap the note with a fingertip. "How far from here?"

"I dunno. Five-six miles maybe."

"I don't suppose there're any cabs around?"

"Yeah, sure." He thinks I've made a joke.

"Any chance I can get something to eat?"

"I got some ham and swiss you want a sandwich. Wonder bread. That's about it."

I tell him that'd be swell because Wonder bread helps build my body eight ways and take my beer to a table where I can see the blazing street. All the while I'm thinking, my, my, I wonder why someone living in this two-bit town would need to call to find out where anyone lives? It's an island, for God's sake. No place on it could be more than spitting distance from any other place, which brought up a pretty nasty mental picture. While I'm wondering who the bartender had called I see a familiar figure coming out of the station and I bet my last dollar he's going to come over here. I win the buck from myself, as I expected I would, as the weasily little gink comes trotting across the half-molten pavement and sure enough comes straight to the door of the bar. He tries not to notice me as he comes in and the effort is so obvious he may as well be gawking right in my face. He gets a beer from the barkeep and, even though every other table in the place is empty, he looks around as though trying to decide where to sit. He finally comes, big surprise, over to where I'm sitting. I figure chances are good he's who the bartender called, God knows why.

"Anyone sitting here?"

"Yeah, my pal the invisible man."

Mistakenly taking this as an invitation, he plunks himself down with an audible *squish*. He sucks on his beer for a minute, his eyes self-consciously avoiding me. He's so nervous I begin to wonder if I'm going to see him completely dissolve right in front of me.

"Say, Miss, ah . . ."

I wonder if I ought to try to make things easier for him, but figure, what the hell. So I just stare back at him. His eyes skitter under my gaze like olives avoiding a dull fork. He mumbles some more then finally makes a brave try at getting to whatever his point is.

"Look, ah, Miss, ah . . . Hey! Sorry about, ah, back there . . . didn't mean to sound fresh or nothin'. Just tryin' to be friendly—helpful-like, you know? You bein' new in town an' all. You know?"

He looks up at me hopefully. I don't give him anything back but more stare.

"Ah, uh . . . you gonna be in town for long?"

"Maybe. Maybe not. Why?"

"Well, uh, you wouldn't be plannin' to go out—poke around town or anythin' like that, would you? I mean, not that it's any of my business or nothin'."

"And if it were your business?"

"Nothin'! Nothin', of course! It's just, well, just that, you being a stranger 'round here and all, you might not be . . . I mean, you might like some friendly advice."

"I'm hanging on your every word."

"Yeah. Well. What I mean is . . . if you got a return ticket, well, then, if I was you I'd just stay around here 'til the next bus outta town. It's nice an' cool here. It's a good place to wait."

"Well, that is mighty interesting advice. You make Plankton sound kind of unhealthy for a poor little ol' city girl like me."

"Well, yeah . . . I guess it could get kind of unhealthy."

"You're a healthy kind of guy, aren't you?"

"What?"

"How're *you* feeling?"

"I . . . uh, OK, I guess."

"That's pretty tough, then," I say, reaching across the table. I grab his tie and jerk it so hard his face bounces off the table like a tennis ball. He continues on backwards, toppling chair and all onto the floor. I glance up at the bartender, but he's got his back turned, pointedly polishing a perfectly clean glass. I get up and toss a tip onto the table, next to where a single tooth is embedded in the wood in the center of a wet red circle. It looks like a tiny tombstone. I go to the bar, retrieve my bag and the sandwich sitting next to it, thank the barkeep for his hospitality and insincerely apologize for leaving such a mess. I can't tell if the sarcasm's been lost on him since he still won't look at me, the bastard. I have to step over Weasel's face on my way to the door. He's still out, blowing a big red bubble through a nose that looks like a squashed tomato. I kick the face and the bubble goes *plip*.

Thanks for the advice, friend.

Chapter Two

I'D SPOTTED A MOTEL—THE "COZY HAVEN O'REST", NO KIDDING—I thought it sounded like a pet cemetery—when the bus had crossed the main highway, so I braved a hike of a couple of blocks. I can't imagine why Plankton needs a motel at all. Its existence is about as good an example of wishful thinking as I've ever seen. During the walk I suspect I see about all there is of Plankton: a seedy-looking general store and post office, a two-story place with a doctor's and lawyer's offices, an express agency, a hardware store, a five-and-dime, a branch bank—the usual small-town stuff except that everything was in pink stucco. I thought the buildings looked like a display in a bakery window. There's only two real streets, the main highway that runs from the mainland all the way to Key West and a cross street that runs off into some desolate-looking scrub in one direction and in the other at the beach and wharves on the far side of the bus station. The tourist court is pretty much what I expected but the cabin doesn't look half bad, not that I've got a whole lot of room to be finicky. The owner gives me a little trouble about being unescorted but I get all high-hat on him and he backs down quick enough and gives me a key. I can hear him dialing his phone, big surprise, before I'm even out the door. Sure would like to know who everyone's so anxious to talk to.

The room's OK, like what'd I expect? It's got a bed, a chair and little table with a clock radio on it, a rickety dresser with an electric fan sitting on top, some godawful pictures on the wall and a closet-sized bathroom with a toilet and shower stall squeezed inside. I'm pleased to see a seat on the toilet. It even has a paper band wrapped around it assuring me that it'd been "Sanitized for Your Protection". *Uh huh.* I make sure the door's bolted and the shade drawn and undress. My soggy clothes peel off me like the skin from a scalded tomato. I turn on the cold water in the shower and let it run a few minutes before climbing in. It feels great even if the water really is only tepid. I don't towel off. The water's cool as it struggles to evaporate into the humid air. Still wet, I unpack the few things in my bag. I don't plan to be in town more than forty-eight hours, tops, but I hate living out of a bag for even that short a time.

It takes about twenty minutes in the humid air, but I'm finally dry. My hair only needs a quick brush before I get dressed and the hell with makeup. White shorts, plaid bandana halter knotted behind my back and a pair of sneakers seem like just the ticket, though God knows there's now not much place to stash my .45, which I have to leave in my purse—a nuisance, but fortunately the bag's got an extendable strap so I can carry it over my shoulder. I check the results in the mirror and figure it's not so bad. Fifty-seven percent leg, exactly, according to a pal I had at Slotsky's who was never without a tape measure. Seems funny to be dressed like this while it's still snowing back home. A wide-brimmed straw hat and sunglasses and I'm ready to face the perils of Plankton, Florida, such as they may be, looking like a goddam tourist.

I'd spotted the sheriff's office on the way to the motel. It was in a moderately new brick building set conspicuously among its shabby neighbors. It also, I saw, housed the magistrate, a license bureau, a farm co-op office ("farm"? farming *what?* coconuts?) and a bail bondsman. Hardly anyone had paid me much attention on my way to the motel, but the few people out in the heat—mostly some old geezers in front of the feed store—now gawked at me as though I'd just been dropped into the middle of town from a flying saucer. I don't suppose six-foot brunettes with legs up to *here* are all that terribly common down here so I let them have their fun, hoping that the rise in blood pressure won't do them any harm in this heat. And screw them if it does. I pass a sweating fat woman lumbering along the sidewalk in an Hawaiian-print muumuu, looking for all the world like some enormous Jell-o fruit mold, who audibly *huffs* at me and I almost laugh out loud.

I wonder how I can get what I want to know out of the sheriff without tipping my hand. I not only want this to be a solo job, I'm as sure that it *has* to be solo as I'm sure the sheriff would lock me up for my even thinking of doing what I want to do. He's probably looking for me right now for smashing Weasel's face. Then again, who am I really kidding? In the hour since then everyone in town probably knows I'm here and has at least half an idea of what I'm after. King Noorvik probably owns the damn place, which I don't doubt for a second. As I'm passing a hardware store I have an inspiration, which happens every now and then. I make a right-angle turn and go in. The place has that great smell only hardware stores have: oil and rubber and metal. A little like a new car. The place is narrow and high and dark, with crowded shelves rising to an embossed tin ceiling and a high ladder on a track for getting to the things out of reach. Looks more like a warehouse than a shop and I like it. There's a counter in the back half covered with packages and boxes and displays of jackknives and combination screwdrivers and a big roll of brown paper. I bang on the bell. Someone sounding like Andy Devine yells from the back, "Hold your horses!". But if I'd half expected someone looking like Andy Devine I was disappointed. The old man who pops out of the gloom in the back of the store is more like a garden gnome than Wild Bill's sidekick. His head can hardly be higher off the floor than my diaphragm. He's so twisted and wrinkled he looks like a length of knotted rope with a big turk's head at the top, one made by an inexperienced sailor at that. Grotesque as this apparition is, it's given me my first friendly reception since arriving in town, which is something.

"Well now," comes that fluting, broken voice from one of the folds in the big knot, "if you ain't a sight for sore eyes I ain't got sore eyes!" I take this as a compliment, while at the same time wondering if the old man even *had* eyes. I assume they were what I might have otherwise taken for a pair of oiled ball bearings embedded in a couple of deep wrinkles. "I reckon you're just passin' through?" he went on. "It'd be too much to hope, I s'pose, that you're thinkin' of hangin' 'round?"

"I hope not. I've got some business in Plankton and if I'm halfway lucky it won't take long."

"Business here? That's a rich one!" His laugh was all twangy like a jew's-harp.

"Well, maybe you can help me out."

"It'd be my pleasure, miss, it surely would."

"You think there's anyone who'd have a car I could rent for a couple of days?"

"A car?"

"Yeah. My business is out of town a ways and I can tell you right now I don't want to walk another fifty feet around here."

"Plankton ain't the best place to be in the summer, that's for sure. Ain't so great in the winter, neither, for that matter."

"I've seen no reason to doubt that. But do you know anyone with a car?

"Sure do. I got one."

"You do? That's great! Would you be willing to rent it to me for a day or two?"

"Ain't doin' me any good. I ain't driven the thing in a year. Useta run deliveries with it, when I useta deliver, which I don't no more. If it'll start, it's yours."

"How much?"

"I dunno. Ten bucks sound OK? Use it long's you want. Like I said, ain't doin' me no good."

"Sounds more than OK by me. You want me to sign something?"

"Naw. Purty gal like you? Besides, wait 'til you see it. You're sure not gonna wanta steal *that* car."

"Can I get it now?"

"Sure. C'mon, it's out back."

I followed the old man through the back of the store and into the alley behind. At first it was hard to distinguish the car from the rest of the trash and rubbish, but it was there all right, a De Soto sedan built before I was born.

"There oughta be a can o'gas just inside the door there" he said while excavating the car, "if you wouldn't mind fetchin' it. I'm sure she'll be dry as a bone. Plannin' to go far?"

I wondered how much to tell him and figured, what the hell. "Depends. How far's the Poughner place?"

"The Poughners? What in the world you want out there?"

"It's a personal thing. Just got to see them, that's all."

"You a relative or somethin'?"

"Or something."

"Well, if you're lookin' for a big inheritance, you gotta rude shock comin'."

"Yeah, I guess someone'll have one coming. I was told the place was five or six miles out of town, that sound right?."

"Somethin' like that, yeah."

"Well, I ought to have your car back by this evening, I imagine."

"If I ain't here, just leave it in back here and chuck the keys in the mailbox."

He'd finished emptying the can into the tank so I took the keys and climbed into the car. The inside smelled like a funeral home. I rolled down the window and leaned on the sill. That just about brought me eye level with the old man.

"You really got business out there, miss?"

"Yeah, I really got business out there."

"Well, I was just wonderin' . . . I mean, if you didn't . . . well, the law ain't nothin' to mess around with, 'round here, that's all."

"The law? The sheriff?"

"Aw, the sheriff's OK. He's a new fella and pretty square, I suppose. Ain't heard a word against, at any rate. It's his depitty, Mackanaw. He's a real wrong'un."

"Well, I'll be careful. I gotta get your car back to you."

"Yeah, well you do that now, miss."

I follow the bartender's directions out of town and by the time I get to the second or third turn I begin to suspect that I'd been had. The odometer's already clocked six miles. By all rights I should've passed the place. In a couple more miles I'll run out of island and be in the Bay of Florida. I wish now I'd shown the directions to the old man instead of just confirming the distance. Well, hell, it's past noon already but I figure I can get back to Plankton, get the right directions from the old man and still have the time I need at the Poughner place, wherever the hell it is.

The island beyond town is just dried-out scrub and sour-looking marshes, flat as a pancake. The air is dead still and the only motion in the landscape is from the heat waves rising from the road. It smells like someone's frying lizards somewhere.

I find a dirt side road to turn around in and I'm just starting to back out onto the road when I hear a siren. I wait for the cop to pass, but instead he pulls over ahead of me. Somehow I feel no particular surprise: the coincidence would be obvious even for *Highway Patrol.* The cruiser looks only maybe five years newer than the car I'm driving and I bet myself it's the only one the county owns. A big red-faced man with a gut too large for his sweat-stained uniform climbs out and ambles over to me, jerking his baggy trousers up as he comes. He's no Broderick Crawford and Broderick Crawford's no beauty, as we all know. He puts a pair of hands the size of catcher's mitts on the roof of my car and leans down toward my open window. I can hear the sweat from his palms sizzling on the metal, but he doesn't seem to notice. I give him my best Pepsodent smile and say, "Good afternoon, officer. Anything wrong?"

He just stares at me for a moment, chewing his cud. I get the impression that I might as well have been speaking Chinese. A glistening droplet of amber spit rolls out of one corner of his mouth and immediately gets caught in a thicket of coarse whiskers. I watch it dull as it dries in the heat.

"You think somethin' *might* be wrong, lady?"

"Me? Not at all. I'm as happy as a lark on the wing."

"Yeah? Kinda lonely place fer a lady to be. This road don't go nowhere. Where might you be headed?"

"Nowhere particular. I'm new around here. Just thought I'd take a look around. That OK?"

"Yeah? Well, lady, it just might not be OK."

"No? I don't see why not, officer. It is a public road and all."

"Yeah. You'd think so, wouldn't you." He steps back from the door a pace. "Want to climb outta there a minute?"

"Well, I'll tell you, officer, unless there's something wrong, I'd just as soon get back to town. There's . . ."

"And I'd just as soon not have to ask you again."

I get out of the car.

"Jesus Christ, you're a long one, ain't you?'

"Why, yes, officer, I guess I am, now that you mention it." He was a full head shorter than me, but about twice as thick.

"And a little bit of a smart mouth, too, eh?"

"My friends have hinted as much." Hell, most of them have told me that outright.

"Well, you so smart you know what happens to uppity wimmin round here?"

"I hate to imagine."

"Yeah, you sure would hate to," he said as without the slightest warning his right hand whips up from his belt and catches me across the mouth. The blow is so unexpected that it throws me off my balance and my back bangs against the car door behind me. He backhands me with a left before I've even bounced back from the metal and this time I can feel the blood rush from my mouth. It was like being hit with a brick wrapped in sandpaper. Before he can slap me a third time my right foot shoots out at the end of a long, straight leg like a battering ram. It catches him on a kneecap but I don't hear the pop I'd hoped for. It was like kicking a tree trunk and I can feel the jolt along the full length of my spine. Given the damage I've failed to inflict on the cop, I'm taken entirely by surprise by what he does next: his fist slams into my face like a cannonball. What kind of Southern hospitality is this?

I'm only out for a second. As soon as the stars go away, encouraged by the pain in my scalp, I realize I'm being dragged into the grass by my hair, like a cave woman and her favorite Neanderthal. I can all too easily imagine what the fat bastard has in mind, so I grab a chunk of coral and smash it into the back of his hand. This time there's an entirely satisfying *crunch* and the cop yells out in pain. That's good. What's not so good is that I've just barely gotten to my knees when he plants a kick in my ribs that lifts me entirely off the ground. But it also throws me far enough away from him that I get a chance to jump to my feet before he can get another kick in.

I face him, crouching tiger-like, or at least I hope so, ready to spring in any direction circumstance or good sense might dictate. The fat cop just stands there facing me, casually confident in his weight and masculinity, both of which he possesses in abundance. One of his hands is blue and puffy, seeping red from a broad abrasion. It doesn't seem to bother him much, more's the pity. He's got a gun, but I suspect—and hope—he's too sure of himself to think of drawing on a mere l'il ol' fee-male. I plan on doing my best to disabuse him of the wisdom of that assumption. I don't know what he thinks I'll do, but I'm betting that preemptive attack is not high on his list. So, acting on that thought, I spin and plant the side of my foot against his ear. I think that's a new one for him. Thank God for HAWKSHAW'S BOOK ON DETECTIVE WORK, *Volume Seven: Unarmed Self-Defense*, to say nothing of three years of practicing high kicks in the Follies. There's a hollow *thonk* like I'd just kicked a watermelon. Not stopping to see the effect of my kick I use my momentum to slam my foot into the same spot again. He staggers back a pace, as much from surprise, I suspect, as the pain. His left ear has been smeared across his cheek like an overripe tomato. I step in and jab the ends of my rigidly-held fingers into his windpipe. I finally get to hear something go *pop*. He goes purple almost instantly, his tongue sticking out as he tries to suck air through his crushed larynx. Unfortunately, I underestimate the man's sheer animal endurance and make the mistake of just standing there, enjoying the sight of him choking, distracted by the pain in my ribs, at least one of which I'm sure is cracked, dammit. Although he can hardly be consciously aware of what he's doing—like a mortally wounded dinosaur—he suddenly pile drives a fist at me that connects with my jaw like a sledgehammer snapping a two-by-four in half. At least that's what it sounds like. There's a blinding flash and I don't even feel my back hit the ground.

The sensation of having the skin flayed from my shoulder blades brings me back around. The cop has both of my feet tucked under one arm as he's dragging me through the saw grass, away from the road and into the low ditch paralleling it. The grass has cut through my shorts like broken glass and my halter's been dragged up around my neck and I'm half afraid I'll strangle on it long before the cop can do whatever he has in mind, not that the "whatever" should be hard to guess. I'm sure it's nothing good, for even from the back I can see that one side of his face is caked with blood and I can hear his breath whistling through a bruised esophagus. I suppose he must resent that. He seems like a man who would harbor a grudge. I'm bitterly disappointed, though, since I'd been sure that I'd hit his throat hard enough to kill him.

I can think of no reason for being taken out of sight of the car that augurs well for my girlish dignity.

I'm just thinking about what I might do, since he's as yet unaware that I'm conscious, when he drops my feet and turns around. I like what I see from this side even less. He'd been no beauty to start with and now he looks as though someone has hit him in the face with a fistful of raw hamburger. As I push myself up on my hands he draws his gun and holds it at his side with a disturbing *non chalance*, if thatmeans what I think it does. People who handle a gun like others would handle a cigarette lighter scare me.

"You shoulda kep' your big fat mouth shut, lady," he says with a gentleness that sends a chill down my back that would have been welcome an hour earlier. "You shoulda jus' turned around an' gone back to town, like I asked. You shouldn'ta smart-mouthed me."

I saw no reason to argue with him: he was absolutely right. Whatever had I been thinking of?

"So what now?" I ask, probably unnecessarily.

"So now I gotta make you sorry."

"You wouldn't just take my word that I am?"

"No ma'm, I don't think I'd believe you. You don't look like the type who feels sorry very often."

Well, he was dead wrong about that, anyway. I was sorry all right, but only that he wasn't on his knees coughing up blood. I knew exactly what he had in mind as punishment for me. Even though he outweighed me by a good hundred pounds if he thought he'd get away with rape entirely unscathed he had another think coming.

It's no surprise, then, when he starts fumbling with his belt buckle with his free hand, but it is when instead of unfastening his fly he pulls the two-inch-wide leather strap from its loops. The significance has only a second to register before I feel the makeshift lash cut into me with the sound of a pistol shot and the pain of a red-hot poker.

He tries it again, but this time I hold my forearm up and the belt whips around it. I give a hard jerk and the buckle snaps out of his hand, taking a chunk of flesh with it so big I think it must be an entire finger. I sure hope so. I'm on my feet before the surprise has scarcely had a chance to register on his face, but I don't have a chance to do anything. The gun is already pointed squarely at the bridge of my nose.

Chapter Three

SO WHAT THE HELL WAS I DOING GETTING THE SHIT BEAT OUT OF ME ON Plankton Key, Florida for God's sake? Me, a would-be private eye from New York who's never been further south than Atlantic City? Don't think I wasn't asking myself that very same question, because I sure as hell was. Well, it all began (to take a tried-and-true opening line from the very best women's magazines) not more than a month ago . . . not in the office of the Bellinghausen Superior Detective Agency (which had been temporarily closed due to non-payment of rent), but in my own apartment building, the Zenobia Arms—eight flats, two to a floor—on Pith Street in the Village. A new family had recently moved into one of the top floor apartments—an occurrence unusual enough to have caused some considerable discussion among the other tenants. There'd not been anyone new in the place since I'd moved in three years earlier. And before that, for all I could tell, the others had been waiting on the sidewalk, suitcases in hand, while the last brick was being laid sometime, I think, during the Garfield administration. I'm sure they'd been there at least that long. It was like living in some old folks' home, not that I'm really complaining you understand. My rooms are on the third floor, on the right side to someone standing on the street looking at the place, not that anyone would be likely to do that. Like every other apartment in the Arms its rooms are lined up one after the other like those in a house trailer: a living room/parlor that opens directly onto the hall at the top of the central staircase, a kitchen, a bath and a bedroom at the back. A fire escape landing is right outside my rear bedroom window. It's a nice place to sleep in the summer. The rooms on either side of the stairs are identical, except for being mirror images of one another.

The first floor apartments are occupied by the Schoenfelds, a nice old couple who run a candy store a few blocks away and who also act as the resident managers of the building and who are unvariably lenient when my rent is late which is almost always, and a pair of nice old spinster ladies—the Clarence sisters. They exist on the income of some kind of trust, which is apparently just enough to pay for their rent and utilities and the single, meager-looking bag of groceries that's delivered every week by the boy from Carlton's down at the end of the block. Mr. Myagkov, who plays the violin and cello for a symphony orchestra and also moonlights for several recording studios, lives in the rooms directly beneath my own. He is very good (at least I think so, but what do I know about music?) and his playing never bothers me at all. In fact, I kind of look forward to the weekends and evenings he isn't working, especially in the Spring and Summer when all the windows are open, because he spends the afternoons and evenings practicing, though I don't know what for since he sounds plenty fine to me. But like I said, what do I know? I can't even whistle. Across the hall from him are the Leonis, a nice Italian couple with about seventeen kids. He's a steam fitter in a boiler factory and she takes care of the kids and I can tell you who I think's got the better half of the deal and so would you if you ever meet the Leoni spawn, God forbid. Across from my place on the third floor is Mr. Arkady. A tall, thin, pale man in the creepy mold of John Carradine, he's always been civil enough to me when I've run across him, but prefers to keep to himself which is just fine by me. I can't see him but what I wonder if he's thinking how my blood would taste, for which I can hardly blame him since he looks like he's definitely shy a couple of quarts. He's a dealer in old books and whatnot who works out of his apartment, which is filled wall to wall and floor to ceiling with musty, leather-bound volumes and precious little else, even his refrigerator had a book in it, for Pete's sake, between the goat cheese and a half bottle of red wine (I'd just gotten my new set of lock picks and had to try them out, so kill me). The place on the top floor right—that is, just above my own—is home to Miss Birdwhistle, a Broadway star in the making (not that I think she has a chance in hell, but why not give the kid a break?). She waits tables nights at a restaurant about six blocks uptown and spends her days and weekends auditioning. So far as I know, the only stage jobs she's ever gotten are gigs in the burlesque houses yet she always seems to think that her big break is coming with the next interview. One has to kind of admire that sort of optimism, stupid as it might be. Kind of like watching a moth bashing its head on the outside of a window, trying to get to a light bulb. The apartment opposite hers used to be occupied by a nice old Jewish man named Goldberg who headed the embroidery department in an apron factory over in the garment district. He died and the apartment wasn't even vacant a week before someone new moved in.

Needless to say, the newcomers ran a gauntlet of curious eyes as they carried their belongings from the street to the top floor. My eyes were among them, of course, but I'm supposed to be a detective so what did you expect me to do?

There seemed to be just the two of them (though I was wrong about that as it turned out): a mother and her daughter, I figured (I was on the money there). The former was a tall, thin, frail-looking bird who I suspected was nowhere near as old as she looked. She had one of those fine-boned, fragile English faces you see on women in FSA photos of Okey families during the Depression, the ones with the hopeless, empty expressions. The kid was maybe fourteen or fifteen, I guessed, tall and thin like her mother though it looked better on her. That and the lean face with the huge black eyes and the hank of black hair hanging over the high, white forehead made her seem very esthetic—I figured her for a poet or some such thing, probably a philosophy, literature or sociology student at NYU. Someone whose scribblings the beatniks in the basement coffeehouses would get all shaky over. She was probably figuring that since she had edited the high school literary magazine and the class yearbook and everyone in Duckanus, Arkansas thought she was the cat's pajamas because she'd written that editorial for the Duckanus *Weekly* that'd gotten the big civic prize from Mayor Cornball, that she'd give the Big City a shot, show the *New Yorker* a thing or two and maybe set off-Broadway on its ear if she had the time and inclination. Either that or she was a consumptive come for treatment at one of the big sanitariums. She sure looked the part, I can tell you that. One way or another, anyway—our building being filled to the brim with nosy Parkers—I was sure I'd be finding out more than I'd ever care to know about the new tenants before the week was out. If one thing is certain, being a detective in the Zenobia Arms is a redundancy.

As it turned out, it didn't take a week at all.

It was one of those weird balmy days in late March when the weather tries to lull you into thinking winter was finally over. I knew better, having just listened to the radio. Buffalo and Albany had just been socked with the worst blizzard in ten years and the thing was rolling down toward New York like an avalanche. In the meantime, I was enjoying the respite—maybe even more so knowing how short it was going to be. It must have been hardly sixty degrees outdoors but it felt a lot warmer in the sun. Since the front of my building faces south, I was lounging in shorts and halter on top of the wide sloping wall that flanks the front steps, soaking up the warmth from the sun and the hot stone and not doing much more than idly watching people walk past. Sounds nice—which it was—though what it really meant was that I didn't have anything much better to do, like work on a job, for instance. Business had been a little slack since New Year's. It had actually been slack since Labor Day, but I was just counting the current year in order not to depress myself unduly.

Anyway, I was about halfway through a bag of peanuts and a Blue Ribbon—my lunch—well, my breakfast *and* lunch for that matter—when I saw the new kid coming up the block. Not hard to spot since she stood out like a sore thumb. She was half a head taller than most anyone else on the street, looking even taller because of her thinness. She looked like one of those East European refugees you see in the newsreels or that skinny, waif-like actress in the movie I'd seen last week, *The Secret People*—Audrey Hepburn. She was dressed as though she were on her way to a Sadie Hawkins dance, wearing only a calf-length gingham dress, bobby socks and sneakers, and a ratty cloth coat even the Salvation Army wouldn't have wished on anyone. There was an overwhelming sense of unhealthiness on first impression, but she walked with a springy step, her jet black hair bouncing around her pallid face like the wings of a crow, her expression intensively alive, her enormous dark eyes as alert as a deer in hunting season.

I took off my sunglasses and greeted her as she swung toward the steps.

"Hi! You must be the new kid from upstairs."

She looked at me for a moment—just a heartbeat too long, enough to make me feel as though I just called her some awful name and she was deciding whether to ignore me or call a cop. But instead, she smiled and said, "Sure! I just moved in with my mother and brother, up on the top floor." She had a pleasant voice, softened by a slow, gentle Southern drawl, the kind that sounds genteel instead of uneducated. The smile had made all the difference, transforming what on first sight had looked like a walking tuberculosis case into something else entirely. She really was a good-looking kid, after all, I decided. Pretty in a fragile sort of way. The kind of kid the French call a *gamin*, I think, if gamin is the word I want.

"Welcome to the Zenobia Arms. My name's Bellinghausen, Velda Bellinghausen." I held out my hand and she took it without any hesitation at all this time. Her grip was firm but cold as ice.

"Hi. I'm Maxie."

"Maxie? That's an interesting name. Want to sit with me for a few minutes? It's too nice a day to be indoors. We ought to enjoy it while we can . . . going to get cold again this week and probably stay that way until Easter. I hear there's snow on the way."

"Sure."

She sat down beside me, carefully tucking her skirt around her long legs, and said, "I'm kind of glad to hear there's going to be snow. I've never seen snow before."

"You'll be thinking twice about that a week from now."

"Maybe, I guess."

"Have a peanut?"

"Thanks." She took one and shelled it, then said, as though I'd just asked her a question, "Everyone calls me Maxie, but that's not really my name, not my given name, I mean."

"What *is* your real name, then, and why does everyone call you Maxie?" I already knew that her last name was Fort. That was no big trick: the name was on the mailbox. "If I'm not being too nosy that is."

"No! Not at all! Well, you see, people actually call me Max more often than Maxie, which is short for Maxine. It's just a name I—I like, I guess. You ever hear how Indians had two names? The one that everyone called them and their secret name, the one only they knew? Something like that, I guess, but turned around backwards kinda, if you see what I mean. I like being called Max because, well, because it just seems to—to fit me better. My Christian name is Cleo—for Cleopatra—you know, the Egyptian queen? Funny, if you think about it, that my Christian name is the same as a pagan queen. She was pagan wasn't she? I'm pretty sure she was. The Egyptians worshiped all those gods with bird heads and all. But like I said, no one ever calls me Cleo except my mother and brother."

"Cleo's nice, though. Very unusual. Very classy."

"Yeah, I guess. I think it sounds like that goldfish in *Pinocchio.* But I hardly ever hear anybody call me that. Not since I was kid. I just tell everyone my name is Max."

"So how do you like New York, Max?"

"It's fine. Awful big, though, and cold."

"Wait until summer, you'll be wishing it was winter again. You liked it better down south?"

"How'd you know where I was from, Miss Bellinghausen? How'd you know I was new to the city?"

"Please call me Velda, since we're neighbors after all. How'd I know? I guess it's just my business to figure out things like that."

"Your business?" She screwed up her face in thought and then brightened. "Miss Bellinghausen! I mean . . . Velda—you, you're not that lady detective they said lives here?"

"Well, there're a whole lot of people who'd argue about the 'lady' part, but, yup, that's me."

"Golly! A *detective*! Just like in the movies?"

"Well . . . not so's you'd notice all that much."

"Gee . . . it must be awful exciting. Being a detective and all! And in New York City! Golly!"

Why disabuse the kid? Besides, it'd been too long since I'd been hero-worshiped to want to spoil the sensation. In fact, no one had ever hero-worshiped me, God knows.

"You have a gun and handcuffs and everything?"

"Sure. I even have a trench coat . . ."

"Oh, just like Venus McFury!"

"Venus McWho?"

"Oh, *you* know! Here," she said, pulling a rolled-up magazine from her school bag. Handing it to me, I unfurled it to reveal an uncommonly lurid comic book. The cover featured a woman of unlikely proportions, who I assumed was the eponymous Venus McFury, in an even more unlikely situation. She did, indeed, have a trench coat, though what little was left of it was being torn from her by a gang of bearded Bolsheviks who did not seem terribly concerned that slugs from the brace of blazing .45 automatics she clutched in her hands were tearing their comrades to shreds. Venus appeared to not be wearing anything under the coat and I thought the men looked more anxious to settle that question than in maintaining their personal safety, let alone overthrowing America by violence or subversion. Cleo's comparison of me with Venus was supposed to be flattering, I guess. The comic book detective appeared to be tall and leggy enough—like I've already said, I'm six foot even—but with more curves than the reptile house at the Central Park Zoo—most of which seemed to be concentrated in her bosom. In fact, most of Venus seemed to be chest which I can tell you right now is no description of me. She had a billowing mane of blonde hair, too, where my dark locks are sheared off in a Buster Brown cut. Well, if Cleo wanted to think I was the living embodiment of her comic book heroine, who was I to disenchant her? I rolled the comic book up and handed it back to her.

"Well, yeah, I guess. Something like that, I suppose. Stop by sometime and I'll show you some of my souvenirs."

"Thank you, Velda, I'd love to come visit."

"What brings you to the big city, anyway, Max? Going to school up here?"

"No, nothing like that. Well, I mean, yes I'm going to school, or will, anyway, soon's I get registered, but that's not the reason we came up here. I . . . I . . . I gotta see some doctors." Her voice had dropped at that last sentence, as though she were sharing some dark, embarrassing secret.

What could it be? Pernicious anemia? Tapeworm? TB? Sure,

why not TB? After all, she looked like she could audition for the lead in *Camille.*

"Doctors? You look plenty healthy to me," I lied.

"These, these are special doctors. They're—they're about my—spells."

"Spells?"

The girl had whispered this as though people passing on the street were going to stop and ask her what in the world she thought she was doing, a nice girl like her, having spells, for God's sake! She looked uncomfortable and I was afraid that I'd touched on something perhaps a wee bit too personal and sensitive. It was dead clear it was something she didn't like being reminded about, and sure as hell not by a total stranger.

"Have another peanut, Max. You come on down to my place anytime at all—it's apartment three-B, and I'll tell you all about what it's like being a detective." I'd have to dig out all my old pulps and memorize some good adventures for her. God knows I hadn't had many of my own. She just struck me as the type who probably wouldn't quite understand that the only cases I'd had since putting up my shingle had for the most part involved sneaking photos through hotel windows of people doing things that surely would have shocked their mothers. And those were the cases that *didn't* embarrass me. The ones I really didn't want to tell her about involved me being on the other side of the window.

"I'd like that just fine . . . Velda. I gotta run, now. It was really nice meeting you and I'd sure like to hear all about being a detective sometime."

"Any time at all."

She uncoiled her lanky prolongations from the steps—for all her apparent gawkiness, she was as sinuous as a cobra—and ran into the building.

Cleo showed up at my door the following afternoon. I was surprised. I hadn't really expected her to take my invitation seriously, but I was pleased to see her and asked her in and offered her a coke. While I got a couple of bottles out of the fridge and popped the caps off, she looked around my place with the kind of slack-jawed incredulity you see on tourists gawking at Rockefeller Center. I guess the fact that it was the apartment of a private eye gave it a sort of glamour in her eyes. It just looked like the same old dump to me, but far be it from me to disabuse a budding fan.

I handed her a bottle and said, “Have a seat, Cleo—ah, Max. Make yourself at home.”

She chose a chair and sat gingerly on the very edge of the seat, tidily tugging the hem of her skirt over her knees.

“Gee, thanks, Miss—I mean, Velda.”

“Where you been all day? Getting ready for school?”

“Oh, no, not yet. I’ve been looking for a job. I mean, a real one. I had lots of part-time work, especially over the holidays, in the stores, but that’s all over now. I’ve been trying to get into some classes, but that’s awful hard this late in the school year. It’s expensive, too, which is why I’m trying to find something to do.”

“Did you have a job back home?”

“Yes—no, not really. I—I stayed home most of the time, when I wasn’t in school that is. And I—I was sick a lot. That’s why we came to New York, you know—so I could see a doctor. But I did make lace, to sell to the tourists, I got real good at that.”

“Tourists?”

“Yeah. Lots of tourists went through town, on their way to Key West.”

“That’s right, you said you were from Florida.”

“Yeah, a little place called Plankton Key. I’m sure you’ve never heard of it.”

“You’re right, I haven’t. Sorry.”

“Oh, that’s okay. No one else’s ever heard of it, either.”

“Did you like it there? Do you miss it?”

“Sometimes—” A strange, distant look came to her face for a moment. I wasn’t sure what it meant, but it wasn’t homesickness. Then her face cleared and she said, perhaps a little too brightly, “I sure miss home when it’s this cold out! Boy! Winter in New York is sure something!”

“Yeah, it’s something all right.”

“Do you work from here, Velda, or do you have an office somewhere?”

"Ah—yes—ah, I've had to stay away from my office lately. Ah—commie agents have the place staked out and I don't want them to get a tail on me."

"Wow! Real communists? Gee, Velda, that's really something! A big case, huh?"

"Yeah, sure."

"I guess you can't talk about it, huh?"

"No, not really. Maybe I can tell you something about it later." As soon as I got a good plot out of *Thrilling Detective Mysteries,* I would do that very thing.

"Gee, Velda, are these pictures of *you?*"

"Uh, yeah—" She'd found the framed photos of me from when I'd worked the stage at Slotnik's. I'd forgotten all about them. If I'd remembered, I'd have taken them down before inviting the kid in. I don't know if they're the sort of thing a teenage girl ought to see.

"Gee . . . that's a pretty swell costume in this one. Gosh, it must've been grand to wear something that beautiful. I've never had anything with sparkles on it like that."

"Well, yeah—" I didn't know what to make of this. I never thought anyone would ever think that anything I'd had to do with Slotsky's was grand. I mean, I was more than a little embarrassed by those years—not that I'd really had any choice in the matter—and this kid was admiring me!

"Didn't you ever get cold, Velda? This one's kinda, well, kinda skimpy—and, gee, are those your—"

It was about time to change the subject while she was still gawking at the pictures from the earlier part of my stage career. I wasn't sure what she'd make of the ones further down the wall, so I said, "Have you made any friends yet, Max?"

"No—not really. Well . . ." She looked down at her coke and blushed.

"You've met a boy?"

"Gee, Velda, how'd you know that? Oh, that was a silly question to ask a detective, wasn't it?"

"I know all."

"It's—he's a fellow I met while I was working in an art supply store just after we moved here last Fall. He's taking classes at Pratt, the big art school, you know? He's studying to be an architect. Isn't that wonderful? He's going to design houses and skyscrapers and things like that."

"What's his name?"

"Bill. He's really nice—a gentleman, you know?"

"Well, I'm glad you met a nice fellow. Let alone a gentleman. It can be hard finding a friend in this city sometimes, especially for someone new in town. The place can be kind of intimidating. I'm not surprised, though, that you've met a boy already. You're a very pretty girl."

"Aw gee, thanks, Velda!" And by God, she was blushing! It was the only color in a face that looked like a black and white woodcut.

"Want another coke? I've got some potato chips around here somewhere that probably haven't gone limp yet."

"Thanks, but I can't stay too much longer. My mother worries when I'm late coming home. Can—can I ask you something personal?"

"Sure. Ask me anything you like."

"Well, I was just wondering—I've never heard of a lady detective before. I mean, outside of TV and things like that. I didn't know that a lady would want—I mean—"

"You mean why would any woman *want* to be a detective?"

"Yeah, I guess so."

"Fair enough. I wish I had a good answer for you. I guess it's just something I want to do. I'm not really very good doing anything else. You should see me try to type." Which was as good an evasion as any, I suppose. I don't know why, but I would've felt kind of weird telling her it beat undressing in front of five hundred strange men every night.

She glanced at the clock on my side table and squeaked. "Oh gosh! I'm going to be late. I'd better run, Miss—Velda. Thanks for the coke. I hope I haven't been a bother?"

"Not at all. You're welcome to stop by anytime you like."

"Thanks, Velda."

As it turned out it was nearly a week before I saw Max again and it wasn't quite under the circumstances that either of us had anticipated.

It was two o'clock in the morning when I finally realized that the banging in my ears wasn't the radiator next to my bed. It was some idiot at my front door. I climbed from under the covers, threw the first thing I could find around myself and went to the front room.

"Who the hell is it?" I asked through the door.

"Miss Bellinghausen?"

I recognized Birdwhistle's voice and groaned. The little moron had probably just been propositioned for the seventy-eighth time and wanted a shoulder to cry on. Someone needs to tell her that she really has only two marketable talents and if she knows what's good for her, she'll stick to waitressing. I told her to hold her horses and fumbled the chain from the door. Birdwhistle looked surprised to see me. Who'd she expect? Senator McCarthy?

"Did I wake you?" she asked.

"Not at all. Some people think it's strange, but I often spend entire nights leaning against my door, just in case someone might knock at two o'clock in the morning."

"That *is* strange."

"Come on in. Want some coffee? Might as well start the day now and get it over with."

"Thanks, Miss Bellinghausen, but coffee makes my teeth yellow."

"Sorry. Should've thought of that. And for God's sake please call me Velda. 'Miss Bellinghausen' sounds like a third grade grammar teacher."

"Sure, Miss—I mean, Velda. Thanks."

"Come on in the kitchen. You can watch me caffeinate myself. I need to see in color before I can talk to anyone. Want some orange juice? I think it's still orange anyway; it's been a while since I looked."

"Sure, thanks. And Miss—Velda, you can call me Iphigenia if you want. That's my given name, but I'm going to change it, of course, when I get on the stage. Iphigenia sounds kinda like some sort of stomach medicine. What do you think of Olivia de la Rue?"

"Never heard of her."

"No, I mean for *me,* for my stage name. Doesn't it sound nicer than Iphigenia Birdwhistle? Kinda elegant-like?"

I thought that a frying pan dropped down the fire escape would sound more elegant than "Iphigenia Birdwhistle", but, on the other hand, Iphigenia Birdwhistle might be better than sounding like a cheap stripper. It was at least unique. So I said, "Olivia de la Rue is a lovely name."

"Yeah, that's what Mr. Lupine said, too."

"Mr. Lupine?"

"The manager at the Bijoux Theater. He said he thought it sounded like the name of a real headliner."

"Uh, Iphigenia, is there any particular reason you wanted to see me? Or were you just in the mood for a chat?"

"Oh! I'm sorry! I completely forgot! I do that all the time and sometimes it's really embarrassing, as you might imagine since you know I'm a waitress—well, just a part-time waitress, of course, just to make ends meet until I get a break. Just the other day, Mr. Spool, he's the short-order cook at the coffee shop, he said—"

"—he said, 'Ipheginia, why don't you get to the point?'"

"Oh, yes! Those new people who moved in upstairs? The ones across the hall from me?"

"Uh huh. The Forts."

"Yeah, well, the kid's really sick and they need someone to come up and help."

"You should've found a doctor, then. I can't even get a BandAid on right."

"It's not like that. I think they need someone like you."

"Someone like me?"

"Yeah. A detective."

I glanced at the clock. One-thirty, it sneered. *Oh, what the hell.*

"Let me get something on first."

I went to the bathroom and shucked my robe. As I was pulling on my jeans, Iphigenia, who was watching me from the kitchen, said with the hushed awe most people reserve for fireworks displays and bad traffic accidents, "Gee, Velda! You oughta go talk to Mr. Lupine yourself! With a figure like you got, he'd give you a part easy, I'm sure. Everyone's always looking for tall girls for the chorus and jeez what I wouldn't give for legs like yours if you don't mind me saying so. They ain't as easy to find as people might think, tall girls I mean, leastways ones that don't look like horses."

"I'm sure he'd be glad to offer me a part, but I'm afraid he might not like what I did with it."

"Aw, you're just being too modest, Velda," she argued, completely missing the point. Sometimes my humor is just too subtle. Just as well, I suppose—Iphigenia would only be hurt if she thought I'd been laughing at what she'd offered as an honest compliment. Besides, I didn't think there'd be anything gained from telling her that because I knew all too well what it was like being a chorus girl, that's what'd made me want to be something else. *Anything* else. Obviously. But just because I wasn't cut out for the business didn't mean that other people weren't—Iphigenia being a perfect case in point. If anyone was destined to be a burlesque queen she was. If she just weren't so damned sweet.

I pulled on my sweatshirt and sneakers, shook my hair into place and said, "All right, Iphigenia. Lead on."

I followed her upstairs and she tapped on the door of 4A. It opened instantly, which was kind of creepy, particularly since it was Max's mother who stood there in the half shadows. It was the first time I'd seen her up close and I was shocked. The woman was obviously a nervous wreck. Anyone could see that she'd probably never been in any great shape to begin with, physically, looking under the best of circumstances like she'd been cobbled together from bits and pieces of beef jerky and coat hanger wire, but now something had worried her to the point of cadaverousness, if cadaverousness is a word. I'd seen healthier-looking heroin fiends.

"Miss Bellinghausen?" she said.

"Call me Velda," I replied and followed her into the room, which was exactly like mine, except laid out in a mirror image like I said before. "How can I help you?"

"I don't know. I didn't know what else to do. Cleo's . . . Cleo's cries disturbed Miss Birdwhistle—"

"That was OK," Iphigenia protested. "I was already awake. I'd just come in and probably wouldn't have heard anything at all if I'd been asleep. I sleep like a log when I've been out all—"

"—and she came over to see if anything was wrong."

"That was kind of her, I suppose."

"It was she who suggested that you might be able to help us."

"Yes, that was *very* kind of her."

"I apologize if she woke you. I'm sure you must've been asleep."

"Me? Naw. Country girl like me gets up with the pigeons, squirrels and garbage collectors."

"I just didn't know what else to do."

"Well, why don't you tell me what's wrong first? That'd help a lot."

"It's Cleo, my daughter."

"Well, yeah, I kind of figured that."

There was a yell from the rear of the apartment, a kind of plaintive bleat that had the same effect on Mrs. Fort it would have had on a mother sheep, whatever those are called. She gave a nervous little frisk and hustled off toward the bedroom. Birdwhistle and I followed.

The bedroom was dark, the only light being what spilled in from the kitchen and a dim blue glow from the window that cast a distorted rectangle across the bed. Still, I could see clearly enough the figure that lay twisting on the bed, writhing like a landed fish giving up its last gasp. It was the kid, Max, and she gave another low moan and Mrs. Fort scuttled over and took one of her hands. The kid was sick, all right, anyone could see that much, and I wondered again what the hell I was doing there.

"We really oughta call a doctor," I told Iphigenia.

"No . . . listen a minute."

The kid—Max—had thrown off most of her bedclothes and was lying on the rumpled sheets in nothing but a pair of cotton panties that looked like hand-me-downs from someone a lot older and bigger, probably her mother, an awful enough thought. Although the room was cold—a light snow had started falling just before midnight—the girl was drenched in sweat. Her blue-white body glistened like a firefly in the dim light. She was lot older than I'd originally thought—maybe more like eighteen or nineteen. Her lanky body and thin face had misled me. She was even skinnier than her mother. I could see her ribs plainly, her breasts sitting upon them like overturned saucers. She was writhing and twisting and moaning like someone who'd just eaten the leftover salmon salad from yesterday's picnic.

"I don't know about this," I said. "It sure looks to me like she needs a doctor."

"No," replied Mrs. Fort, wringing her hands together with a sound like dry leaves. "No—she's been like this before."

Just then, the kid gives out another low moan, like a cat in heat, and I felt my nape go all bristly, which had never happened to me before and I didn't like it one bit. I went closer, to where the light from the window fell across her face. It looked like it was made of suet. The lips were tightly clenched, as were her hands, but the spookiest thing was her eyes. They were wide open, the pupils dilated to black pools, the whites showing all the way around. They looked dull, like bread pills, and stared right through me. When I waved my hand in front of her face the eyes didn't waver. Her expression was a Godawful mixture of horror and fear, like she was seeing something utterly unbearable.

I felt her chest, face and hands. They were cold as ice. I touched her wrist and was astonished to feel a regular, though faint, pulse. It seemed as though she were hardly breathing at all—you had to watch for a minute to see her thin chest slowly rise and fall.

"She's done this before?" I said to the mother, wondering why she needed me, let alone anyone else, if this were a regular item on the Fort program. "What the hell's wrong with her?"

"I don't know. I don't know. She's done this off an' on since she was six. Hardly's had a spell at all since she was sixteen, but now they've started again."

"Well, Jesus, you really ought to have a doctor take a look at her."

"Yeah," added Iphigenia. "I saw someone have a fit once, right on the sidewalk. God, it was something awful to see! Bit his tongue right off. Jeez, you shoulda seen all the blood!"

"She's perfectly healthy," Mrs. Fort protested. "Never had a sick day in her life, other than these spells. They don't seem to do her any harm—she hardly remembers them when she wakes up."

Max suddenly jack knifed straight up in her bed, screaming at the top of her puny lungs, "For God's sake! *Don't hit him!*"

I jumped, not from the sound but because the kid had made the warning sound so . . . so real. Her eyes were wide open, focused on a point somewhere beyond my shoulder, and the impression was so strong that she was looking at someone I instinctively turned to see who it was. There was nothing there but an empty chair.

"Don't kill him!" she shrieked, and kept repeating that until I could hear people stirring in the floors below us.

"Come on," I said, "we better get her calmed down or someone's going to call the cops."

Mrs. Fort brought a pan of cold water from the bathroom and she and Iphigenia got the kid quieted down some by bathing her face and chest with wet hand towels. Max lay back on her pillow, mumbling and crying, but at least not so's you could hear her a block away now. As I'd been half expecting, there was a knock at the door. I recognized the discreet tapping of either Mr. or Mrs. Schoenfeld. I knew it well. It was the apologetic knock they used when they came to remind you that your rent was overdue. I took the liberty of answering the door. Both Schoenfelds stood there, huddled together with their eyes bugging out, as though they'd been certain they were about to witness the bloody scene of an ax murder. They looked vaguely dissapointed.

"Miss Bellinghausen?" Seeing me there instead of their new tenant, they must've been sure that something awful was going on.

"Yup. Sorry about all the fuss. The kid here's just had a kind of nightmare, I guess."

"Nightmare? My heavens, it sounded like someone was being murdered!"

"Nothing like that, I assure you. Miss Birdwhistle and I came over to see if there was anything we could do. The kid's a little sick is all, picked up a fever and it gave her a nightmare. We got her calmed down now and I'm sure she's going to be quiet."

"Well, I certainly hope so. We got a very angry call from Mr. Arkady. He's quite upset about being awakened this early in the morning."

"Early? It's only two o'clock. That's still practically yesterday."

"I wouldn't know about all that, but you should please tell Mrs. Fort that this is a quiet place, with respectable people, and we just can't tolerate this sort of thing."

"I'm sure it won't happen again. Go on back to bed. Everything's going to be all right now."

"Well, if you say so, Miss Bellinghausen. We certainly hope you're right."

When I got back to the bedroom, I was glad to see it didn't look as though Maxie were about to put the lie to the promise I'd just made. She was under a blanket now, just laying there, her eyes like ball bearings, muttering to herself while her mother wiped her forehead. I took her wrist in my hand. Her pulse was still weak but steady.

I sat on the edge of the bed opposite Mrs. Fort and held the bowl for her while we chatted quietly about nothing in particular. Finally, I suggested to Mrs. Fort that she ought to get some sleep herself. She looked like hell, though I didn't put it exactly like that. For all I knew maybe she always looked like hell. She didn't take much convincing but only nodded wearily and stumbled off into the living room where I guess she bedded down on the sofa seeing that the kid was occupying the only bed I'd noticed in the place.

"You might as well get to bed yourself, Iphegina. You don't want to miss much more of your beauty sleep if you've got auditions tomorrow."

"It's okay. I'm used to being up all night anyway. I'd like to hang around if you think it'd be okay."

"It's no skin off my nose."

"Swell. I'll just curl up in that big chair in the living room. You need me, you just call, okay?"

The only chair in the bedroom was a cheap wooden one, which I pulled it over to the bed and slouched in, leaning the back against the wall behind me. I could see that the kid wasn't sleeping too well. She seemed to be as rigid as a board and her breathing was shallow as she panted and clenched and unclenched her fists.

Around about two-thirty, Max sat up again with a kind of little whimpering cry. I went to put a hand on her shoulder when she suddenly launched from the bed like a startled deer, nearly knocking me over backwards. She wasn't screaming this time, thank God, but it took all my strength to hold her down. I was startled by the strength she showed—she felt like a bar of spring steel. Her eyes had that glassy stare again, focused somewhere beyond me. It was like wrestling a blind lunatic and it was a damned uncanny sensation.

Max, meanwhile, was talking. The same stuff she'd spouted before, about someone being hit, being killed, about blood being everywhere, and new things, things that my skin go all cold and pimply. She talked about running down dark alleys, hiding in doorways, wondering where the river was so she could throw herself into it. She whimpered, "My feet! Oh, my feet!" and when I felt them they were as ice cold as the pork chop in my fridge downstairs. Then some very weird stuff about having a baby taken from her. This went on for about half an hour, her voice getting weaker and weaker until she finally fell back onto her clammy sheets, this time (I hoped) completely exhausted. At any rate, she was soon asleep, breathing deeply and regularly.

I pulled the blanket back over the slender figure and as soon as I felt sure she was going to be quiet, I made myself as comfortable as I could in the chair and watched her. I must've fallen alseep for the next thing I remember was hearing the front door open and close and heavy footsteps coming toward the bedroom. I glanced at the clock. It was nearly five—I'd been out for more than two hours. The window was a lightless rectangle. I glanced at Max and saw that she was still sleeping soundly. Suddenly, the room darkened. An enormous figure was eclipsing what little light had been coming from the front of the house. Behind the colossus I could just make out the figure of Mrs. Fort and beyond her the silhouette of Iphegenia.

"Oh, Ruben!" Mrs. Fort said, seeming to be happier to see King Kong in her bedroom than I would have been. "Ruben, Cleo's had another spell."

"Yeah." Ruben's voice sounded like someone talking into a coffee can. *Ruben?* Who's going to show up next, for God's sake, Pappy Yokum? "Looks like a bad'un."

"Worse she's had in a long time, Ruben."

"Who th' hell're all these dames?"

"They're neighbors, Ruben. Be polite. They came 'cause they thought I needed some help. This is Miss Birdwhistle, from 'cross the hall, an' this is Miss Bellinghausen. Misses, this is Ruben, Cleo's big brother."

"Bellinghausen, huh? You th' bird thinks she's a shamus, huh? Long drinka water, ain't ya?" He said all this without looking at me at all, being too busy ogling Iphigenia like some geek in front row center at Minsky's waiting for Sally Rand to molt her last feather. "The kid'll be out for hours. I seen it before. Don't see no reason for you t' be hangin' 'roune any longer." A great big thank-you from Mr. Ruben Fort, you're welcome.

"I can take a hint," I said. "I'm sensitive that way."

"Yeah." He chewed an idea around for a minute or two, then said, "So you're some kinda detective, huh? That's funny."

"Yeah, it sure is."

"Well, I can tell you right now Ma ain't paying you nothin'. You came up here on your own hook. You wanta charge someone, get that bimbo invited you in here to pony up, you wanta make a buck outta this. You ain't gettin' a penny outta us."

"Calm yourself, Ruben. I was just being neighborly."

"Neighborly! Hmpf. Yeah, sure."

There was little point in arguing with the big lummox, or in letting him get my goat, which he was well on his way to doing. I wanted to find out more about Ruben, who I could tell was bad news from way back, but for the time being I just shrugged my shoulders and walked out. As Ipheginia and I passed through the living room, I saw Mrs. Fort draped on a ratty sofa that must have come with the room, out like a light. I closed the door quietly behind me, said good night to Miss Birdwhistle and went back to my room, showered and got dressed. I badly needed to go out and get some coffee. I'd stopped seeing in color around five a.m. and it was annoying me.

I didn't really want to, having had about as much of the Fort family as I could take in one sitting, but I was dead curious about the kid and, besides, maybe the old lady'd like me to bring back some coffee and something for her and the kid to eat, seeing as how it looked like neither had had a square meal since VE Day. Heart of gold, that's me. Brain of gold, too, if you get my drift. I went back upstairs and rapped on the door of 4B, hoping that Ruben the Ox wouldn't be there. When Mrs. Fort opened the door, looking as though she hadn't slept in weeks (which was unfair since she was the only one who *had* gotten any sleep last night), I could see that her son was nowhere in sight. Good. Probably gone back to his job braining cows at the slaughterhouse.

"I just thought I'd look in and see how the kid was doing."

"That's very kind of you, Miss Bellinghausen—"

"Please, call me Velda."

"Yes. Well, that's very kind of you, Velda. Won't you come in? That was so nice of you to look after poor little Cleo last night. I can't tell you—"

"Don't bother. What're neighbors for, anyway?"

"Would you care for some coffee?"

"I was just on my way out to get some and I thought maybe I could bring something back for you."

"I couldn't possibly ask you to do anything else. You've been much too kind already."

"Is Max—Cleo—still asleep?"

"Yes, thank God. She's been sleeping like a log all morning, bless her heart."

"Just what *is* the kid's problem, anyway?"

"I don't know, I really don't. Our doctor back home had no idea. The problem's that Cleo's in perfect health otherwise. You have to see her having one of her spells to tell how sick she really is, and the doctor never saw that."

"Doctor back home? Just where *is* home, Mrs. Fort?"

"Oh, we've come all th' way from Florida. Just a little backwater town no one's ever heard of. We only had one doctor there, just an old country MD. Awful good man, but t' tell th' truth anything beyond a broken leg or a childbirth is a little beyond him. He told us about a doctor in Tallahassee who might be able t' help. Took every penny we had an' it didn't do no good at all. Said we should be grateful we had such a healthy girl."

"How'd you get up here, then? New York's a wee tad further away than Tallahassee."

"Oh, I got a little inheritance when my granddaddy passed away, and Ruben, he got a job 'cross the river that pays the rent."

"What's Ruben do, anyway?"

"He works for a meat packer."

Ha!

I strolled down the block to Joe's place, a hole-in-the-wall diner where I've had my morning coffee and donuts for the last four or five years. It'd snowed all night and there was a couple of inches on the sidewalk and streets. There hadn't been enough traffic yet to turn it all into grey slush and everything was still quiet and pretty. Captain Joe grinned as I came in, as he always did. He was a castaway from the Merchant Marine, a hugely powerful man gone to flab. He was always there behind the counter no matter what time I'd wander in, which was as likely to be one o'clock in the morning as noon. It was now about six thirty which split the difference pretty closely.

"You look like someone kicked you down a flight of stairs, Velda," he said not unkindly, pouring me a cup of his infamous coffee. "You're getting too old to party like that any longer. Here, have an eye-opener." I've known Turks who consider it a variety of paint remover and as such an affront to Allah but I always found it hit the spot. This time it hit it good and hard.

"Take care, Joe. You open my eyes too much and I'll remember how ugly you are."

"Got a hot case cookin'?" Joe's fascinated by my line of work, apparently thinking I'm some sort of female Mike Hammer. As automatically as he'd poured my coffee he placed a plate with four plain cake donuts—the only kind I can bear to eat with coffee—beside the cup. I hate being so damned predictable, but there you are.

"Wish I did. But no—just a case of neighbors."

"You oughta find a place where you can get some sleep. Nice girl like you needs all the sleep she can get."

"Yeah. If I ever got the all beauty sleep I need I'd be in a coma." I winced as a police cruiser roared around the corner, its siren sawing the top of my head off.

"Aw, you're too hard on yourself, Velda."

A customer had just come in and as Joe went to see what the newcomer wanted he tossed the morning paper onto the counter.

"Help yourself, kid, hot off the press."

I unrolled the paper and flattened it next to my plate. I scanned the headlines, hardly reading them, until one caught my eye. "Prominent Socialite Found Murdered." I was vaguely aware of the name mentioned in the text, a self-proclaimed "man about town" who I'd briefly met once or twice for no particular reason, so I couldn't really say I knew the man. So far as I knew, though, his passing would be no great loss to the world at large. Getting both of my eyes into focus simultaneously, I read the article to see who'd done the city such a big favor. It was brief, just a paragraph evidently slipped into morning edition at the last moment.

Jackson Sline, well-known patron of the arts and clubman, was found dead in his bedroom in his penthouse at Sheridan Square Square in the early hours of this morning. Police report that Sline's skull was fractured and his body savaged in what was apparently a violently brutal attack. An artist's model known only as "Max" is currently being sought in connection with the murder.

The story was continued on page 12 and I flipped the paper over. I didn't read what it said because there was a photo of the suspect, the artist's model known only as "Max". It was a photo of Cleopatra Fort.

What the hell?

Chapter Four

When I got back to the Arms, the cops had come and gone and Maxine with them. I was astonished at the speed with which the police had acted, but there you are. Sometimes they're a lot more efficient than I usually give them credit for. Mrs. Fort was incoherent with shock and there wasn't much I could do with her except to get her into bed. Apparently she hadn't yet been able to get word to her son, who was still in Jersey whacking cows in happy ignorance, and no one had told her where they were taking her daughter. I told her I'd find out what I could and that seemed to calm her a little. I then went down to my own place and made a couple of calls. The first was to Dr. Finlayson, a retired MD who lived a few blocks east and who owed me a couple of favors. The second was to Chip Finney, my pal at the *Graphic*, who I'd known since he was just a publicist for Maxim Slotnik's Follies and All-Girl Revue and I was just one of the Girls.

"Morning, illiterate," I greeted when I heard his voice on the line.

"Good morning to you too, beanpole." We love each other. "I take it you must want something since I never hear from you otherwise."

"That's unfair! When was the last time I ever asked you for anything?"

"Let me think. How about the last time you called?"

"I was doing you a favor letting you take me to dinner. Think of the prestige you gained from going out with an attractive girl for a change."

"Well, if it is another free meal you are after, forget it. I'm broke."

"Tell me what you know about the Sline murder and I'll spring for lunch."

"That will be the day! What fuels this burning interest in Sline, anyway? I would hardly think you were his type."

"No interest at all, so far as I know. And what do you mean, not his type?"

"If you do not know who Sline is, then take that as a compliment. So what is the deal? You are usually not so concerned about current events."

"All I know is what I read in the paper this morning."

"What paper?"

"The *News*."

"Traitor. No wonder you do not know anything."

"Yeah. I'm real ignorant. So why don't you do something nice and educate me?"

"I have been trying to educate you for years, Slim."

"Yeah? Well, I already took biology in high school, thank you very much. Look, we can rehearse our revival of *Front Page* later. All I know about this Sline is that he got bumped off last night. You know any more than that?"

"Listen—if you are on to something, I want to know about it."

"If and when I am, you'll be the first to know."

"Uh huh, sure."

"Come on—give."

"There is not all that much to tell right now. Sline was beaten to death. Looked like someone had set out to break every bone in his body. His head was hammered clear into the carpet, which I understand had been a very nice carpet indeed. Cops think robbery was involved since his apartment was torn to pieces. A clock knocked off a table was stopped at two twelve, so they figure that is when the attack occurred. They also found a pair of wet woman's shoes and a syringe wrapped in a handkerchief that had the name 'Maxine' embroidered on it. The super remembers admitting a girl, whom he had seen there before, at around one o'clock in the a.m. on the night of the murder. As the super was going off duty, he saw Sline and a young man entering the elevator. The night man showed up late, so we have to depend on other witnesses about who came and went during the next fifteen minutes or so. About ten minutes after Sline had gone up, an artist who lives in the place was coming back from a party and saw a young man leaving the building. From the description it was the same bird the super had seen earlier. Apparently this bird seemed to be very upset, nearly running the witness down he was in such a hurry. Sometime around one forty, one forty-five, the newsie on the corner saw a young woman running from the building. He noticed her particularly because she was barefoot and coatless which seemed a little unseasonable given the current weather conditions. Sline's neighbors say they were disturbed by the sounds of a violent argument between Sline and another man over a woman named Max. The other man threatened Sline. Last I heard, only one arrest has been made. They found the girl at her place this morning. I got the address here someplace . . ."

I could hear the next part coming as the sounds of paper rustling stopped and there was what is known in literary circles as a pregnant silence. When I again heard Chip's voice, it had a cautious edge to it.

"Say, Slim, what's going on? The cops picked up this Max frail at your place."

"Don't get in a swivet. I don't know anything more about her than you do. She and her mother only moved into the Zenobia a little over a week ago."

"That is long enough for someone as nosy as you to learn everything about them back to the Flood."

"It's true. I mean, its true I don't know anything about them. Not much, anyway. I only met the kid a couple of times and the mother not at all until last night."

"Yeah, like I trust you further than I could throw you."

"You couldn't even pick me up, you puny runt, let alone throw me."

"Just give me a chance sometime and I would be most glad to give it my best shot."

"Yeah, well, bring a friend to carry you home. Who was it went in with Sline? Anyone recognize him?"

"Oh, yeah. Yeah, they got an ID on him. You will like this. It was Bill Noorvik."

What? What? What? Bill *Noorvik*? The DA had a son named Bill, from one of his several marriages, I have no idea which one.

"Not the DA's kid?"

"Yup. Met him a couple of times, a decent-enough lad, unlike his pop who is a first-class rat as we all know very well. A student at Pratt, I think, studying art or architecture or something useful like that."

Pardon? *That* Bill? Bill the would-be architect? *Max's* Bill? Couldn't be! Could it?

"Noorvik," Chip was saying, "was the reason they found the twist this morning. He had been running around the past few weeks with a girl named Max who fits the description to T. Half a dozen people knew exactly where she lived since he had made no special secret of it.

"You are awful damn quiet, Velda, which is quite unlike you. What is going on?

"I have no idea, Chip. I'll have to get back to you."

"You damn well better. You owe me."

"That's why I can't sleep nights, worrying about my debt to you."

I hung up. "What's going on?" he'd asked. It beat the hell out of me, but things were getting a little too strange to entirely suit me.

How in the world could so many people have identified Cleo as the young woman who was at Sline's apartment last night? Shoot, even *I* identified her if that photo in the paper was anything to go by. It had been of Cleo all right, there was no mistaking that. But I'd been with her all night. I knew *exactly* where she'd been from one o'clock in the morning until about an hour before her arrest. But then, there were those witnesses and that handkerchief—and her nightmare . . .

My thoughts, such as they were, were interrupted by a discrete tap at my door that I recognized as Dr. Finlayson's. I invited him in and offered him a drink. Finlayson, I knew, never took a drink before four o'clock—and it was always four o'clock somewhere on the planet. He carried a little almanac with him at all times, just to prove that this was so. It was this misuse of the international time zones that had indirectly led to the suspension of his license and to the favor I'd done for him a few years ago. Since it'd kept him from not only spending the rest of his life in prison, but from losing his license altogether—though only by the skin of his teeth—he seemed to feel that he owed me a debt. Far be it from me to argue with him. I have no problem at all with people who think they owe me something. If nothing else, it's a nice change of pace. While he sipped at his tumbler of gin, I told him what I could about the events of the previous night.

"Strange," he said after I'd finished. "I've never heard anything quite like it. I wish I could've examined the girl."

"Well, you may have your chance yet. In the meantime, think you can take a peek at the kid's mother? She's not looking so hot."

"Be my pleasure, Miss Bellinghausen. Lead the way. Onward and upward."

I delivered him to Mrs. Fort, who didn't seem to think there was anything amiss about a doctor showing up at her door with a glass of gin clenched in one shakey paw. I knew he was a damn good doctor in spite of appearances and did my best to radiate confidence like a hundred-watt bulb. She asked him if he'd like a cup of coffee and I left as he was wincing at the blasphemy.

Chapter Five

I met Chip on the front steps of police headquarters. It'd been two days since I'd talked to him. I hadn't been able to get into see Cleo. Her lawyer was some shyster the court had appointed who'd given me a runaround on the phone that I hadn't liked at all. In the meantime, I busied myself checking up on the Fort family. That was easy enough since there wasn't all that much to find out. The mother and daughter had arrived by train in late November. The lummox brother had already been working for the meat packer in Jersey for nearly a year. He'd lived in a rooming house a few blocks from where he worked until his mother and sister arrived. Mrs. Fort and Max stayed at the YWCA until they'd been able to find an apartment that Ruben could afford, which turned out to be the Zenobia. Then they all moved in together. I hadn't yet been able to find out much from Plankton Key, Florida, other than the fact that yes, indeedy, ma'am, theah shorely was a family o' Forts alivin' down heah, sho nuff. Took off foh th' big city mebbe a month ago or thereabouts and ain't heard from 'em since, no indeedy, ma'am.

"So King Noorvik's kid was running around with Cleo Fort. Is that true?"

"Yeah," Chip said. "I knew Bill had a new girl, but I had no idea who she was. Someone he had met around NYU somewhere, that is all I had heard."

"But you don't know for sure it's our Maxine?"

"Nope, but I do not know who else it could be. Sline had met her a couple of months ago—around Christmas, so far as I can tell—somewhere around the school."

"That was before she moved to the Zenobia."

"Yeah. She and her mother were still at the Y then. Bill seemed to be very much in love with her, if that means anything. I mean, really in love. I do not think I had ever heard him talk about anyone the way he talked about her. Bill, you gotta understand, is a whole nuther ball of wax from his daddy."

"The DA."

"Yeah. King Noorvik is a first-class scumball from the word go but Bill is a decent kid, go figure. Anyway, there is no doubt it was Maxine he was seeing—the girl you say is really named Cleopatra Fort. Look, that is really her name? You are not kidding me?"

"It's Cleopatra Fort all right, but she told me she prefered to be called Max or Maxine, though she never did tell me why. Just that she'd prefered it that way as long as she could remember. Like a nickname or something. Which doesn't help our case one iota. Say, I'm starving. Let's get something to eat and I'll tell you what I know, such as it is."

"Fine by me. I will gladly substitute a breakfast for that lunch you owe me."

Dammit. I was hoping he'd forgotten about that.

There's a decent lunch counter around the corner from the jail, where the bail bondsmen hang out and the cheap lawyers who hover around the courthouse looking for scraps. They all nodded sullenly at Chip as we came in, warily and resentfully, like too many carrion crows around too little road kill. We found a booth in the corner and ordered something to eat. At least I did, since I wasn't kidding when I told Chip I was starving, and asked for ham, eggs, home fries, toast and coffee. Chip distractedly picked something at random from the menu. I hoped it'd turn out to be something he'd like. I also hoped it would be something cheap.

"So . . . how you been, Velda? It has been a long time."

"Yeah." It'd been six months since the last time I'd seen him—and more than three years since we'd, well, been together. Once upon a time we'd seen a lot of each other. I'm not sure what happened, not exactly, even after all this time. I'd gotten fed up to here with the cheesy life I'd been living—bored silly, to be perfectly truthful, in much the same way I imagine a hamster must feel when it finally realizes it's just going to spin that little wheel until it drops dead. I wanted more than anything I could imagine to be doing something clean and decent and useful. I know, I know, so look what I picked for my new career. Well, my dad had been a cop and it just seemed like the thing to do, so what can I say? Chip'd been offered a job on the *Graphic's* theater section and took it without even a glance behind him. Beats me why the paper wanted him—he was no more literate than it took to write a press release for a new strip show. One day I realized we hadn't been seeing each other much any more. Then, after a while, we didn't see each other at all. It'd just happened, that's all. C'est la guerre, if that's the phrase I want.

I must've been frowning because Chip misinterpreted my expression and asked if I was worred about the Sline murder, so I told him about what happened at the Arms two nights earlier.

"See? I spent practically the whole night with the girl right there in front of me. From one o'clock, more or less, until five in the morning I was in the same room with her, holding her hand half the time, for Pete's sake. It's flat-out impossible she could have been a mile away abetting a murder. At two twelve, the time Sline was supposedly having his brains beaten out, I was taking Max's pulse, for Christ's sake."

"That is just fine and dandy so far as Max is concerned, but it does not help Bill. In fact, if she really was not there it only makes things worse for him since he is the only other suspect."

"Tough on Bill, then. I take it Noorvik had a fit when the kid was picked up?"

"Well, that is just it. That is one of the things I wanted to tell you. The cops have not found Bill Noorvik."

"What d'you mean, haven't found?"

"I mean Bill Noorvik has skipped."

"Jesus. So what's going to happen to Cleo?"

"I do not know yet. She is going to be indicted as an accessory at the very least, but I will bet you anything that Noorvik tries to pin the whole thing on her. The hearing is this afternoon. That ought to tell us more about what really happened."

"How soon can we get the details from that?"

"Immediately. We can sit in on it, if you want. It is a public hearing. I will be there for the paper."

"When's it going to be held?"

"Four o'clock."

"Then let's eat and then we'll see if we can't get in to see Max in the meantime. Or Cleo or whatever the hell her name is."

That proved to be no big deal. All the cops knew Chip and they just waved him through. They all knew me, too, but even though my dad had been a cop—and one of the best, too—I got a warier reception. They knew they owed me respect for Dad's sake, but the cops, especially the old-timers who knew Dad, never did approve of what I'd had to do to earn a living after he'd been killed. Well, the hell with them. If they hadn't turned their backs on him when he'd really needed them I'd have gotten his pension and wouldn't have had to scrounge to pay all the bills—since I didn't get anything from the insurance company either—and keep myself alive besides. Some pals Dad had. No wonder they can't look me in the face.

Max—I couldn't help but keep calling her that—was even paler than usual. She looked like a statue made of milk, if such a thing were possible. Yet for all of that she seemed strikingly beautiful. Her huge black eyes were opium brilliant and she seemed uncannily calm and in perfect control of her emotions. She was certainly aware of where she was and under what conditions. She had risen from her cot when we entered the cell. She was a head shorter than me but her slimness made her look taller than she really was. The bare lightbulb hanging from the ceiling cast sharp shadows across her chiseled face. Just for a brief moment, until she stepped back out from under the light, her face looked like a bare skull. I felt Chip suddenly stiffen and give an almost inaudible gasp. He took a half step backward, but otherwise didn't make a sound. I think he was as shocked by her appearance as I was. I'd forgotten it was the first time he'd ever seen her in the flesh.

Max came to me and I took her outstretched hands. "Oh, Velda! My mother—Ruben—do they know where I am? Do they know what I've done?"

"Calm down. This is my friend, Mr. Finney. He's one of the best reporters in town. He's going to help me get you out of here. I know you didn't do anything."

She turned toward him, her face almost phosphorescent in the dim cell. She looked like Joan of Arc interrupted in mid vision. "Why hasn't my mother come? Why hasn't anyone been here to see me? Where's Bill?"

Chip and I looked at one another and tossed a coin with our eyes. I lost.

"No one knows where Bill is, Maxie. He's gone."

"He's gone? What do you mean? He's left me to go through this alone?" I'd seen kicked puppies who looked less hurt than she did at that moment and I added another level to the hell I hoped her precious Bill would burn in.

Chip took out his notebook and changed the subject. "What is your full name, Miss Fort?" he asked, was all business-like. This matter-of-factness seemed to shake her out of her hysteria and she replied with a brave show of calmness. "Max . . . I mean, my given name is Cleo. Cleopatra Fort. But I've always liked to be called Max or Maxine since I was a little kid."

"Why is that?"

"I—it's just a name I like, that's all."

"And your mother's name?"

"It's Cleo too."

He gestured for her to sit on the cot and sitting there with her, he began his interrogation. I listened to her answers with ever-increasing horror. The girl incriminated herself with every word she uttered. It was dead clear she was trying to protect Bill Noorvik, but didn't she realize she was trading her life for someone who obviously was too cowardly to come forward and save *her*? It was pretty clear to me that whatever sterling qualities Bill might have he was an acorn that hadn't rolled very far from the tree.

"Bill wasn't there when—when it happened," she said. "I didn't see him there at all. It was—someone else. I saw it all, as plainly as

I see the two of you. Miss Bellinghausen knows I saw everything. She'll tell you so. I was there in *that* room, asleep on the bed, and someone shook me and called me an awful name and I woke up."

"Woke up in your bedroom, you mean?"

"No . . . I woke up in—that man's apartment."

"For God's sake, Cleo," I said, "do you have any idea what you're saying? You were home in your own bed. I was there, with your mother and brother and Ipheginia. I saw you. We all saw you."

"I *know* I was there in that apartment! I know I saw that, that awful thing happen. I have to tell the truth, even if I die for it. I was in that big house. I've been there dozens of times. I've been in that room, that awful room, so—so many times . . . and in other rooms, too. I'd—I'd done things there. Awful, shameful things. I could take you to see the rooms if you want me to, I know my way around them like my own home. I went there that night. I *know* I did. Mother and I were in the kitchen doing the dishes, waiting for Ruben to come home and then all of a sudden *I went*. It was just like that, in a flash I was there, and a red-headed man named Sandy let me in. He said to me, 'Don't stay Max, don't. He's not here and won't be here 'til one. Besides, you're not going to get what you're after. He told me that himself.'

"'He told you that?' I said. I was furious and I said, 'I'll kill him if he doesn't give it to me! I'll *kill* him! I ought to have killed him long before this!'

"'Go on,' the man said, 'get out of here. Go 'way before you do something you'll be sorry for. You'll never get what you want from him. Let me try an' see what I can do—but you, you get away from here.'

"'No,' I said, 'I told him I'd come and I'm here. I've kept my word and if he fails me, *so help me God I'll kill him!*'

"Then the man shook his head and took me up to that room. I took off my coat and sat down on the bed by the fireplace. My shoes were wet and I took them off so they could dry. I put them beside the fire.

"I didn't feel afraid at all. I put my hand in my purse and took something out of it. It was a syringe and I stuck the needle into my arm and pushed the little plunger. I don't know what it was, but I felt better and then it made me go to sleep. When I woke up, the man, the man I'd come to see, was shaking me and calling me awful names. His face was red and his spit flew at me as he shouted. He jerked me from the bed and started to shake me. He slapped me in the face and just then someone, another man—not Bill—someone else, came out of the shadows and with one blow of his fist—"

"Just a second, Cleo," I interrupted. "This other man, the one you say killed Sline. Who was he? Did you recognize him?"

"No—I mean, I never saw him clearly. He was just a big shadow. Just a big, black shape. I—I—whatever it was I'd injected myself with, it—I just wasn't seeing things clearly. I know it wasn't Bill though! I *know* that!"

"All right. We'll let it go for now."

"The other man hit Jackson and he fell to the floor. He was dead. His head was all crushed in and there was blood and, and awful stuff everywhere. It was just horrible. The man started kicking the body and beating at it with his fists. 'Don't kill him! Don't kill him!' I screamed and when I tried to stop him, he threw me into the corner and everthing went black. When I came to, I was all alone in the room with—with the dead man. I—I searched the apartment, but couldn't find what I'd come for.

"I couldn't think of anything else to do but get away from that place. I ran from the building, as fast as I could in the snow. I'd left my shoes in the apartment and had completely forgotten I was barefoot until I was on the street and then it was too late. I didn't dare go back. I was afraid that the man who'd killed Jackson was still there. I finally found a place to hide, a place I knew. I wanted to die . . . but I—I don't think I had the courage. I found a safe place to curl up in and I, I just went to sleep. When I awoke, Miss Bellinghausen was sitting beside me and my mother was holding my hand and Ruben was sitting in the chair in the corner of the room, asleep.

"This is true, isn't it?" she said, turning to me. "Isn't it true? But—how could it be? When I start to think too much about it, my—my head starts to burn and—and I feel myself going out of myself again, in the old way, and I try not to go, I really, really try. I know I can stop if I can only try hard enough. If I want to badly enough."

I didn't know what to make of this speech. Was she completely nuts, or what? I could only conclude that she was either totally batty . . . or was an awfully canny girl who'd concocted a pretty slick basis for an insanity plea. But what was I thinking? It was impossible for her to have been involved in the murder of Jackson Sline. However else she might be involved, however nutty she might be, she was *not* at Sline's apartment the night he was bludgeoned. She *couldn't* have been.

I glanced at Chip, wondering what he was thinking, but I got nothing from his expression.

"What were you looking for, Max," I asked, "when you went through his pockets?"

"I—I was looking for something, some clue as to where—where my baby is."

"A what? A *baby*?"

"There's a child, didn't I tell you? He took her from me. He knew I wanted her. He knew how badly I wanted her—and he promised I could have her back if I would—come to him that—that night. I remember how I felt. I'd do anything—*anything*—to get her back. If I went there and he refused me, I'd kill him. I would, without a moment's hesitation. But—but it wasn't me who killed him after all."

What the hell? I asked myself, but couldn't think of anything to answer but to say *What the hell?* again.

The indictment hearing was held in the courthouse across the street. I met Chip in the foyer and we found places in the gallery As they brought Max into the courtroom I heard Chip mutter, "Oh hell!"

"What is it?"

"I did not know who was Cleo's mouthpiece."

"It's Wilmer Flan. She couldn't afford an attorney of her own so the court appointed a lawyer for her. Why?"

"Court-appointed my eye tooth. He was hand-picked by Noorvik himself. Wilmer Flan, Esquire, is one of King's most loyal toadies. She might just as well plead guilty and get it over with as have that shyster represent her."

I watched the proceedings with an ever-increasing sense of unreality. The facts as they came out were damning . . . yet I knew,

I knew!, that Max or Cleo or whatever she wanted to call herself, was innocent. I felt as though I'd been dropped into the middle of one of those science fiction stories, the ones about alternate universes, where everything seems familiar but is really all mixed up and backwards. Where your friends are really your enemies and everything you think you know isn't true.

Alexander MacHinery, aka Sandy, the janitor of the building that held Jackson Sline's apartment, testified first. It was obvious that he was the red-headed man Cleo'd described and a chill ran down my spine at that small confirmation of her story.

Sandy described how he'd found Sline's body on the floor of his (Sline's) bedroom, beside a sofa that had been moved near the fireplace. Jackson's pockets had been rifled and drawers and cabinets had been opened and their contents spilled willy nilly everywhere. He naturally figured someone had tried to rob the place. On the hearth was a pair of woman's shoes, still wet. Near them lay a small clock that had been knocked from the mantle. It was broken, the hands frozen at two twelve. On the sofa lay a hypodermic syringe wrapped in a handkerchief on which was embroidered the name "Maxine". The only other odd thing MacHinery noticed was a man's right-hand glove lying just inside the front door.

MacHinery admitted that he'd taken a girl to Sline's apartment. Sline had told him to do so. Taking girls upstairs was hardly anything out of the ordinary, he'd done so dozens of times and at all hours of the night and he hadn't thought twice about it. MacHinery knew who she was, too, a well-known local model who'd worked for any number of Village artists, including several in the same building as Sline's penthouse. Yes, a number prominent commercial artists had their studios there and models were always coming and going. He had no idea what the girl's real name was—everyone seemed to have a different name for her, but, yes, he had heard her called "Max" or "Maxine".

At one thirty, he'd left the building for home. On his way out he'd seen Sline entering with a young man whom he recognized as Bill Noorvik. Was the girl he'd seen anywhere in the hearing room today? Yes, he said, pointing directly at Cleo, she's sitting right over there.

Next on the stand was an artist named Moldauer who maintained a studio on the floor below Sline's penthouse. On his way in he had met a highly agitated Bill Noorvik leaving the building. This was about one forty in the morning, he recalled. "He looked angry—or maybe very ill. It would be hard to say which. I suppose at the time I just figured he was drunk. Nothing unusual, I can tell you, coming from upstairs. I did notice, though, I have no idea why, that he had only one glove on. Just looked funny, I guess. Just one of those funny things you notice for no particular reason."

"Which glove was missing?" asked the coroner. "Do you remember?"

"The right one, I believe, but I wouldn't swear to it."

"Have you ever seen this girl before?" he asked, gesturing toward Cleo, who was sitting with Flan.

"Sure. Max's modeled for me many times. Not the last few months, though, not since last summer, in fact, but plenty of times before that. I'd recognize her anywhere."

The prosecutor called the witnesses who'd seen a girl leaving the apartment building sometime around one forty-five in the morning. She'd appeared, they said, to be obviously distraught and had run across the street into Sheridan Square. They wouldn't have noticed her particularly if it hadn't been for the fact that she'd been barefoot and there was at least an inch of snow on the ground.

Finally, the coroner called the doctor who'd examined Cleo after her arrest. He testified that her health appeared to be generally good, though the girl seemed to be exceptionally high-strung.

"Was there anything unusual about her?" asked the coroner. "Anything, I mean, out of the ordinary physically? Something that would make an identification positive?"

"You mean like a birthmark or tattoo?"

"Yes, something like that."

"Well, it's not something that would normally be easy to detect—that is, by someone who wasn't specifically looking for it."

"And that would be?"

"One of her feet is slightly deformed. It's smaller than the other one, nearly a full shoe size, in fact. She required a special orthopedic shoe on that foot to correct her posture and gait."

"These are the shoes found at the crime scene, Doctor. Do you notice anything unusual about them?"

"Yes. One of the shoes is noticeably smaller than the other, with a built-up sole and heel. It is obviously a correctional prosthetic."

The court found sufficient cause to indict Cleopatra Fort for first-degree murder. Her lawyer had not said a single word during the entire proceeding.

CHAPTER Six

I INTERVIEWED MRS. FORT AND RUBEN AGAIN THAT NIGHT. THE MOTHER was in another world, answering me in distracted little dollops like a vending machine dispensing jujubes. The brother, on the other hand, spent the entire hour standing in the middle of the room with his thick arms crossed, glowering blackly at me. I had no idea what his problem was—I was, after all, only trying to help his sister, but he seemed to actively resent my very presence. Well, the hell with him. I wasn't exactly enjoying the sight of the big ape myself.

Mrs. Fort didn't tell me a whole lot that was new. She did confirm Max's mismatched feet, which I was embarrassed at not having noticed while I'd chatted with her on the steps, her feet not a yard away from my nose. Mr. Hawkshaw would have been ashamed of me.

"She was born that way," Mrs. Fort said, a little defiantly, as though I were about to accuse her of something, "but it never bothered her none at all. She ran an' played just th' same as all th' other kids. No one'd even notice th' little difference 'less it was pointed out t' them."

"I never saw it myself."

"Some detective," grunted the hairy ape, but I disregarded him. He had a point, but I wasn't about to give it to him.

"Why haven't you been to see Cleo yet, Mrs. Fort?"

"Oh, I just couldn't bear it," Mrs. Fort replied, wringing her hands. They made a sound like someone crumbling dried leaves. "I just couldn't bear it. My poor little Cleo."

"'Poor little Cleo'!" snorted the brother. "You know what *I* think?"

"Surprise me," I said.

"I think she did it."

"Pardon?"

"I said I think she did it."

"Oh, Ruben!" cried his mother. "How can you say such a thing?"

"Why not? The kid's crazy, nuts, always has been. How d'*you* know where she went every day? D'you know who she hung out with, what she was doing? How d'we know she *wasn't* involved with this Sline boob?"

"Look, Kong, I was here with your sister the whole night—she was right here in front of me the whole time the murder was supposedly being committed."

"Yeah? Says who? Ma says she was asleep here in the living room. And that bimbo was out, too. There was no one in the bedroom for hours but you and Cleo. No one knows what she said in there but what you claim she said. There'd've been plenty of time for the two of you to've cooked somethin' up. And how do I know you didn't? Sline's place's less than a mile from here. You could've been there and back in plenty of time."

"Are you even more stupid than you look? Because if so, I can tell you right now I wouldn't have thought it possible."

He just sneered at me. "Sure. Insult me all you like, but it don't change nothin'. For all I know, you bumped off Sline yourself and're trying t' pin th' whole thing onna poor mental case like Cleo."

"Mrs. Fort says she's been having spells like these for years."

"So? She never had one where she said she killed no one neither."

There was no point in trying to untangle the negatives in that sentence. The man was obviously a low-level moron. I turned back to the mother.

"I'll only bother you with a few more questions, Mrs. Fort. Is

Max—Cleo—your only daughter? I mean, she hasn't got any sisters, anything like that?"

"Oh—no, no . . . I've only the two children. Ruben here, the oldest, and Cleo. Their father, Mr. Fort—Edwin—he died just before Cleo was born. He worked in a sponge-packing plant. He was a good man."

I also talked to the Schoenfelds. They would gladly testify to the disturbance on the night of the murder, but, they pointed out all too reasonably, they hadn't actually *seen* the girl, they'd just heard a lot of noise. I didn't bother with Arkady, not really being in the mood to listen to him bitch. Besides, what could he say other than that he'd heard a girl yelling? That was no proof that it'd been Cleo. Even Iphegenia wouldn't be a big help, though better the others, I had to admit. Still, she'd been asleep in the living room much of the time and, besides, I could just imagine what a prosecutor would do to a dumb little chorus girl like her. These witnesses pretty much took care of anything I hoped to get out of the Zenobia. That left Sline's place.

I knew the building, of course: an antique mansion that'd been turned into warren of big flats and lofts just off Sheridan Square, mostly given over to various artists *du jour* and assorted sports who wanted a home away from home. Sline was one of the latter and had the entire top floor, which he liked to call his "penthouse", to himself. Sandy MacHinery was no harder to find than the building was. I just went around to the back and down the outside stairs into the service area. I only had to find the warmest place in the basement, which was not surprisingly the furnace room, to locate Sandy. He was a dull-looking Scot whose entire head, with its mangy, rust-colored hair and beard, looked like something a cat coughed up and was damn glad to be rid of, too. He was slouched in an overstuffed chair someone much more discriminating than he had wisely discarded. He had been engrossed in spelling out the words in the captions of a pornographic magazine he held in one hand, while the other hand (I was relieved to see) was wrapped around the neck of a half-empty fifth of something with a mimeographed label. He blinked at me, trying to get both eyes to swing in my direction at the same time with no great success.

"Jeezus," he said, glancing back at his magazine and back to me again, with the dim idea, probably, that some bizarre fantasy he'd been entertaining had just materialized, which must surely beat the pink snakes he usually saw. I figured he'd have to be drunk to confuse me with one of those hyperpituitary holsteins.

"Mr. MacHinery?"

"Jeezus."

"Mr. MacHinery, I'd like to ask you a few questions about the night Mr. Sline was murdered. That okay?"

"Jeezus. Yeah, sure. Okay. Sure."

"It's awful hot down here. Mind if I take my coat off?"

"Jeezus."

I shrugged myself out of my coat. Beneath it I had on black capri pants, a wide red cinch belt, a red jersey sweater and the red silk scarf that Chip had given me for my birthday five years ago tied around my neck. While I was pleased that I hadn't misjudged my man, I feared that I may have overdone it, given that he looked as though he were in the first stages of a stroke or an embolism or something.

"Mr. MacHinery, are you all right?"

"Sure, sure. Jeezus, lady. Y'don't wanna oughta do that t' summun, outta th' blue like that an' all, wit' no warnin' er nothin'."

"I'm sorry, Mr. MacHinery. Do you think you could answer a couple of questions?"

"Questions? Questions 'bout what?"

"About the night Mr. Sline was murdered."

"Like t' shake th' man's hand."

"Sline's? Why?"

"Naw, not *him*. Th' one what knocked 'im off, that's who. Whoever it was did th' world a helluva favor."

"So I understand . . . but why? I mean, why's the world a happier place with Mr. Sline's presence no longer gracing it?"

"Would ya like a slug, Ma'am? Don't wanna seem a poor host er nothin'."

"No, thanks—though it looks mighty delicious." I'd sidled up closer to him, licked my lips when I said "delicious"and was delighted to see his Adam's apple bobble in response. "You were about to tell me about Mr. Sline . . ."

"What? Sline? Yeah. Real bastard he was, pardon me for bein' so frank."

"That's quite all right, Mr. MacHinery. Words like that only sound bluff and hearty and honest coming from a big ol' rough man like you."

"Uh, you c'n call me Sandy if ya like. Ev'ryone else does."

"Why, sure, Sandy. They call you that because of your red hair?"

"No, not exactly, ma'am—"

"Call me Velda." I pronounced it "Vvvellldaa" just to watch his eyes roll.

"—it's more on accounta my dandruff, ma—Velda. It's kinda chronic-like."

"Bet Mr. Sline didn't have dandruff like yours. Takes a real man to have scales like those."

"Yeah, but he got th' babes anyway, I c'n tell ya."

"Had lots of girlfriends, huh?"

"Don't know that I'd call 'em 'girlfriends', if y' get what I mean, but oh, sure, in an' outta th' place all th' time, all hours. Mosta them models f'r them artists what live here, but lotsa dames from th' burlycue—th' strip joints, you know?"

"Was the girl the police arrested a show girl, then?"

"Her? Nah! Too skinny. No meat on 'er at all. She just modeled. Never saw what them artists saw in 'er, myself. Looked like one a them magazine models—all skin an' bones. No meat to 'er. Them artists took to 'er, though, God knows why. All pansies anyway, I swear. I think that's how Sline met 'er, through one a th' artists."

"You saw her coming to the studios?"

"Sure. In an' out all th' time, *in an' out*, heh heh heh. Started comin' here, oh, I dunno, 'bout a year ago I guess."

"A year ago, huh?"

"Mebbe longer. Sure ya don't wanna drink? Cold night out fer a lady dressed like—I mean without much, I mean—"

"No thanks, Mr. MacHinery, I don't know if I could control myself if I had very much to drink, you know what I mean?"

"Uh, yeah, I think so." He licked his lips, something I found chilling to watch.

"This girl we're talking about, her name was Maxine, right? Maxie?"

"Sure, sure. In an' outta here all th' time, in an' out. Modelled fer all th' artists in th' place. Saw 'er doin' it once, too."

"Doing what?"

"Modellin'. Fella on th' third floor does calendar work, ya know. Got babes comin' in day an' night, day an' night, lucky stiff, comin' in an' out all th' time. Tol' me his sink was backin' up an' all th' girls was complainin', couldn't bear t' lookit all th' hair floatin' roun' in it. I wen' on up an' knocked all reg'lar like an' he said c'mon in an' I went on in—"

"Naturally."

"—an' there she were nekkid as th' day she was born."

"Who was?"

"This Maxine, who else?"

"You saw Maxine modeling?"

"I don' know *what* she was doin' I jus' know she was *nekkid.* Stark nekkid."

"What happened?"

"Nothin' happen'. I went an' fixed th' sink an' Maxine an' th' painter they din pay me no 'tention tall. He jus' kep' on paintin' an' she jus' kep' on . . . on . . . whatever ya call stayin' nekkid."

"When was this?"

"When? Oh, I dunno, not long after she started showin' up roun' here, I guess. Las' winter sometime, mebbe Feb'rary, mebbe March. I 'member she din look cold an' th' heat weren't on yet."

"And you're sure it was her? Maxine?"

"Sure. Too skinny for my taste—not like, not like you, fer instance—but it were her all right. See fer yourself."

"What do you mean, see for myself?"

"Th' calendar, over there on th' wall."

I turned in the direction he had waved his bottle and there, between a cold water return pipe and the main fuse box was sure enough a calendar. I went over to it. It was the usual sort of thing found in every garage and welding shop in the country. March was a girl on a sand dune who was cleverly symbolizing the month by having her skirt blown over her head by a gust of wind while a musclebound gink leered at her. Below the picture was a poem:

March is a month with too much breeze.
So I follow the sun and take my ease;
It's nice and warm beside the sea,
For the son of a steel mill follows me.

It stunk, but I didn't suppose the calendar was meant for people who normally preferred Shakespeare.

"May," Sandy wheezed. "She's May."

I flipped up a couple of the pages. There was May all right . . . and there, dammit, was Cleo. What the hell? I *knew* Maxie wasn't in New York last winter. She wasn't even in New York last *fall* . . . but there she was. Miss May. She was supposed to be on a beach, I guess, wearing only a bandana-diaper bikini and a gauzy top tied under her breasts. Her verse read:

> *Young lady doesn't favor the country.*
> *It's the city sunlight she craves;*
> *She doesn't want a home where the buffalo roam—*
> *Just one where the playboys play.*

Ugh. I looked closely at the page. It was a painting, not a photograph, I realized, but . . . The artist had fleshed her in some—she wasn't as gaunt as the Maxine I'd seen writhing on the bed a few nights ago—it was a gorgeous body, in fact: long, lissome, leggy, probably just what Cleo'd look like with a few square meals under her belt . . . but the face—the face was the same. The same black hair, the same prominent cheekbones, the same full, sensual lips, the same enormous, steel-grey eyes. There was no mistaking that face. It was Maxie all right, but a Maxie radiating a raw sensuality I'd never have dreamed she possessed. So like I said, what the hell?

"Thas 'er, that's Maxine," said Sandy. "Tol' ya. Thas 'er. Rec'nize'er anywhere."

Yeah. So would I, dammit.

"There's on'y one thing thas weird." Sandy, I noticed had finished his fifth, which surely had not been his first.

"What?"

"Th' kid."

"The kid? What kid?"

"*Maxine's* kid, what kid d'ya think?"

"What?"

"Th' kid. Maxine had a kid. A lil girl, I dunno, mebbe coupla years old. She'd bring th' kid with 'er. That day, th' one I'm tellin' you 'bout, th' kid was right there, right there in th' studio with 'em, her mother right there in front of 'er nekkid as a jaybird. Say! Where ya goin'?"

Where I had gone was to interview the artists who had studios in the building. There were three of them—two pinup painters and an "art" photographer—and every one of them had used Maxie as a model at one time or another. They all spoke highly of her and were anxious to show me work for which the girl had posed, and I was just as anxious to look at it.

The first one I talked to was a little butterball of a man, maybe sixty, sixty-five years old. His name was Lester Gint and his fringe of greying hair and gold-rimmed glasses made him look more like a banker or businessman—a solid pillar of the community and deacon of his church—instead of a pinup artist. I discovered that my first impression was not so far off. He treated his profession strictly as a business and no nonsense, no sirree. And it was a business that certainly kept him busy, I decided, when he began showing me his collection of printed work—there must have been calendars going back to the turn of the century, to say nothing of clippings from every men's magazine ever published and God knows how many advertisements. Big-time clients, too, and the magazines weren't sleazy rags, either. There was plenty of quality stuff like *Esquire* and *Pic*. And every one of them featured a spectacularly beautiful woman painted even better than lifelike.

Wow! I thought as I flipped through the big scrapbook, these are *Gint Girls!* This is *the* Gint! The Gint Girl Gint. He didn't even have to sign his work—those long-legged corn-fed all-American beauties who were his trademark were as recognizable as a Coca Cola bottle (in fact, there was a rumor that the Coke bottle had been inspired by an early Gint Girl). There were Gint Girl cosmetics, Gint Girl bathing suits (I had one myself, God knows), Gint Girl cocktail glasses, Gint Girl hood ornaments and Gint Girls in every stage of undress had sprawled across the noses of half the bombers that flew over Germany and Japan. Jesus, he was one of the most famous artists in the whole world. I smoothed my hair down while he wasn't looking and made sure I wasn't slouching, but he hardly even glanced at me, the crumb.

If Gint didn't look like I'd expected, neither did the studio. Except for a big easel off to one side of the big room, it looked more like the lobby of a very conservative insurance company, or maybe the lounge of a snooty men's club. Lots of big oriental rugs and lots of bookcases and heavy leather-covered furniture. He did offer me a sherry, which I thought was pretty elegant.

I told him I was interested in anything he could tell be about Max, the model, or Jackson Sline.

"Sline I scarcely ever saw," he said with a disdainful sniff, as though I'd just asked him if he was late taking out the garbage. "He really didn't appear to be the sort of gentleman whose company I would normally solicite or with whose associates I would have cared to mingle." He actually talked like that.

"So you never went to any of his parties?"

"I should think not. I thanked God I had a club I could retire to on the evenings Sline held his ridiculous orgies. I'd complained to the management of the building, of course, but I never really expected them to do anything. It's my understanding that Sline controls a large portion of the realty company that manages the place."

"Really? Who'd ever have thought he had so much dough? Do you have any idea where he got his money from?"

"Hardly. I never thought enough about him to ever wonder. To tell you the truth, I suspect the owner of the building overlooked Mr. Sline's—peccadilloes, shall we say?—in exchange for certain . . . favors."

"Favors? Like what?"

"I think you might be able to imagine, if you are familar, as you seem to indicate you are, with the sort of riff raff he associated with."

I suppose I did.

"Just who *is* the owner of the building, Mr. Gint?"

"King Noorvik. I'm sure you've heard of him."

"Indeed I have. Did Noorvik ever show up at any of these, um, soirées?"

"I'm sure I wouldn't know."

"How about Max, then?"

"Did she attend Sline's little soirées? I would have no idea, but I wouldn't doubt but that she did."

"She modeled for you, though?"

"Yes, indeed. She modeled for me quite often. I was quite pleased with her. She was excellent, very expressive, very sensual but very professional in every way. She appeared to take her work quite seriously. I wish I could have used her more often, but she really wasn't the, um, type most of my clients appreciate."

"I can imagine."

We chatted for a bit longer and I struck every pose I could think of, but Gint looked at me with all the interest a boa constrictor who'd had just eaten an entire pig would have in an after-dinner mint, so I thanked him for his help and moved on.

The other artist's studio took up the other half of the same floor as Gint's. His name was Roscoe L. Moldauer and was a lot more like I'd expected a pinup artist to look like. Maybe forty years old, sleek-looking, wearing a red velvet smoking jacket and a white silk cravat (really! honest to God! though it might have been rayon, I suppose). A straight-stemmed briar pipe was clenched between two rows of perfect teeth on the lip above which languished a moustache that bore a striking resemblance to one of Marlene Dietrich's eyebrows. His studio was a little more like I'd expected, too. Lots of blonde oak and indirect lighting and streamlined stainless steel-and-glass Swedish furniture that even I knew was damned expensive. Another difference was that Moldauer wasn't the least bit shy about displaying his own work and a dozen large framed paintings hung on the walls, all carefully lighted by little lamps sunk in the ceiling, just like in a museum. They were no big surprise, either—he was no Gint, but it was good, competent pinup work. They were the real thing, too. Cheesecake, but very high-toned. It was all pretty impressive, but the girls in the pictures made me feel even more inadequate than Gint's did. I told myself that the important thing was that he was the artist who had done the art for the calendar Sandy'd shown me and I tried to keep my mind on that.

Moldauer certainly showed me a lot more attention than Gint had done. He didn't just offer me a little glass thimble of sherry, he offered me a whole grown-up martini. I accepted it gladly because it was nice to have a martini in a real martini glass for a change, with an olive and everything, just like in the pictures. When he handed it to me, I noticed that the olive had been skewered by a little plastic stick with a naked girl on the end of it. That settled the *deja vu* I'd been undergoing since first walking into his place. I knew right then what Moldauer's apartment had reminded me of: a cocktail lounge. It just lacked a guy in a tuxedo playing "Smoke Gets In Your Eyes" on the piano over in the corner. Moldauer made up for that by putting some pretty nice jazz on his combination radio-phonograph console. It was blonde oak, too.

I'd let Moldauer take my coat and so of course it was some time before I could get him to focus on the reason I was there. I suppose his reaction was not noticeably different from Sandy's. I mean, I do look good in capris and a sweater, if I do say so myself. Moldauer's drooling was a little creepy, though—I almost prefered Gint's bland indifference—but I figured if it kept him off guard it was probably worth while. He would answer my questions long before they registered in his brain, which might be a good thing. I let him follow me all around the room as I gazed with feigned admiration at his work, using my best runway walk and ignoring his every effort to turn the conversation to the subject in which he was obviously most interested. It was fun, but he finally put his hands on his hips and said with no little exasperation, "Well, Miss Bellinghausen, suppose you tell me then just why you *are* here?"

So I told him.

As I'd figured from my first impression, Moldauer'd not missed any of Sline's parties if he could possibly have avoided it.

"Ol' Sline wouldn't fool around," he said. "When he threw a party he threw it into the next county."

"So I heard. What sorts of things'd go on up there?"

"What *didn't* go on, you mean? You name it, Sline had it or did it or could get it. Jeez, but I'm going to miss him. Why would anyone want to kill a swell guy like that?"

"I couldn't begin to imagine. All that must've cost a bundle—this place, the way he entertained—where'd he get his money?"

"How would I know? I certainly never asked. Never even *occured* to me to ask, for that matter. Wouldn't have been very neighborly to get real nosy—looking at the old gift horse's tonsils, you know?"

"Who went to these things?"

"Who didn't?" His style of answering my questions was beginning to annoy me. But then, everything about Moldauer was beginning to annoy me. "Everyone in the Village. All the poets and musicians and writers anyone was talking about and, of course, all the best artists. And models and showgirls, naturally, plenty of 'em. Say . . . *that's* why you look so familiar! I couldn't figure it for the longest time. Didn't you used to be—?"

"No. Did Maxine ever go to these parties?"

"Did she! And how! You wouldn't think she'd be much to look at when you first met her—I mean, she's no Mamie van Doren, God knows—but she sure knew what to do with what she had, and how. She looked like a mouse most of the time—I mean, she'd show up here for a modeling session dressed like someone straight off the boat, but Jesus, once she got her clothes off . . . bodda boom! There sure was something about her. I mean, it wasn't the *way* she posed, she didn't do anything any of the other girls hadn't done a million times, but I tell you there sure was something extra. I dunno what. I can tell you, though, if I could of caught even a tenth of what she had on canvas I could of been bigger than Gint."

"Was Gint able to . . . to express this, um, quality of Max's?"

"Him? Ha! Hardly. Are you kidding? He hasn't done anything new or original since the WPA stopped handing out post office jobs. Instead of seeing that ten-thousand-horsepower sexuality of Maxie's, he just turned her into one more of his damned patented Gint Girls."

"Did you know Max well?"

"I only wish." He slumped into a curvy Soren Hansen chair and gazed wistfully into his martini. "I only wish. But no, she flitted in and out of here like a, like a will-o-the-wisp. Never even found out where she lived. I don't think anyone knew that."

At my urging he pulled out the original painting of May that was in the calendar I'd seen in the basement. It was about two and a half times the size of the calendar page and the colors were so clear and brilliant they were like an electric current. No, I take that back—what hit you with 110 volts of household current was the intensity of Max's sexuality. The picture could have been done with Crayolas and she still would've had it. Jesus, she made me feel like a turnip.

And you could see how she'd drawn something out of Moldauer that I bet he'd never suspected he even had. No wonder the girl drove him crazy. When I compared his painting of Max to those of the other girls in the calendar . . . well, it was like comparing the Mona Lisa with "Little Lulu". She'd obviously inspired him. I think Moldauer knew this, too—knew that he'd seen his one and only greatness come and go just like *that*.

Moldauer talked me into another martini while he showed me some of his other drawings and paintings of Max. The girl in his and Gint's artwork was undeniably Max, but an idealized Max, one made to fit the expectations of the artists' publishers, so I had to discount any minor discrepancies between the two impressions. These guys weren't police artists, after all. The photographer on the next floor, on the other hand, I was much more interested in.

It took another fifteen minutes to tear myself away from Moldauer. When he realized I was going to leave, he turned up his charm to "kill" and did his damnedest to get me to stay. And to tell you the truth, I really thought about it. I mean, wouldn't it be great to be in a calendar? I'd never had my picture painted by a real artist before and the idea was awfully attractive. I just wish Moldauer had been, too.

I took his card with me, anyway.

The photographer's name was Chester Conklin and he'd come east from LA only two years earlier. He'd gotten a pretty good reputation shooting classy publicity photos of movie stars, but got sick and tired of being called the "second Hurrell". He was interested in pursuing more creative stuff, he said, and since there wasn't much call for that kind of thing in Hollywood, figured the New York gallery scene'd be more amenable to his work. It was. He had photos in half a dozen toney galleries and even one in the Museum of Modern Art, which I have to admit even I thought was pretty impressive. He did a lot of magazine work, too, stuff for *Vogue* and *Bazaar* and other equally high-toned outfits.

Conklin was a nice enough fellow—something of a cross between Gint and Moldauer, the best features of both taking the edge off the worst. A smallish, slender man, about thirty-five or forty, dressed with a kind of casual indifference that looked good on him. No three piece suit, no smoking jacket and cravat—just an old cardigan sweater, a flannel shirt and a pair of rumpled trousers and rope sandals. He reminded me a little of John Garfield and I liked him right off. He took me pretty much as I was, with neither Gint's snooty disinterest nor Moldauer's randy lust, and I liked that, too.

Like Conklin himself, his place was neither pretentious nor overtly arty. It was just a vast room that'd been subdivided into separate areas by a clever arrangement of the furnishings and judicious lighting—the whole place wasn't lit, just pools of light here and there, like islands. Conklin was neither so snobbish that he offered me a sherry nor so obvious as to hand me a martini—but instead just asked me if I wanted anything to drink and if so, what. I didn't really want anything after the stiff drink I'd just had at Moldauer's, but asked if he might have a Pabst on hand, just to be sociable. I thought a relaxed atmosphere would be more conducive to conversation. He surprised me by coming back from the corner he used for a kitchen with a bottle of beer—and a Blue Ribbon, too! Handing it to me, he invited me to sit in what passed for his "living room", which was just a half dozen plain but comfortable sofas and chairs arranged in a square around a low glass-topped coffee table. When you were sitting in one of them you were hardly aware of the rest of the studio. I was impressed when Conklin didn't automatically sit beside me but instead took a place on the other side of the table.

"I only used Max as a model a couple of times," he told me. "I was a newcomer to the Village art scene and I didn't know who the good models were—I mean, the kind of models I wanted to use. It's easy for the guys downstairs to find them—half the showgirls in town are dying to take the clothes off for some spare cash—but they're not what I'm looking for. There's nothing, well, subtle about them, if you understand what I mean."

"Yeah, I think I do. When you've seen them once you've seen all there is to see."

"Exactly, and I'm usually sorry I saw them the first time. There's more to taking a photograph of a woman than just dumping a hundred pounds of flesh in front of the camera. The model's got to have something that goes beyond her mere carnal existence. When that happens, when you get that special combination—well, then you have something."

"I take it Max was like that?"

"Indeed. Here, let me show you."

He got up, went to some dark corner of the studio and after a few moments brought back a large black portfolio—a spiral-bound thing with big cellophane sleeves in it. Placing it on the table between us he opened it to reveal a dozen or more black and white photos, one to a page. They were big prints, big as a magazine page, and they were good, real good, a lot more artistic than what the two painters did, even I could tell that. All shadows and strange angles—sometimes you could hardly even tell it was a nude woman you were looking at—but for all of that, a hell of a lot more erotic than any of the other boys' pinups. The last picture anyone'd taken of me had been glued to a big cardboard cutout in front of a ticket booth. I found myself wondering what I'd look like in one of Conklin's photos.

"Here's the best portrait," he said, turning to the last page. "It was the last photo I ever took of her."

I got up and took the portfolio over to a window and looked closely at the face in the photo he'd turned to, trying to find any differences between it and the one I'd seen on the girl in the cell downtown. There was no difference. It was the same face down to the last eyelash. The same jet-black hair, the same enormous eyes. Unmistakable. The body maybe wasn't as gaunt as the Max I'd seen writhing on the bed. The figure was a little fuller, a little sleeker—but the photos had been taken months ago so that proved nothing, even if I knew what I'd been hoping to prove. Just before I closed the book, I remembered what Max had said about her feet, about one being smaller, a little deformedk, so I flipped through the rest of the book. Half a dozen of the remaining photos were full-figure, so I took a good look at the feet in them. A felt a chill go down my back like my spine was a harp string someone had just twanged. The feet of the girl in the photos didn't match. One was a little smaller, a little twisted-looking maybe, not quite right. Not enough that you'd particularly notice if you weren't actually looking for it, but there it was. Damn it.

"When was the last time you saw Max?" I asked.

"Oh . . . hmm . . . it's been a while, now that I think of it. Six months. Maybe as much as a year. No more than that. At least, that is, since she last modeled for me. She may have been modeling for somebody else in the meantime. I'd have no way of knowing that."

"I'll ask around and see."

"Say, ah, Miss Bellinghausen . . ."

"Mm?" I closed the portfolio and looked up at Conklin, who was leaning against the wall, staring at me with an oddly appraising expression, like he was trying to decide whether or not to buy the new car the salesman had just pitched him.

"I was wondering . . . You've modeled before, haven't you?"

"Me? Well—not exactly."

"Really? I was sure you must have at some time. The way you carry yourself, you know. And you have—well, you have a, um, a unique look. It's quite different. I'm amazed that someone hasn't taken advantage of it before."

"Oh, people have tried to take advantage, no fear there."

"No—" and damn me if he didn't look embarrassed! "I mean—well, I hope you don't take offense, this is really just a professional opinion you understand, but I think you'd make a sensational model."

I raised my right eyebrow as far as it would go.

"No, really. I take it that neither of those two hacks downstairs looked at you twice? They didn't ask you to pose for them?"

I didn't tell him that Moldauer was interested in me all right, but instead said: "Hacks they may be, but they're obviously not fools. They're pinup artists, remember? Do I *look* like a pinup?"

"No, you don't, but that's *exactly* my point."

"Hm. Well, look here, Mr. Conklin—"

"Chester, please—"

"Yes, well, Chester, look—"

"No need to say anything now. It's just a suggestion. Think about it and let me know sometime if you're interested. We'll do some test shots. I think you might be surprised. We could do some very interesting things together."

"Um. Well. Yes, I'm sure. Um, yes. Well, look, Mr.—Chester. I really appreciate your time, and letting me look through these photos. Which are really very excellent, too, I might add."

"And?"

"And? Oh. Well . . . well, I'll just have to let you know."

"Well, I hope you'll agree. You have such wonderful facial planes. Just how tall are you, anyway, if you don't mind me asking? You look like you must be at least five-eleven."

"I'm six feet even, in my stocking feet. Look, I was wondering. About those photos—I mean the photos of Max Fort. You wouldn't have one I could take with me, do you? It'd be a big help, it really would."

He said, sure, there were some rejected prints. He'd been cleaning out the files recently, but hadn't yet discarded the test prints from his last session with Max. If I wanted one of them, I'd be welcome to it. He found a manila envelope full of photos and I chose one of the full-figure shots. It featured her face clearly as well as the mismatched feet. Conklin scribbled his name on the back of the print and when he handed it to me he included one of his cards.

"Give what I said some thought, Miss Bellinghausen. Please. Call me anytime and we'll talk about it."

I said sure, I'll do that, as I slipped the photo into my bag, but I was just being polite. Me a *art* model. Right. I only wished.

About Max herself, Conklin hadn't been able to tell me much more than the others had. She had been a quiet girl, friendly enough but reticent about talking about herself. Still, what few comments she let drop during the time she worked for the photographer allowed me to piece together the history of the person I was beginning to think of as "the other Max". She'd begun life in the gutter. At ten she was living off trash in the Jewish quarter. At twelve she was haunting stage doors and studios. At fifteen she had been convicted of theft and sentenced to a juvenile home somewhere upstate. At seventeen she'd become a mother. Everyone in the building assumed the father was Sline and the girl never denied it.

A far cry from what I knew about *my* Max, about Cleo. But who was this "other" Max? Was she real, or was she a product of Cleo's imagination?

So now I figured I had someone else to find besides this other Max. I needed to find her kid, too. Jesus, doesn't that figure? I hate kids.

Chapter Seven

I HAD BREAKFAST WITH CHIP THE NEXT MORNING IN THE LITTLE CAFeteria in the basement of the *Graphic* building. His treat, thank God. In exchange, I told him what little I'd learned so far about Max.

"A kid, huh?"

"Yeah. And where's this kid, now? That's what I'd like to know."

"It is a very big city, as we both know all too well."

"This thing's getting weirder every minute, you know? All I've succeeded in doing so far is making the positive ID of Maxie even more positive. It *had* to've been her that night in Sline's apartment . . . but *how*? I was sitting there in her own bedroom right beside her the whole night—I was practically holding her hand, in fact I *was* holding her hand. I might believe there's a lookalike running around the city, a twin maybe, or something like that, but what about the handkerchief with her name on it? And what about that foot? Two people might look alike, but not down to a deformed foot, for God's sake. And there's that dream, or whatever it was. She *knew* what was going on at Sline's pad. I just don't get it."

"Well, the idea of a lookalike is not so bad. I mean, to tell you the truth, Cleo looks a little like a young version of you, in a way. I mean, she could be your kid sister or something. If you were her age you might look a lot alike, I am thinking."

"You're nuts," I said, mainly because he was right. It'd nagged me vaguely from the very start that Cleo looked somehow familiar. Well no wonder. I saw an older version of her every day in the mirror. Or, on the contrary, every time I saw her I saw what I might have looked like in a concentration camp. But it was just a resemblance between us—we weren't twins by a long shot. We were both tall, slender and black-haired, but that's pretty much where it ended. People might think we were sisters, but twins, never.

"Be that as it may, I have been looking into the affairs of our friend Bill Noorvik. At least I have been trying to."

"What d'you mean?"

"I mean I have been stonewalled at every turn."

"Stonewalled?"

"Yup. Someone has been doing their damnedest to keep his name out of this whole affair and I will give you one guess who."

"Could the initials be King Noorvik?"

"A kewpie doll for the lovely lady."

"Well, he's got his eye firmly glued on the mayor's office, so I can imagine that he'd be pretty skittish about the possibility of scandal . . . and having his son involved in a murder would seem to be sufficiently scandalous."

"Even if it turns out that the kid had nothing to do with it, his name would still be involved."

"The guy's got his finger into every mob pie in the city and *he's* worried about who his son is hanging out with."

"Yeah, well, you know he is on the take and I know he is on the take, but so long as the public don't know he is on the take, who cares? He is a charmer and he has got a fabulous conviction record as DA, the best in decades—though no one seems to notice, or care, that while he is the angel of death to every two-bit punk, mugger and pickpocket, that while he will send some poor sap who bludgeoned his brother-in-law to the chair or some frazzled, frustrated housewife who chopped up her abusive hubby with the electric carving knive, Noorvik has never given serious time to anyone connected to any of his, um, special interests. Light sentences or dismissals or acquittals, that is all those hoods need worry about so long as King Noorvik is DA. Imagine what things will be like if—when—he gets to be mayor."

"The mind boggles."

"So the point is: to the public he is a squeaky clean champion of truth, justice and the American way. His son's name gets attached to a murder case and there is nothing he can do to cover that up—even if he could, it would be too late. The damage would be done."

"Bill his only kid?"

"Yeah, and decent-enough, too, which is very surprising. Planning to be an architect and doing pretty damn well, so I understand."

"His mother's dead, right?"

"Yeah. Beautiful woman, too, according to the morgue photos, but took a powder just after Bill was born. Just flat out disappeared, what? seventeen, eighteen years ago? Story was she had a nervous breakdown, but I do not know how true that is."

"I can't imagine a man like King taking that very well."

"The understatement of the century, my love. He was in private practice then, this was just before he started in politics, and he just about went berserk. Had detectives combing the whole country for her, I guess, but nothing ever turned up so far as I know, anyway."

"So you figure she's dead, huh?"

"Dead or living in a cave in Outer Slobbovia. Either way, the upshot is the same. Seven years later to the day, Noorvik had her declared legally deceased. End of story."

"End of story. What was her name?"

"Georgia."

"Georgia? Suhthun gal?"

"Yup, though funny enough she was not from Georgia. She was from Florida. That's where they met, you know: when Noorvik was a law student in Tallahassee."

Well, well!

For the life of me I couldn't figure out why I was getting so involved in Cleo's case. No one had asked me to and I sure wasn't going to get a nickel out of it and I was plenty in need for nickels right about then, I can tell you. So why was I getting so involved? It beats me. I guess, if I had to come up with some reason, I suppose it was Cleo herself. No one could take so much as one look at her without seeing what a sweet girl she really was. And I mean that: she was sweet in the very best sense of the word. Not cloying and sentimental and gushing, not like some drippy little Doris Day with lacy underpants, but just an honest, wide-eyed naïvete that was as refreshing as . . . I don't know. I'm starting to sound like a soft drink commercial. But there it is. It was like when you see someone kicking a puppy. You just don't let them keep on doing that, or at least I hope you wouldn't. Well it was like that, I guess. The world was kicking Maxie Fort in the teeth and I just couldn't stand by and watch, you know what I mean?

And . . . maybe, now that I think of it, maybe there was something to what Chip said. Maybe I *did* see something of myself in Cleo and there were sure things about my life that I'd hate to see the girl go through. Once was enough. Maybe I saw a chance to do things over again but this time right, by proxy. Beats the hell out of me. I mean, who am I? Sigmund Freud?

So what to do, what to do? I had to find the kid, I knew that, but how? Where? Then it occured to me . . . *Cleo*. Cleo herself. She knew what this, this *other self* of hers was doing. Maybe all I had to do was ask her. Maybe it'd be as simple as that.

I went to visit Cleo the next morning, getting in by lying my head off to a desk clerk who couldn't have cared less, apparently not being privy yet to Flan's injunction. The girl seemed glad to see me, but I was shocked at the sight of her. She looked awful. I mean, she had never looked really well, but there was something terribly, awfully different now. When the matron led her into the visiting room, she had to keep a firm hold on one of the girl's arms to keep her from stumbling. She fell like a ragdoll into the chair opposite me, her short black hair lank and lusterless, her big eyes dull and sunken into blue-grey sockets.

"Hi, Velda."

"Howya doin', Max?"

"Fine, I guess. I haven't been feeling so hot lately, though."

"Doctor been to see you?"

"Yeah, but he just gave me some aspirins. I think he thinks I've only got a cold or something."

"Well, take care of yourself. You don't look so hot. How've they been treating you otherwise. Okay?"

"Yeah, I guess so. The matron's been nice."

"Been eating all right?"

"Yeah. The food's pretty good, really."

"Mom been in?"

"Yeah. She comes by every day now, almost. That's nice. Velda . . . have you heard anything from Bill yet? Do you know where he is? Something must've happened to him, I'm sure of it. It's the only way he'd not come for me. He . . . he loves me, Velda."

"I know, I know. Everyone's doing the best they can, Cleo. You've got to trust that."

"I guess so."

"Still having your . . . spells?"

"Yeah. One or two. They've just about stopped though. The doctor's been giving me medicine that helps me sleep."

"Tell me, Maxie . . . do any of your spells, have any of them ever had anything to do with a child, a little girl?"

"Why, yes, Velda! Yes. How'd you know that?"

"Remember, I'm the master detective. Look, Maxie, this is important. This little girl in your spells, do you know her name?"

"Her name? Sure. It's Jackie."

"Jackie? You're certain? Her name is Jackie?"

"Uh huh. Of course I'm sure. She's . . . my daughter. Jackie. It's short for Jacqueline."

"Do you know where she is now?"

"No . . . no, I don't. I, I really miss her . . ."

"Maxie . . . look at me. *Do* you have a daughter?"

"No. No—Yes. I . . . I don't know. I don't know. *She* does, though. *She* has a daughter."

"Who is 'she', Maxie?

"*Me*, Velda. She's me."

I told Chip about my talk with Maxie. He chastised me for sneaking in to see her, which I of course ignored, and concluded that she was just plain nuts. "I think she is going to try to cop an insanity plea," he said. "I can not think of any other reason for such a lunatic story, though to give her credit it is a dilly."

"Maybe she *is* nuts, but who am I to be calling anyone nuts?

Who're you, for that matter? The bottom line is that whoever or whatever Max is, we *know* there's a kid. She's not something Max dreamed up, other people saw her, saw them together. The kid's real."

"Yeah, but so what? The kid has got nothing to do with why Max is charged with murder. The kid was not there, she is not a witness. She is what the shysters call irrelevant. Whether the kid exists or not proves nothing one way or the other."

"I know. But I don't think the kid has anything to do with Max, our Max, I mean—Cleo. That's the whole point."

"What point?"

"Look, Einstein. I don't think Cleo had anything to do with the killing. I think someone else did it, someone who looks enough like Cleo to fool all the witnesses. The kid, this Jackie, belongs to this other Cleo, this Max. We find the kid, we find her. Or, at the very least, we find the kid and she'll at least tell us that our Cleo isn't her mother."

"So how do you explain the fact that Max knows about the kid? How do you explain the odd foot? How do you explain how she knows so much about the murder? Jesus, Velda, she has all but confessed to it."

"How am I supposed to know?"

"There's one more thing and you're not going to like it."

"What?"

"The cops found the place that made the shoes."

"The shoes?"

"The pair of shoes that were left in Sline's apartment. They found the place that made them, a little shop on Amelia Street, specializes in shoes for gimps. Just one old man, makes everything himself by hand yet. He recognized the shoes right off as his work and when the DA showed him a photo of Cleo, he identified her right off, too. And he also tells them that not only did she order those shoes, she has been buying special shoes from him for years."

"Dammit to hell, Chip. What's going on? Cleo's not been out of Florida her whole life, not until she got here last Fall. Did you call the county registrar's office down in Plankton, like I asked you?"

"About the birth records? Sure. And I will be glad when you

can afford to handle your own cases, Velda, instead of foisting your bills onto the paper."

"This isn't a case, Chip. I'm not making any money off it."

"So how is that any different than any other case you have had? You do not even subscribe to the paper, for Pete's sake, you read it free at Joe's."

"Give me a break. You'd've called the registrar anyway for the sake of your story, so just lay off me about it."

"Yeah, well—it would still be a very nice surprise indeed when you start doing your own leg work."

"You never had any problems with my legs before. So consider me chastened, boo hoo. So what did you find out?"

"Nothing Mrs. Fort has not told you already. Ruben was born Ruben Ananias Fort in the town of Plankton, Pine Barren County, Florida, twenty-eight years ago. The only other child was a girl, named Cleopatra Fort, born nineteen and a half years ago at three-fifteen on the morning of August third. Father of both was Edwin Q. Fort, sponge packer, currently deceased. That is all."

"I was figuring on a sister, something like that."

"I know you were. But there is just her and Ruben. No more, no less."

Damn.

I checked my answering service when I got back to my place. The operator who watches my line is a girl named Sally Forth. We've gotten to be friends over the last couple of years even though we've never met face to face. Although I'm probably doing her an injustice, I picture her as being aggressively blonde and composed primarily of bubbles, like a foam rubber pillow. I'd instructed her to ignore anyone wanting money, which usually serves to eliminate any messages at all, so I was surprised to find she had one for me that I was actually interested in hearing about.

"A Mr. Conklin called, Velda. He sounded nice."

"Uh huh. He's nice all right. A photographer who wants me to model nude for him."

"*Really*? Are you going to do it?"

"Sally! What kind of girl do you think I am? Never mind. I

know what kind of girl you think I am and what's worse is you're probably right. Was that all he wanted?"

"I would have thought that'd be enough. But, no, he also said he remembered something about some girl, the one you were asking about, he said."

"Yeah?"

"Yeah. He said he remembered something about her kid."

"What was it, did he say?"

"He wouldn't tell me. He wanted you to call him back, natch. You got his number?"

"Yeah. I got his card."

"Say, Velda, this guy legit?"

"The photographer? Yeah, I guess he is. His stuff's in a lot of pretty posh museums, galleries, things like that. Places even I've heard of. He seemed okay. Why?"

"Lemme have his number, will you? This job don't pay but peanuts. I need some extra dough. I'm not so bad-looking, I'm really not. Fellows are all the time telling me I oughta be in magazines."

"Sure, Sally, why not?" I gave her the number, what the hell. "Wait 'til tomorrow to call him, though, okay?"

"Yeah, sure, thanks, Velda! You're a brick!"

I fingered the hook, got a tone and dialed Conklin's number. He picked it up on the second ring.

"Conklin."

"Bellinghausen."

"Who?"

"Velda. I talked to you the other day . . ."

"Of course! *Velda!* Of course I remember you. You've been thinking over what I suggested?"

"Well, no, not exactly. I was wondering what you remembered about Max?"

"Max? Oh. Yeah, well—I remembered a little thing. It's not much but, I figure, I've always heard that no clue is too small."

"Well, one never knows, you know."

"You like to stop by? I'll be here all day. I could tell you what I remembered and maybe we could talk things over, maybe have coffee or a little bite . . ."

"Well, I'll tell you, Chester, that sounds swell, it really does, but my dance card's pretty full today. How's about you tell me now what you remembered about Maxie and I promise I'll come by as soon as I can?"

"So long's you mean that, Velda—"

"Yeah, sure."

"Well. It's not much, like I said, but you know Max brought her kid with her almost every time she modeled? Cute little girl, too, maybe two years old, three, thereabouts. I didn't mind if Max didn't. The kid was quiet, never said a word, just sat in a corner by herself looking at picture books, fooling with a doll, kid things like that. No problem. Well, one day Maxie shows up without the kid. It kind of surprised me, so I asked, 'Little girl not sick today, I hope?' and she just looked at me for a second and I thought she wasn't going to say anything like she usually did when I asked her something personal and then she said, 'She's with Maggie today'."

"Maggie?"

"That's it. That's all she said. 'She's with Maggie today'. She got undressed, took a pose and didn't say much of anything else the rest of the morning."

"She didn't say Maggie who?"

"Nope. Not another word about her. Just 'she's with Maggie'."

"Well, thanks. I really appreciate this."

"Think it'll help any?"

"I don't know yet. I hope so."

"So . . . when do you think you might be able to come by? I mean, no pressure or anything, whenever it's convenient for you. Maybe we could try some face shots for starters, tests, just to see how you photograph. How you light. I've got a new panchromatic film here I'm anxious to try out. . . I'd think you'd look terrific in black and white."

"I'll call you, Chester, as soon as I can. I promise. I really do."

"All right then. I appreciate that. I don't want you feel pressured."

"Not at all. I'll call you soon, promise." And, you know, I think I really meant it.

So the person I'd been thinking of now as "the other Max" had a daughter named Jackie *and* a friend named Maggie. That was something, but what? What could I do with those scraps of information, if they even *were* information? Well, I had an idea, which was a start at any rate. I glanced at my watch. It was only four o'clock, still time to get an ad in the personal section of the *Graphic* and maybe some of the other papers as well if I was quick about it. I called three of them and placed the same notice in each: "Maggie. Call Excelsior 1506. Maxie misses Jackie."

It was two days before the ad payed off. In the meantime I'd bullshitted my way into see Cleo twice and she looked worse with each visit. I talked to the police doctor and he had no idea what was wrong with her, though I suspect he didn't really care very much either. It took some finagling and bullying—and the laying on of plenty of guilt on cops who used to work with my dad—the ones who hadn't deliberately screwed him that is, the others probably couldn't even spell the word guilty so why bother—but I was finally able to get permission for Dr. Finlayson to see Cleo. He had to examine her in the cell with a matron watching, but that was okay, she was a right old bird. Cleo's court-appointed lawyer was there, too, glowering like a petulant schoolboy, so it was quite a crowd. Flan hated the fact that we'd gotten around him by having Max herself request Finlayson in writing and there wasn't a damn thing he could do about it.

Poor Cleo looked like hell. She barely stirred from her cot, only moving when Finlayson asked her to. The matron had the decency to look concerned, but the lawyer never did much more than fidget and look at his watch. Finlayson could have sawed Cleo's head off and I don't think Flan would have raised a finger to stop him.

"Are you quite finished?" he said as soon as he saw the doctor rise and start packing his instruments back into his bag.

"Yes, I think so. For the time being anyway."

"All right then, let's get out of here. Matron, I believe we're finished with the prisoner."

The matron, who knew an asshole when she saw one, bored holes into the back of Flan's head with her glare as she locked the cell door behind us.

"You understand," Flan said, "the both you, that the results of this examination are absolutely confidential?"

"Of course!" replied Finlayson, mustering all of his considerable dignity. When at his best he looks positively Shakespearean.

"I know that you—" he was pointing at me now "—are in tight with some of the *Graphic* crowd. If one word of this exam leaks to that rag I'll not only have your license pulled, I'll have you up for charges. Understand?"

"Oh, my, yes sir, indeed I do, sir!" I batted my eyes at him ingenuously, but I don't think it made a very good impression. Flan just glared at me and turned his sneer onto Finlayson.

"So, *Doctor*. What's your opinion, then? What's wrong with the girl?"

"It's hard to tell . . . malnourishment, certainly, though I'm told that she eats most of her meals. I'm going to request that the warden transfer her to the prison infirmary, where she can get better care. But that's not the half of it. I'd say that most of her symptoms would seem to be those of someone suffering from exposure."

"Exposure?"

"Yes, dehydration among other things, but, well, hypothermia primarily."

"Hypo what?"

"Hypothermia. She's slowly freezing to death."

The lawyer glared at the doctor for a moment, like a surly drunk in a nightclub who'd just realized he'd missed the comedian's big punch line.

"You're not being very funny, doctor, and if you're serious, then you're as mad as she is."

I walked with the doctor most of the way back to my apartment. The cold was bitter, but I needed to think. Snow was drifting through the streets and the air was filled with flurries of hard little pellets that stung like bits of broken glass. I thought about what he'd said about Maxie freezing to death. I asked him if he was sure about his diagnosis.

"As sure as I can be, Velda. Might be a lot of other things, but it certainly looks like hypothermia to me . . . along with, as I said, malnutrition, dehydration and a general malaise. I certainly don't think there's anything organically wrong with her. Nothing disease-related, that is."

"But her cell's not cold. Far from it. If anything, the place is too warm by half."

"I agree. The conditions don't match her symptoms, but there you are. Her condition speaks for itself."

"Yup. There I am, all right. Let's take a cab the rest of the way. I'm hypothermizing now, myself."

When I got back to my place, after dropping the doctor off, I put some water on to boil for coffee and called Sally to check my messages.

"Hey Velda! You know what?"

"Probably not."

"I called that photographer friend of yours, that Conklin guy, and guess what?"

"What? You're going to be cover girl on the next *Field and Stream*?"

"Naw, silly! I got an appointment to test with him next Tuesday. Whattaya think of that? Maybe this is the break I need to finally get untied from this damn switchboard."

"Well, I certainly hope so."

"Me, too. Oh! Say! I almost forgot . . . you got a message from someone."

"Yeah?"

"It was an answer to some newspaper ad you ran. Hold on a sec . . . here it is."

"Was it a man or woman?"

"Woman. Nice voice, kinda low and husky, like Lauren Bacall, you know?"

"She leave a name?"

"Nope, just a phone number. Got a pencil? Okay, here it is: Arsenal five three two four. Got it?"

"Five three two four. Yup. Thanks a load, Sally."

"No sweat, kiddo."

The Arsenal exchange included the Bowery. Not all that far from my place. I dialed the number and waited. It rang seven, eight, nine, ten times and I was about to hang up when I heard a woman's voice say, cautiously I thought, "Yes?" She sounded like Lauren Bacall all right so I knew at once it was the person who'd left the message. I thought I detected a slight accent of some sort, or maybe not so much an accent as that careful way of pronunciation people have who haven't spoken English all their lives, or who maybe haven't always lived with English speakers.

"This is Velda Bellinghausen. You left a message for me?"

"Are you the person who ran the ad? The one about . . . Jackie?"

"Yes. Are you Maggie?"

"What do you know about Jackie?"

"I know she's Max's daughter and that Max wants to see her."

"Who are you?"

"I'm a private detective. I've been helping Max. She's in a lot of trouble. I don't know if you know that."

"Yes. I've been reading the papers."

"She's going to be tried for murder."

"I know."

"She wants to see Jackie."

"All right. Where do you want to meet?"

"Anywhere you like. Do you want to come here? Or I can come wherever you are."

"No, I'd rather meet someplace else."

"You know the diner at the corner of Pith and Wellspring? Joe's place?"

"Um—yes. I think so. Across from the tobacco shop? I can be there in forty-five minutes. Will that be all right?"

"It'll be perfect."

“How’ll I know you?”

“Look for a tall woman wearing a long camel coat and a red head scarf.”

“In forty-five minutes, then.” She hung up.

Well, well! I had a good half hour before I had to leave, so I made myself a sandwich and gulped it down with the coffee. Then I made a couple of phone calls. Things were going places now! Hot dog!

The woman arrived at almost the same time I did, though I spotted her first. She was small (though it’s hard for me to judge such things, since most people look small to me), with a slim figure, so far as I could tell under her overcoat, dark hair, olive skin. Her face was oval, with dark, almond-shaped eyes. She was young—no more than twenty, I guessed. Her looks and vaguely slinky way of moving made me think of a cat. She looked at me for a long, wary moment and then said, “Miss Bellinghausen?”

“Velda. And you’re Maggie, I presume?”

“Maggie Belasco, yes.”

“Want to come in? Be glad to spring for a cup of coffee.” I’d noticed she wore neither gloves nor boots and that her tatty coat was too light for this weather. The wind coming off the river was like a razor and the streets were ankle deep in slush. Her face was pale under the olive tint.

“That’d be swell. Thanks.”

We took seats in my regular corner booth and Joe automatically brought over a pair of steaming mugs of coffee. Maggie put her hands over hers to warm them.

“You ladies like something to eat?”

Maggie looked uncertain, embarrassed, so even though I wasn’t the least bit hungry I said, “Yeah, Joe, bring us a couple of grilled cheese sandwiches. It’s my treat, Miss Belasco.”

“Thanks, Miss Bellinghausen. That sounds great.”

Joe toddled off to take care of our order and I turned to Maggie, leaning toward her on my elbows. “You know something about Max’s daughter, Jackie?”

“Yes. I know where she is—at least I think I do.”

“Let me check something first.” I took a snapshot from my

bag and placed it on the table in front of Maggie. It was a photo of Cleo Mrs. Fort had given me. "Do you recognize this girl?"

"Sure. That's my best friend, Maxine."

"Maxine what?"

"Maxine Polketta."

"You're sure?"

"Of course. I'd recognize her anywhere. I've known her most of my life. More than fifteen years, I guess. We're practically like sisters."

"Ever meet a girl named Cleo Fort? Cleopatra Fort?"

"No, never."

"Max ever mention a girl named Cleo?"

"No—not that I can recall."

"Does Max have a sister?"

"No. She's an only child."

Well, so much for that hope.

Joe showed up with our sandwiches about then and we ate the first few bites in silence. I could see that Maggie wanted to wolf hers down whole and was consciously restraining herself. I didn't think she'd had much to eat lately.

"Tell me what you know about the kid, Maggie."

"Jackie? Jackie's Max's little girl. Jackson Sline was the father. Max named her Jacqueline because of Jackson, she was so much in love with the lousy bastard, may he rot in hell."

"You didn't care for Sline much?"

"Are you kidding? I'd call him a rat if I didn't like rats more than I did him. He used their baby as a lever to make her do what he wanted and he wanted, well—he wanted some awful stuff. He knew Maxie was devoted to the kid, the bastard. I don't know what was going on at the end—Max had disappeared completely late last year. I didn't see her for nearly six months. She only showed up again shortly before Sline was killed. I'm sure he had something to do with her disappearance and I'm sure it had something to do with Jackie, but I don't know exactly what was really going on between them. Being Sline, it couldn't've been anything good."

"Have you seen Maxine since the murder?"

"No. The last time I saw her was the day before. I haven't seen her since."

Damn.

"Did Sline have the little girl? Was that what Max wanted from him?"

"No, but he knew where she was. He wanted something from Max in exchange for Jackie."

"Do you know what that was?"

"I'm sorry. I don't have any idea."

"Do you know where he was keeping Jackie?"

"I do now. After the murder, the . . . the people Sline'd left Jackie with got scared and called me. They knew I was Maxie's best friend. They didn't know what they'd gotten themselves into and didn't want to get involved with the police. They thought they'd just been doing a kindness, taking care of the kid, and now they were afraid they might be accused of kidnaping or something."

"Who are they?"

"Do you really need to know? They're really a nice old couple who had no idea they were doing anything wrong—Sline'd told them they were taking care of the kid for Maxie. I'd just as soon keep their names to myself."

"I guess that's all right. Do you have the kid now?"

"Yes."

We finished our sandwiches in silence.

I'd made an arrangement with Maggie to meet me at the infirmary the next morning and I was waiting for her on the steps outside the jail. It was bitterly cold, but I didn't have to wait long. Just like the day before, Maggie was dead on time. With her was a little girl that looked to be about three years old or thereabouts who I knew immediately was Jackie. The resemblance to Cleo was striking—too striking to suit me, I can tell you.

"Good morning, Maggie. This is Jackie?"

"Yes. Jackie? This is Miss Bellinghausen. She's a very nice lady who is going to help you find your momma again. You want to see your momma?"

"Oh, yes! Please!" said the child, clapping her little mittened hands together, her huge dark eyes sparkling in the morning light. "I want my momma!" I tell you, she'd break anyone's heart she was so cute.

"All right," I said. "Everyone's waiting for us upstairs. Ready?"

When we arrived on the third floor, I told the matron who we were and she told us that Cleo was waiting and led us to a small room just off the main ward. I was pleased to see that they'd granted at least that small kindness. Dr. Finlayson was already there. So was Chip and Mrs. Fort. I'd asked him to bring her along separately since I hadn't wanted her to meet Maggie or the child until the last possible moment.

"Flan is going to have a fit," Chip said as I approached. "He reports directly to Noorvik, you know. This could be dangerous for all of us. The head sawbones here is taking a big chance on this thing."

"Flan and Noorvik can just go and—" I glanced at Maggie and the kid. "—and, and go jump in a lake," I finished lamely.

"Maggie," I said, "this is Dr. Finlayson. He's a friend of mine who's been looking after Cleo for me. He's the one who got the warden to transfer her to the infirmary here. And this is Mr. Finney, he's with the *Graphic*, but you can trust him anyway, and Mrs. Fort. Mrs. Fort, this is Maggie Belasco and Jackie. They're here to see if they can help Cleo."

There had been absolutely no sign of recognition between either of the women, who merely looked at one another with that kind of wary curiosity any pair of strange women have upon meeting. Nothing more. Even more curiously, Mrs. Fort barely glanced at the child. The kid obviously meant nothing to her.

I glanced inside the room and could see Cleo just inside the door. She was in a wheelchair, humming softly to herself. I turned to Chip.

"You haven't talked to her yet?"

"No one has, and I do not think she even knows we are here. She has been in a kind of swoon ever since they wheeled her in. I thought maybe she had been drugged but the matron assures me she has not. She says Cleo has been like this for a couple of days."

"Do you recognize her, Maggie?" I asked. "You know the girl in that room?"

"Yes, of course I do. That's Maxine Polketta, my best friend. I'd recognize her anywhere."

"You're sure?"

"If nothing else, I recognize what she's humming. It's a gospel song she sung at her mother's funeral."

Mrs. Fort swung around on that, her eyes focusing for the first time on the small, dark girl beside me.

"What'd you just say?"

"Poor little Maxie," Maggie continued, still talking to me, "she's thinking of the day her mother died. It was terrible being in that old room all alone, so cold, so dark . . ."

"What are you *saying*?" Mrs. Fort interrupted shrilly. "*I'm* her mother! Who is this, this woman? What does she mean?"

"This is someone who knew Max," I explained. "She's come to see her."

"*Cleo* never knew this—his person. She was always a good girl, she'd never been away from home, she never went anywhere I didn't know about, never had friends I didn't meet. She certainly never knew anyone like, like this!"

"Well, look, it'll do no harm for her to see Cleo. If it's a mistake it's a mistake and no harm done."

"How do you know? How can you know that?"

"I don't, Mrs. Fort, not really. But I think there's someone out there who people are mistaking for your daughter. If we don't find who it is, Cleo could end up going to prison for a long time for something she didn't do."

"She couldn't do that! No! It would kill her! Just look at my baby! It's killing her now, being in a place like this! Just killing her!"

"That's right, Mrs. Fort, that's why we have to try everything we can. I think the girl Miss Belasco knows is *another* Cleo. That is, I mean a girl who looks a lot like your daughter, enough like her that people can't tell the difference. She can maybe tell us that if we give her a chance to see Cleo."

Asking the others to remain outside, I took Maggie into the room. Cleo was in a wheelchair, her lap covered by a blanket, facing the tall barred window opposite us. It was snowing and the blue light streaming though the glass made her look like a porcelain doll. I could hear her singing softly to herself. I recognized the song immediately. It was "Nearer My God To Thee". I mean, who could see *A Night to Remember* and ever forget that tune? I'd cried like a baby.

"That's what Max sung," Maggie whispered, "the day her mother died. She sat by the body all day singing it over and over and over, until the city people came and took her mother away."

"Cleo? There's someone here to see you."

There was no response from the girl. She kept on humming softly to herself.

"Maxie . . ."

She half turned her head so we could see her profile. She stopped singing and smiled. Before any of us could say anything, Jackie broke free of Maggie's grasp and ran to Cleo, crying, "Momma! Momma!"

With a glad cry, Cleo embraced the child, who buried her face in the girl's skinny bosom and bawled with relief and happiness. Cleo looked up at us—first at Maggie and then at me. "It's true then? There *is* a child? Am I really her mother?"

"I don't know. Is she? Are you?"

"No! *No*, it's not possible," said Mrs. Fort, who'd come into the room behind me. "It's not possible! How could it be? Cleo's not been away from home a day in her whole life. How could she have a child? No—no—this is, this is indecent! How could this child, any child, be hers? What are you *saying*? What are you trying to do? What does this woman want with Cleo? What is she after?"

Cleo looked up at us with a tear-streaked face. "Is she mine? Is she really? I—I seem to remember . . . I . . . she's so familiar—I know her, I *know* I do. This is my Jackie, isn't it?"

"No, Cleo," said Mrs. Fort with more gentleness than I would have credited her with. "No, you don't know her. You're only dreaming again. You're just imagining you know her. You don't know this child. You can't."

"But—but look!" The child had been sitting in Cleo's lap and Cleo pointed to the little girl's shoes. All chill of disbelief creeped down my spine but there was no mistaking it. One was smaller than the other, with the same built-up sole and heel that Cleo's shoes had.

"Let me see this," I said as I kneeled by the wheelchair and untied Jackie's shoes. I pulled them off and then her stockings. I could only stare at the exposed feet, one of them as pretty as could be, for a kid's foot anyway, and other—well, it was funny-looking. What else was there to say?

"See?" Cleo said. "See? Her feet . . . they're just like mine. Just like them."

"Maggie?" I said. "Go around and take a good look at Max—Cleo. Take a good, hard look. Is she your friend or isn't she?"

She circled the chair, getting between Cleo and the window so the light fell fully upon the girl's face. She smiled when she saw Cleo and I could see not only the recognition but the concern and shock behind the smile caused by the sight of that dreadfully pale countenance. Then I could see the uncertainty—first as two little lines between Maggie's brows as they drew together slightly. Then her eyes narrowed almost imperceptibly. The corners of her mouth twitched and then, catching herself, she smiled again.

"Max," she said, gently. "Maxie . . . do you know who I am?"

"No—no, I, I don't think so. You look . . . familiar, I think, but I don't . . . Who are you? I think I must know you. You brought Jackie back to me, didn't you? How can I ever thank you?"

"You don't recognize me, Maxie?"

"No . . . no, I—I don't think so. There's something very—I'm sure I've seen you before, but . . . I'm sorry, I really am. Should I know you?"

"I'm Maggie, Max. Maggie Belasco—your old pal, Maggie?"

"I—I'm sorry . . ."

Maggie stood and looked at me for a moment without saying a word.

"This isn't Max. At least, she's not the Max I know."

"Are you sure about that?"

"Of course. This isn't Maxie. She looks almost exactly like her—they could be twins, but no, she's not the same person."

"How can you tell? Just because she didn't recognize you? That probably doesn't mean anything in the condition she's in—"

"No, it's not that. It's her eyes. This girl's eyes match, but Max's don't. It's hard to see, the difference isn't very striking, but they're not the same. One of Max's eyes is green, the other is a kind of grey—hazel, I think the color's called. Both of this girl's eyes are green. The same, exactly, no difference at all. No, this isn't my Maxie."

"But her feet, Maggie! One is deformed, and the shoes found at the crime scene, one was for a foot exactly like hers. And Jackie, she has the same deformity."

"You think so?"

I looked, but I couldn't see what she was talking about. Jackie's odd foot had the same slight inward twist that Cleo's did, the same slight mismatch in size, not enough to be immediately noticeable and not enough to affect her walk much if at all, but there all the same. Jackie's left foot was exactly . . . Then it hit me with a jolt that was almost painful.

"What is it?" Chip asked. "You look like you just swallowed a worm."

"The shoes. The shoes they found in Sline's apartment. Where are they?"

"Where? Probably in the evidence locker at police headquarters. Why?"

"I need them. Can we get them here?"

"Are you kidding? Not likely! But do you need the shoes or do you just need to see them?"

"Pardon?"

"I mean, if it will help whatever it is you have in mind I have got a photo of them here, in the file in my briefcase. The paper got it the day of the inquest."

"Yeah, sure! That'd be perfect! Get it!"

I followed him as he went to where he left his case out in the ward and as he fumbled the thing open, I asked. "Did anyone ever have Cleo try the shoes on?"

"What do you mean?"

"I remember the doctor being asked about the shoes and Cleo's feet and all, but did he ever actually try them on her? I don't think anyone asked him that."

"I have no idea, but I do not think so. Probably did not see much point to it. She identified them herself as her own shoes. And there was that one gimp shoe. She could hardly have mistaken that. Who else's would they be?"

"Well, that's just the point. Did anyone ever actually *show* her the shoes? More to the point, did anyone ever have her try them on?"

"I have no idea, but now that you bring it up I doubt it. For one thing, Noorvik would not be likely to do anything that would remotely give the girl a break. I mean, she could have pretended they did not fit or that she did not recognize them or something. He wants a scapegoat for Sline's murder and the girl is it. Besides that, you are forgetting that they found the shoemaker who made them and besides that he identified the girl."

I took the photo he handed me and looked at it closely. The shoes had been photographed on a black surface, probably some table in the crime lab. A wooden ruler was laying beside them for scale. It was pretty clear that the shoes were a mismatch. I got my purse, took out one of the photos that Conklin had given me and held it beside the first one.

"Well, I'll be damned."

"What is it?" Chip asked, taking the photos from me. "Where'd you get this?"

"That's one that Conklin, the photographer in Sline's building, took last year."

He whistled. "It's sure Cleo all right, no mistake about that."

"Yeah, I know. If you can tear your eyes away from the rest of her for a second, take a good look at her feet."

"So? Left one looks a little funny—and I can see what has got you so upset. Odd left foot, odd left shoe. You were hoping for a mismatch, weren't you? Too bad."

I took the photos back into the room with me and squatted down in front of Cleo. She was still holding Jackie, who was now blissfully half asleep in the girl's arms.

"Cleo, I'd like to take your slippers off so I can see your feet. Is that okay? Do you mind?"

"No, Velda, of course not."

I took the slippers off and looked at her feet. Small, slender, white, with one just slightly smaller and twisted in toward the other in an odd way. Nothing really deformed-looking and hardly noticeable if you didn't see both feet together. I looked up at Jackie. Her little feet were just at my eye level, the left foot twisted and slightly smaller than the right one. But—and this is what had gotten me so wound up—it was Cleo's *right* foot that was the odd one, not the left. That's what I'd been failing to notice all along. It's what everyone else had failed to notice, too, or, more likely, I thought, anger welling up inside me, what everyone else had consciously avoided noticing.

"Chip, come over here a moment and look at this." I handed him the photo of the shoes and asked, "Which one's the orthopedic shoe?"

"This one. You can see the difference."

"And it's the shoe for the left foot isn't it?"

"Yeah, so?"

"And the photo—the girl in the photo, her left foot is the odd one, right?"

"Again, so?"

"Well, dummy, look at Cleo. It's her *right* foot that's deformed."

"Pardon?"

"These aren't her shoes and that's not her in the photo."

"I will be damned. And the kid?"

"Jackie's not Cleo's daughter."

WELL, MY HUNCH HAD OBVIOUSLY BEEN ON THE MARK. THERE *WAS* another Cleo out there somewhere, I was sure of it now, and it was *that* Cleo, the girl known as Maxine Polketta, who was tied into the murder of Jackson Sline. But now what? That fact might conceivably get Cleo off the hook so far as the murder rap was concerned, though I more than halfway doubted it since it was pretty obvious that Flan and Noorvik wanted a scapegoat and Cleo had been unanimously elected, but what about her wasting away? She was dying . . . no—no, the *other* Max was dying and our Max, linked somehow to this other girl, was dying with her. Knowing she was out there was no real help. She could be anywhere—and I could hardly imagine her hanging around after the murder, especially when there was someone else to take the fall for her. But I didn't have forever to look for her. And Finlayson wasn't exactly excited about Cleo's prospects. The care the nurses at the infirmary were providing was as good as humanly possible, given the circumstances, Finlayson was seeing to that. No one could've turned their back on that pale, wasted figure, even if she was a cold-blooded murderess, which she wasn't.

The only living link I had to the other Max was Maggie, though she was as much in the dark as I was so far as the missing girl's present whereabouts. It was a complete surprise to her that there present whereabouts. It was a complete surprise to her that there was another Max running around town. I invited her and the kid back to my apartment after the meeting in the infirmary. I sent out for Chinese, we ate, rolled Jackie up in a blanket and put her in the care of the Schoenfelds, who cooed over the kid like she'd just been dropped into their laps by the Good Fairy of the North, made some coffee and martinis and talked through the night. I was a little embarrassed that I only had jelly glasses to drink from, but Maggie was nice enough not to notice.

"It's a swell place you got here," Maggie said as we slouched in the only two armchairs I own and propped our feet on the windowsill over the radiator.

"It's okay, I suppose. Some nice people live here, except maybe for Mr. Arkady. I like that."

"I didn't know there were any women detectives. It must be interesting work."

"A few of us kicking around, I guess. More on the west coast than here, I suppose. Yeah, it's okay work when I can get it."

"I take it you haven't been getting much?"

"However you meant that, the answer is no, not really."

"So why do it then? What's in it for you?"

"My dad was a cop—a homicide detective. The best."

"That him?" she asked, leaning over the arm of her chair to get a good look at the photo on the wall not far from her elbow. "Nice-looking guy—tough, but nice-looking, like Pat O'Brien. What happened to him?"

"He was killed, well, gee, I guess it's eight years ago, almost nine now."

"Sorry."

"The department screwed the whole thing up. I still haven't got it all straightened out yet, but there was a big coverup of some kind and, well, it left a black mark on his record—on the cleanest record any cop'd had in thirty years. It kept me from getting any benefits—I've never yet gotten a penny of insurance and I was pretty desperate by that time, I can tell you."

"You were alone?"

"Yeah. Mom'd passed away a few years before that and it was

just me and Dad. When he died, I had to drop out of school and take whatever jobs I could get. I sort of fell into the burlesque racket by default—I really didn't have the training or experience to do anything else. One day I was delivering Chinese food to the manager of the Follies—you know the place?"

"Sure."

"I was delivering Chinese to him and he offered me a job in the chorus right then and there."

"That you in that picture over there? Nice outfit, what there is of it. I guess there must've been a shortage of sequins that year."

"Yeah."

"I take it you didn't care over much for the work?"

"You got that right. I hated it, but on the other hand I wasn't bad at it, either. I just figured, if I had to do it I might as well make a good job of it. It wasn't long before I graduated from the chorus line. I made more money but I can't say I was very proud of the way I was making it."

"But that's where you met Chip, wasn't it? He worked in the theater, too?"

"Yeah. He was Slotsky's press agent—wrote up all the ads, figured out the publicity gags, all that kind of crap. He and I, well, we had kind of a thing going, I guess. But he always thought he was destined for something better and was always trying to get work on some paper or another. Finally got a job on the *Graphic* writing reviews and covering gossip for the theatrical section and you'd think he was working for the *New Yorker* to hear him. Our paths, well, they kind of stopped crossing much after that."

"You're not seeing anyone? I can hardly believe that!"

"Yeah, well. Burlesque kind of, you know, sours you on guys, you know what I mean? You think they're all after one thing and it's kind of hard to get that out of your mind when some guy is giving you the glad eye. I mean, it kind of prejudices you against them right off the bat. But, you know, I don't get asked out as often as you might think. Yeah, I see your look, but it's true. I know I look good on stage, but on the street, well . . . most men's dream girls aren't skinny six-footers. I look a lot better in sequins in a spotlight than I do fully dressed in daylight. After Chip moved out, I can tell you I got pretty low."

"Well, I think you're a little too hard on yourself. I'd give two pints of my soul to have even half your looks. So you decided to become a detective, of all things?"

"One day I was down in the dressing room with the other girls when I happened to notice a matchbook that said, 'Be A Detective!'. It was like it was talking to me personally, you know what I mean? Like those voices Ingrid Bergman heard. I filled out the little form on the inside, sent in my dollar and got a book in the mail. I still got it, see?"

I pulled a ratty, dog-eared little paperback volume from the magazine rack next to me and tossed it to her. She looked at the lurid cover that depicted a mustachioed man shooting someone who looked vaguely like a streetcar conductor, I have no idea why, under a floridly lettered title that read: HAWKSHAW'S COMPLETE BOOK OF DETECTIVE WORK, or How and When To Adopt It As A Profession.

"Looks fascinating," she said, politely, turning it over and over in her hands.

"It's great. It was a whole course, a book like that one came every month. Taught me just about everything I know, everything I hadn't already picked up from Dad, of course."

Which really hadn't been much. I loved and respected my father, but he was an unemotional, private man—as square and honest as a set of Johannson blocks and just about as easy to warm up to—a man who rarely brought his work home with him. I admired the hell out of him, but did he inspire me? I don't know, but it's Dad's nickel-plated forty-five automatic I carry. Make of that whatever you want.

"See here—" I took the book back from her "—it's got chapters on the Sweat Box, Shadowing (two chapters on that), Deduction, The Detective and the Law . . . everything. There's one whole book just on fingerprints."

"I can see why Cleo feels she's in good hands."

"I sure hope she's right. Speaking of Cleo—how do you know Maxine?"

"I hadn't seen Maxine for nearly a year," Maggie said. "neither her nor Jackie. Then she popped up out of nowhere. This was a few days before the murder. I don't know where she had been staying or what she had been doing, or where she'd been for so many months, although I'm pretty sure she was seeing Sline somehow. He had her practically hypnotized. Anyway, the last time I saw her was the day before the murder. She wouldn't tell me anything, just that she'd see me in a few days and explain everything. She said, 'Everything's going to be okay from now on'."

"Did you know what she meant by that?"

"No, not really. I know there was something bad between her and Sline, but I never knew exactly what it was."

"Before you go on, I've been wondering: did Max ever have dreams, dreams of being someone else?"

"Oh, sure! All the time. For as long as I've known her, ever since we were kids in Hell's Kitchen. She used to dream she was a kid living in some sunny little hick town. Wishful thinking, I always figured, I mean, who'd not rather live someplace like that instead of Hell's Kitchen? I just figured she'd seen one too many Shirley Temple pictures."

"Do you know if she ever met anyone named Cleo Fort? Cleopatra Fort? Anything like that?"

"That kid we saw in the infirmary? No . . . I'm sure she didn't. If she did, she never mentioned it to me. I mean, she met a lot of people at the colleges when she was modeling for art classes and I don't know how many at the parties the artists and photographers held. We were still close, we were always best friends, but in the last couple of years we kind of drifted into different circles. But if she ever met your Cleo, she sure never mentioned it to me. It'd be a hard name to forget, you know, Cleopatra Fort. And it'd be hard to overlook someone who looked so much like you, too. I'm sure she would have said something on that count, if for no other reason."

"Here, let me freshen up your glass."

"Thanks."

"You say you've known Max since you were kids?"

"Oh, yeah—I mean like, I dunno, like since we were five or six. We were practically raised together."

"Did she have any sisters?"

"No, she was an only child. No brothers, no sisters."

Damn.

"You're sure about that?"

"Unless they were raising a kid in a closet and feeding it through the keyhole, I'm sure. Maxine's mother'd nearly died while giving birth to her. Tore her all up inside somehow. She couldn't have any more babies after Maxie. There was just the one kid and that was it."

"What about her father?"

"He died before she was born. His name was Max and Mrs. Polketta named her after him, God knows why. He was shot during a longshoreman's strike."

"He worked on the docks?"

"No. He was a scab and crossed the picket line once too often. He didn't have any regular work, just what he could find when he ran out of booze. Max's mother, I think, was happy to see him go, even though it meant a lot more work for her.

"You have to understand how we had to live then. There was just the one room for the three of us above a thimble factory on the lower East Side. I had no family at all, you see. I don't even remember any more exactly why that was. It was just the way things were, I figured. My earliest memories are of playing with Max in the alleys. I would go back to her room with her, first to play, then to eat—and I know now how it must have strained Mrs. Polketta's resources to feed even that small extra mouth—then to sleep. Eventually, I was living there all the time, just like I was Max's sister."

"What'd the mother do to support the three of you?"

"She was pretty nearly crippled all the time I knew her. Partly, I think, from the beatings that Polketta'd given her. He was dead, you know, long before I came along, like I said, so I only know what Mrs. Polketta let slip and what I could guess. I'm pretty sure he beat her real bad once and messed something up inside her head. I couldn't have known then, of course, but now I don't think Mrs. Polketta was—well, was all there, you know what I mean?"

"You mean she was nuts?"

"I don't know about that. But looking back on it, I don't think she ever quite knew where she was—how she was living. Anyway, the only work she could do was at home, making lace and embroidery for the notion shops in the garment district. As her fingers gave out she taught Max and me to make the things. We were just kids, though and couldn't make stuff as fast or nearly as good as Mrs. Polketta so we had a much harder time selling it. Sometimes the shopkeepers wouldn't take our stuff at all and then it was really hard. We depended then on Maxie, who's a couple of years older than me—I don't know if I mentioned that yet. She'd always manage to scavenge something for us, enough to keep us alive at any rate. She got food by begging, by stealing, by going through the garbage cans behind restaurants if she had to, any way she could. By the time I was ten and she was about twelve, Maxie'd developed a, well, a pretty independent personality. She was strong, awfully strong—not just in her mind, you understand, but in her body, too. At fourteen she was as old in just about every way as any twenty-year-old. She looked it, too, and took advantage of it. I—I don't much like to think in what ways she must have done that.

"It wasn't long after that that our—her mother died. I'm sorry, I've never been able to think of Mrs. Polketta as not being *my* mother, too. Mrs. Polketta'd been sick for a long time—probably for as long as I knew her, now that I can look back and see all the signs. I think she'd always been sick in the head and gradually became sick in her body as well. Max told me that from the day she was old enough to go out on her own, she'd never known her mother to leave her room, not once Max was able to take care of herself and her mother too. Max—and eventually me, as well, to a lesser extent—became her only contact with the outside world. We ran all her errands, fetched food, took her lacework to the buyers. Like I said, she eventually became as sick in body as she was in mind and she began to just waste away. And soon she just wasn't there at all. Max took it pretty hard—I couldn't get her away from the body, she just sat there beside it, crooning that damned hymn for hours on end. The city finally came and took the body away and neither Max nor I ever knew where they buried it. Something changed in Max then, something became—hard—but I didn't notice until later, when I looked back on it all.

"It was right after her mother died that Max saw an ad for figure models at the Art Students' League, so she gave it a shot. She lied about her age and although I don't know if anyone really believed her, no one ever questioned her either. She liked modeling—it was good money for easy work—and I guess she was good at it, too. It wasn't long before word got around and she started posing for artists and photographers all around the Village. I know some of the things she did weren't very, well, nice—I've seen some of the magazines—but she always got paid. She demanded more than most of the other models and got it, too. I think she might have been paid for other things, too, but I never asked her about that and she never talked about what she did and I don't think I really wanted to know. I still don't. We were eating a lot better in those days and that's all that really mattered.

"It was while she was modeling for some pinup artists that she met Jackson Sline. He made her stop modeling—he didn't like it. Do you want that egg roll?"

"Please, help yourself."

"Thanks. I haven't seen much of Max in the last couple of years, not since she started modeling and hanging out with that awful beatnik crowd around Sline—not that I have anything against the beatniks, but these were such phonies, in it for the dope and booze and sex—and then not at all for most of last year. I know she got sent up for shoplifting, spent a year in a reformatory upstate. When she came back, well, that's when we started to drift apart. I mean, we were still best friends, of course. We've always been like sisters, we just didn't go around in the same circles any more. She'd always had a, well, I guess you could call it a pretty subjective interpretation of honesty, but she was never truly a bad person, not really. She did what she had to do for us to survive—but something in the reformatory changed her. She came back—different. Something was missing from her, leaving only the cold, hard parts. More coffee?"

"Thanks."

"What's your interest in all of this, Velda? What're you getting out of it, if you don't mind me asking?"

"I don't mind. Unfortunately, the answer is 'nothing'. I mean, nothing so far as making any money. I've just kind of butted in, I suppose. Max seems to appreciate what I'm trying to do, but no one's actually asked to be my client. Flan assumes I'm officially working for the Fort family and I've not disabused him. I hope he doesn't decide to actually ask one of them or I'll be out on the street in a heartbeat."

"But just what *are* you trying to do?"

I'd wondered about that myself and was pretty sure it had nothing to do with altruism. I *think* it's because I had something to prove but what I told Maggie was: "I'm trying to keep Maxie out of prison. I guess I ought to start calling her Cleo all the time now, shouldn't I? *Your* Max is the real Max, isn't she?"

"If you want to put it that way, I suppose she is."

"It's just that I can't for the life of me figure out what the connection is between the two girls. There's gotta be one and it's driving me crazy trying to figure out what it is. I mean, the first thing anyone'd think is that they're sisters—they're dead ringers for one another—even Jackie was fooled—but you tell me that Max was an only child and Mrs. Fort says that Cleo is her only daughter. So what's going on?"

"You must be right. There has to be some link between them, but I don't know what it could be. Max used to have dreams, too, I told you, dreams of being someone else."

"I know. Her dreams sound like Cleo's life. It's too weird for me. Like something from *Lights Out*."

Maggie yawned and stretched, actions that made her look even more catlike than ever. "I'm going to be dreaming myself in about five more minutes. I'd better gather the kid up and go."

"No need to do that. She's fine where she is. You take my bed, I can camp out on the sofa."

"I couldn't—"

"Sure you could. Besides, it's nearly midnight, you don't want to take the kid out this late. Listen to the wind, it's freezing out there."

"Yeah, well, all right. I don't think I could stand for very long anyway. It's been a long while since I've had a drink."

Everyone was still unconscious when I woke in the morning, not that "woke" is really the right term—I hadn't done much sleeping that night. My brain kept whirling the same questions around, over and over again, and I couldn't stop it. It was like an engine racing, spinning its wheels and getting nowhere fast.

It was still dark outside as I pulled on my slacks and a sweater. There was an all-night grocery around the corner and I thought I'd get some milk and cereal for the kid, since I'd have to fetch her back from the Schoenfelds before they left for the candy store, and maybe some donuts for Maggie and me. I let myself out as quietly as I could and locked the door behind me. It was as crisp and clear as cellophane out on the street, the frozen slush crackling beneath my boots and my nostrils pinching shut with the cold. I'd not quite gotten to the corner when I heard a car door open and shut behind me. I'd only just registered the approaching footsteps when something slammed into the side of my head with a sound like Mantle making a solid connection with a fast ball.

Chapter Ten

I didn't go out, but everything went red for what couldn't've been more than thirty seconds. When my vision cleared, I was in a narrow passageway between two buildings not more than twenty feet from the sidewalk. I must've been dragged there. I was on the ground, my back propped against a brick wall. My coat had been pulled down and back, effectively pinning my arms behind me. It was damn cold, with only my sweater between me and outside. But that wasn't my immediate concern.

There were two of them. The big one was kneeling across my legs, his hands on my shoulders, pressing them against the wall. The skinny one was standing, slapping a stumpy club of some kind into the palm of his free hand. Both were backlit by the streetlights and with my vision still shaky I couldn't get a good look at either one. They'll be damned sorry if do, I thought.

"Who the hell are you?" I demanded, but the tough tone I attempted was spoiled a little by coming out in a kind of falsetto croak.

The standing man leaned over and swatted me across the ear with his club. It was a rolled-up newspaper and it hurt like hell, too, the bastard.

"Shut up," he said.

"Screw you."

"I said shut up." He hit me again and I shut up. "If you're half as smart as you think you are, you'll keep your big trap shut and listen good. You only got two words to remember so it shouldn't be too hard for you: *lay off.*"

"Lay off what?" I said just as I realized that I'd made a mistake in speaking so I really didn't need him to hit me in the face with the paper again, but he did anyway. This time I tasted blood and I just hate that.

"I told you to shut up and listen. That's all you gotta do. Shut up and listen. Unless you're stupider than I think, which maybe you are."

I didn't say anything, just to prove him wrong.

"I'll tell you just one more time and I ain't going to tell you again. Lay off. Keep away from the kid and keep your pretty little nose outta the Sline business. That's it. That's all there is to it.. Should be very easy, too, given the only alternative you got."

I raised an inquisitive eyebrow (I was afraid that if I opened my mouth all my teeth would fall out).

"Give her a sample of the alternative."

"It's not really necessary—"

"Gladly," said the goon sitting on my knees as he punched me in my right breast with his fist. I gasped from the pain and caught the same fist in my open mouth. My head bounced off the bricks behind me with a *clonk* that sounded appropriately hollow. He got off my knees, which was something anyway since the thug must've weighed two-fifty and was breaking my legs. It was only a momentary relief, however, since he'd only stood up to make it easier to kick me in the ribs. The skinny guy watched him do this two or three times.

"That's enough. We don't want to kill her, do we?"

"Well—I guess not."

"I think she got the message. I think she'll behave herself."

"I almost hope the bitch don't. I could have some fun with a dame with looks like this one's got."

"Now, now, don't be over-anxious, you may get your wish yet." He stooped down to where he could almost look into my face. His breath puffed at me in cigar and garlic-scented clouds. "You *are* going to behave yourself now, aren't you Miss Bellinghausen? There's worse things my esteemed colleague can do to you than kick your ribs in, of that I can assure you. In fact, he was looking forward to being a little more creative with you and I really feel bad about having to disappoint him. I wouldn't want to do that to him again—he'd be very hurt. So I do hope you get the idea since it's the only time I'm going to tell you."

He got to his feet, tugged on his gloves, straightened his hat and said, "Come on. Leave her alone. With any luck, she'll freeze to death."

I laid there for I don't know how long, but I was thinking that if I didn't get to my feet his prediction about me freezing to death was going to come true.

This is one stupid way to make a living, I thought, *except that I'm not making any money.* Realizing that this didn't make me sound any smarter, I decided I'd better get back home.

The sky was getting steel-colored with what passed for dawn in late March and a few cars were beginning to show up on the street. I wanted to get back to my place before anyone saw me and called a cop. Using the wall as a support, I got up and nearly passed out as waves of pain shot through my chest. Jesus, they must've broken some ribs for sure. I pulled a glove off and wiped my hand across my face. It came away bloody. All right. Time to get home for sure.

I made about twenty feet before I was leaning over a railing puking my guts out into some poor slob's basement entrance. Each heave set my ribs on fire. My head was spinning like a 45 playing at 78.

Another twenty feet and a rest against a helpful tree. God, anyone sees me they'll think I'm some drunken slut weaving her way to her next john. What'll I say if a cop stops me? That I was mugged? Why not? I had no idea where my pocketbook had gone. Oh Christamighty, was my gun it it? I couldn't remember. That'd be asking too much.

Fortunately for me, the Zenobia's in the middle of the block. It seemed to have taken an hour to get there, even though it wasn't more than a hundred yards from the corner, but I was finally climbing the steps and fumbling for my keys. *Dammit*! Why do I have so many keys? What are all of these keys for? I don't own anything, God knows.

Then I was going up the stairs, which was just about as difficult as anything I've ever done. See if I ever get a third-floor walkup again. By the time I got to my door I was on my hands and knees. I had to knock four times before I heard Maggie's voice. It sounded frightened. She must've realized I wasn't in the apartment.

"Who is it?"

"It's me. Velda. Lemme in."

"Velda? What . . ."

I heard the lock click and the chain rattle. I was leaning against the door so I nearly fell into the room as Maggie swung it open.

"Velda! Oh Jesus! What—Velda, what happened?"

She said all of these things, but at the same time was acting quickly. She had me inside and the door locked and chained in a matter of seconds and I was very glad to see that was the first thing she did. I fell into my armchair, crying out in spite of my best intentions not to. Maggie didn't say another word, but instead went straight to the kitchen. She came back a moment later with a pan of water and a dishrag. She started mopping at my face. The water was hot and felt great. I stuck my finger in my mouth and felt my teeth. I couldn't believe it but they all seemed to be intact which was a real relief since I don't have a dental plan. There was a big hole in my lip, though, where the thug's blow had driven my front teeth through it.

I've said that getting up the stairs was one of the most painful things I've ever done, but getting my coat and sweater off was a lot worse. Once she'd gotten me peeled, Maggie took a good look and I didn't like the way she sucked in her breath at what she saw. My right side was one big bruise and it hurt like hell to take a deep breath, and I had a breast that'd swollen like an eggplant.

"You really oughta get to a hospital," was the first thing Maggie said since getting me into the room. "I think a couple a ribs are broken."

"No. I'll call Finlayson later. He'll fix me up."

"You could puncture a lung or something."

"I don't think so. I'm not spitting up blood yet. If I sit here quietly—which is all I want to do right now—I'll be okay until he gets here."

"Who did this to you?"

"I didn't see them, but I'm dead certain who they were working for."

I was laid up for the rest of the week. Fortunately, nothing had been broken, much to my surprise. Finlayson said my coat and sweater had absorbed the worst of it. There really wasn't much he could do for me, he told me, other than tape me up, give me a prescription for a painkiller and order me to stay put for a few days, at least until the swelling went down. Maggie hung around, bless her heart. Neither one of us said anything about it, one way or the other, but I think she was grateful to have a place to stay and, frankly, I was glad to have her there. Jackie, too. I'm not really partial to kids, not being exactly overflowing with maternal instincts, but Jackie was a doll: bright, quiet, polite—all the things I like best in a kid.

Chip came around a couple of times and clucked his tongue over my injuries. He was anxiously curious about my bruises but I knew he just wanted to see my tit so I told him to get lost. He did bring news, though, such as it was. Cleo was still declining and there was serious doubt about her making it through the end of the month. They'd bumped her trial date, figuring, I guess, that if they waited a couple of weeks the city might save itself a big expense.

"Looks like Noorvik is getting a little antsy," he said.

"Yeah."

"I take it from your continued interest in the case that you are going to ignore his advice?"

"Well, hell yeah. What d'you expect me to do?"

"What I expect you to do and what I hope you do are two entirely different things as we both well know. You are doing exactly what I expect, which is to say, being too damned stubborn for your own good. Say, is there anything I can get you? Anything you need?"

"No, thanks. Maggie's taking care of my errands for me."

"How about a nice alcohol rub?"

"I thought I told you to get lost?"

He went over to the window and leaned against the frame,

looking idly into the street below. "How is the old bankbook holding up, Velda?"

"That's none of your business."

"Yeah, I know. You have not had much work lately, though, have you?"

"Didn't know you were that interested in me."

"Do not flatter yourself. But it is true, is it not? Been living off your savings, have you not?"

"What's it to you if I have?"

"Absolutely nothing." He glanced down as something caught his attention. "There she goes."

"Who?"

"Mrs. Fort. They have been letting her stay all day at the infirmary with Cleo. Looks good in the papers, Noorvik letting the dying girl's mother stay with her and all. He does not lose either way. The girl recovers, she gets railroaded through a kangaroo court and sent up to Fishkill for life or worse—or she drops dead in a couple of weeks. Either way the case is closed and Bill's name is never mentioned."

"I take it no one's seen hide nor hair of the kid?"

"Nope. On the other hand, I ca not say anyone has been looking real hard, either. Noorvik has been making sure the investigation stays focussed on Cleo and Sline. If Bill's name ever comes up, woe betide the cop who uttered it. Or the reporter for that matter."

"That reminds me. I'll be up in a day or two but in the meantime I want you to check on someone for me."

"Who this time?"

"Ruben. The brother. He's been just a shadow hanging around in the background, but the big ox looks like trouble squared. I'll be the most surprised girl in the world if he hasn't got a record of some kind. He was pretty free about slinging around accusations about what Cleo and I were doing the night of the murder—but where was *he*? He didn't show up until the following morning. Where was he when Sline was getting his head bashed in?"

"Ruben Fort, huh? The family is from Florida, had a place on one of the Keys somewhere—"

"Plankton Key."

"Yeah. I did a quick check on them last week, but since everything seemed to square with what Mrs. Fort and Cleo told us, it did not seem worth digging any deeper. I can call a buddy at the *Herald*, see what they might have on the lad."

"Would you do that, please?"

"Sure. I do not think it is going to get you anywhere, though. Ruben had only been in town less than a year—lived in Jersey most of the time at that, until a few months ago when he moved in with his mother. When and how would he ever have come in contact with Sline, of all people? Just look at the big oaf. Can you imagine him running around in the same circles as Sline and company? Even if he had had the opportunity to kill Sline, *why* would he?"

"Beats me. Hated poetry, maybe?"

"Well, I will find out what I can."

"Thanks. You'll be careful, won't you?"

"*You* be careful."

"Why, I'm always careful."

"Say," he added as he was about to go out the door, "you did not by any chance notice what paper they used to beat you with?"

"Hardly. What difference does it make?"

"No difference. It would just make me feel bad if it had been the *Graphic*."

"Go to hell."

Maggie volunteered to pick up my grocery-shopping where I'd left off and together we worked up a list. I gave her some money (noticing with no little trepidation how shallow my pocketbook was getting—I was going to be getting *that knock* from the Schoenfelds next month) and she took off with the kid in tow. I now had at least two hours to myself.

I knew the Fort apartment would be empty all day. Mrs. Fort would be at the jail until late afternoon and Ruben wouldn't be back from the slaughterhouse until dark. I'd heard his heavy footsteps at five in the morning, sounding like a bowling ball rolling down the stairs. I pulled on a cardigan, with not a few tears I can tell you, and slipped out of my place. I had to be careful. Too many people in the Zenobia were home all day and had hearing as keen as a sonar operator's. But I had my sneakers on, knew where the bad steps were and, mostly by hugging the wall or railing, made it to the fourth floor without making a sound. The lock was a joke—it was the same as every other apartment's and I'd already had practice breaking into Arkady's place. In two seconds flat I was inside with the door shut behind me.

The place was too warm, the steam heat turned all the way on, not surprising, I guessed, for people not long out of Florida. I took my sweater off, tossed it onto a chair, undid the top buttons of my blouse and rolled my sleeves up. It took only fifteen minutes to search the place, mainly because there was hardly anything there *to* search. The furniture had come with the apartment which meant that it had been there since the Coolidge administration. The living room had only a cheap steel-tube-and-formica dinette set, an overstuffed armchair and a sofa where I guessed Ruben slept since there seemed to be nowhere else. The bedroom had only the one bed, where I supposed both Cleo and her mother had slept together, a plain wood chair and a dresser with its veneer peeling off in long, thin leaves. That was about it. There was nothing in the place that gave a clue about the people who lived there—it'd looked the same for decades I was sure, remaining unchanged while the occupants had come and gone. The furnishings were permanent, the tenants were interchangeable.

I started with the bedroom dresser which was apparently devoted for the most part to Cleo's things. Underwear, socks, all of which had neatly darned heels, a couple of brassieres, God knows why, Bermuda shorts, a couple of neatly folded sweaters, et cetera et cetera, nothing out of the ordinary. The bottom drawer had been claimed by her mother, but it held nothing to interest me, either.

The bed was neatly made. I looked under the pillows. Nothing. I glanced under the bed, but there were only a couple of pairs of well-worn shoes. On the nightstand beside the bed were a couple of romance novels, which I assumed belonged to Cleo, and some pill bottles. These had been prescribed by a doctor in Florida and filled by a pharmacy there. Just pills for sleeping (for Cleo) and for high blood pressure (for her mother).

The closet had a dozen blouses, a couple of jackets and coats, two or three pairs of slacks, a few skirts and dresses. Nothing new by several years, everything washed to colorlessness and linty fragility. I looked at one of the blouses and noticed that it had been meticulously repaired at least a dozen times.

On the floor of the closet were three suitcases. I pulled them out and opened them. The one on top still contained clothes, all neatly folded. They looked like the mother's and I figured she was probably using the suitcase in lieu of a dresser. The other two cases were empty.

There was a shelf above the clothes rod and I raised myself on tiptoe to see what was on it. Just a couple of small cardboard cartons. I pulled them down, set them on the bed and opened them. One had a pretty little hat and a pair of white gloves, the kind of things a nice girl might wear to church on Sunday and that was probably just exactly what they were. Another box was filled with spools of thread, funny-looking needles, lace collars, cuffs and similar gewgaws. I remembered what Maggie had said about Maxie and her mother being lace-makers and wondered if this was the kind of stuff they'd've used. Were either Cleo or her mother lace-makers, too? I almost hoped not, because if so, it would be yet one more inexplicable coincidence. The last box was filled with nicknacks and I got my hopes up. Nicknacks at least looked like something personal and personal things contain information. The rest of the place had given me the creeps, it was so utterly impersonal. There'd been nothing that reflected the personality of the people living there. It was as though a set dresser for a movie had set out to create a tawdry, working-class apartment and had taken the easy way out and gone to the Salvation Army store to pick up everything he needed. The Fort place was like that.

But in spite of all my hopes the box of nicknacks was a dead end, too. Just the stupid junk any teenage kid picks up: costume jewelry, ribbons, junk prizes from carnivals, postcard pictures of movie stars, sea shells, foreign coins, all that kind of stuff. There was a neatly folded handkerchief. I opened it. Cleo's name was embroidered on one corner. It was almost identical, except for the name, to the handkerchief that'd been found in Sline's apartment and an unwelcome chill squirmed down my back. Even the style of script looked the same. I put it aside. At the bottom of the box was a rubber-banded pack of snapshots. Those looked promising, but didn't turn out to be much. Mostly shots of what I assumed was the family home, a not-too-shabby little stucco bungalow with palm trees all around it. Pictures of Ruben, God alone knows way, since he was as thuggish-looking as a kid as he was as an adult, and snaps of Cleo at every stage from infant to teen. I looked at these with some interest. A cute kid, I thought, and a lot healthier-looking than when I first met her. The most recent pictures, which must have been taken just before the family left Florida, showed Cleo at about nineteen I guessed. Without the gauntness that made her look so unhealthy and fragile, she really was a strikingly beautiful girl. I thought she looked a little like Jean Simmons, maybe, like when she played Joan of Arc in that movie. She could have modeled for any top fashion magazine. Her resemblance to the girl in the paintings and Conklin's photos was even more striking than I'd already thought. There was a shot of her in a bathing suit half reclining on a beach that reminded me uncomfortably of Miss May. Jesus Christ. Was I wrong? Were Cleo and Max the same person after all?

I riffled through the remaining photos realizing that maybe the most important thing was what wasn't there: Not one photo showed Cleo with another girl, not even as an infant. If she'd had a sister, wouldn't there've been at least a baby picture of her? But then, I was an only child so what did I know?

I went to the bathroom. There was only cheap soap in the dish and a half-empty bottle of Prell by the tub. There was a glass on the sink with three toothbrushes and a rolled-up tube of Ipana. I looked in the medicine cabinet. A bottle of aspirins and one of merthiolate, a styptic pencil, a man's razor and shaving brush and a bottle of Aqua-Velva. There was a box of BandAids (with only one left) and box of tampons—Cleo's I assumed. A wicker hamper contained only some dirty underwear and socks.

The kitchen cabinets were mostly empty: the basic collection of battered pots and pans, a skillet and some utensils—all cheap Woolworth stuff. The drawers contained mismatched knives, forks and spoons, looking like they'd all been swiped from cafeterias, a couple of clean towels, a can opener, a few tools, all of which, I suspected, came with the apartment. Under the sink I found only a bucket with a mangy brush in it and a box of Ivory soap flakes. The cabinets had a few cans of soup, hash, Franco-American spaghetti, condensed milk, half a loaf of Wonder bread, a half-empty box of corn flakes, a can of coffee, a can of Ovaltine, a half dozen glasses, coffee cups and chipped plates. The refrigerator contained only a half-full bottle of milk, a paper packet of sliced pimento loaf, some slices of American cheese and four bottles of Blue Ribbon. I took one of those. They were probably Ruben's and the hell with him.

I went on to the living room. It was as barren as the rest of the place—more so, if anything, probably because it was where Ruben lived and he hadn't much personality to imprint in the first place. I checked under the cushions and found only some loose change, which I kept. Behind the couch was a pillow and a folded army blanket. There was also a suitcase. I dragged it out onto the floor and opened it. Nothing but flannel and denim workshirts, all well-worn and often-patched, well-darned socks, underwear. I stopped there since I didn't much feel like browsing through Ruben's BVDs. The only other thing in the case were half a dozen pornographic magazines, which didn't tell me anything particularly new about Ruben other than that he was partial to women with breasts bigger than their heads.

Damn it. People couldn't possibly live this anonymously, could they? Everything in the place was as random and anonymous as the contents of a second-hand thrift shop. Ruben and his mother, might be that colorless, but Cleo was a bright girl, just out of her teenage years. Surely *she* couldn't live in a place for even five minutes and leave the same kind of vacuum her mother and brother did.

I went back to the bedroom. I sighed. There was just nothing there. I mean, the room was practically empty to start with. Figuring I might as well scrape the bottom of the barrel, I got down on my hands and knees and looked under the bed. I hadn't done it before because it made my ribs hurt like hell to bend over like that—silly me, because there was something wrapped in a handkerchief tucked up against the wall. Well, well!

I fished it out and untied the handkerchief. Inside was a little book. One of those little pink things with a fake lock you can get at any five and dime. A diary.

I shoved it into the back pocket of my jeans and after a quick look around to make sure I hadn't disturbed anything too much, left the apartment and slipped back down to my place. I made myself some coffee, took a fistful of aspirins and got as comfortable as I could in my armchair.

The first page of the diary revealed that I'd discovered even more than I'd first thought. In the big round letters that seem to be typical of teenage girls, Cleo had written *My Dreams.*

Her dreams.

I flipped back and forth through the pages randomly. "Last night I dreamed I was in the desert," she had written in one of the last entries, "walking through the Sands with bright, colored lights flashing all around me like Fireworks. It was so Beautiful! I had this same dream almost every night for two weeks and I was glad because it was so Lovely!"

On the next page: "Today I dreamed I was dressed in a beautiful red Gown. It was the most Beautiful Dress I'd ever seen. There were people all around me, all dressed in beautiful clothes too, but I was the most beautiful one there. I felt just like Cinderella." But right after that: "Oh it was the most awful Nightmare! I was in my beautiful red Dress but it had all turned to Blood! The dress was melting and running off into big puddles around my feet. My hands and arms were covered in Blood! I screamed and frightened Momma. She came in to see what was wrong. I cried all the rest of the night." The succeeding half dozen pages were each marked "No dream tonight" with nothing else written on them.

I flipped to the middle of the book. "I had the strangest, most wonderful Dream today! I had the most beautiful darlingest Baby Girl! She is so very Precious! And just like me in every way, too, even to one of her little feet being funny like mine. Isn't that the strangest thing?"

"Sometimes," said an entry a few pages later, "I do the most awful, shameful things. I can't write them down they're just so

Terrible! They make me ashamed, the things I do, and I just can't stop crying."

"Sometimes I'm afraid to go to sleep at night," she'd written in one of the final entries. "But sleeping during the Day is a thousand times worse. Sometimes I can't tell which Life is really my own. Am I dreaming, or am I just dreaming I'm dreaming? This last year there has been a change in my dreams—and in me, I mean, the other Me. She's done terrible, shameful things and I am afraid of her."

And on the following page: "After my last Dream, I lay in bed for three days. Momma told me how scared she was. She thought I was going to die. Dr. Goddard said he didn't know what to do. He said I ought to see a Specialist. He is afraid I'll go crazy if the dreams can't be stopped. Sometimes I think he's right."

By the time Maggie returned I'd read the entire diary from the first page. It was the biography of Maxine Polketta, so far as I knew, told as though seen through a kind of veil, or like someone telling you the plot of a movie they couldn't quite remember. I asked Maggie to read it, telling her nothing about it until she'd finished. Her hands were shaking and her normally dark face was the color of putty as she closed the little book.

"What *is* this thing?" she said, trying to control her voice.

"It's Cleo's diary. She wrote down her dreams, most of them at any rate, since she was at least about fourteen or fifteen. She was dreaming Max's life wasn't she?"

"My God in heaven! Every detail! It's like reading Max's own thoughts. The thing is—the thing's uncanny, unholy. Why, she tells about things no one but Max and I could've known. Things we said and did when we were alone. It scares the hell out of me. How can this be possible?"

"I don't know, but it's dead clear to me that it was Max who was in Sline's apartment the night he was murdered, not Cleo. But what good does that do us? The only hard evidence in Cleo's favor are the shoes but that's not much and the DA's going to suppress it anyway in order to railroad her to a conviction—probably won't even have to, everything else being so damning. Your assurances that Max and Cleo are two different people and my testamony about being with her that night aren't going to hold much water, not against all the eyewitnesses, let alone Cleo's own belief that she was there. She's mixed together her life and Max's in her mind so much that she no longer has any idea which world she lives in, which life is really her own. But there's one thing I'm pretty certain of and it scares the hell out of me."

"What?"

"That it's not Cleo Fort who's dying in the infirmary. It's Maxine Polketta."

CHAPTER Eleven

THERE WERE THREE OR FOUR PEOPLE I NEEDED TO LEARN MORE about. I already had Chip checking on Ruben. The next two on my list were King Noorvik and his son, Bill, who'd apparently vanished off the face of the earth. If Cleo's dream represented anything like reality, then Bill was the most likely candidate for being the murderer. The witnesses who saw him enter the building with Sline and, even more significantly, depart in some panic only minutes later, certainly supported that suspicion, to say nothing of his disappearance, which sure looked fishy as hell to me. Fat chance, of course, that Bill's name would even be mentioned at the trial, if there was ever going to *be* a trial. Finally, I wanted to find out more about Jackson Sline.

I went to the *Graphic* and sweet-talked the librarian in the morgue into pulling the bio files on both the DA and Sline. Chip'd probably kill me for going around him this way, but he was off chasing his tail somewhere and I didn't particularly feel like waiting for him. Besides, who needs his permission? This was my case, if it was a case.

Sline was easy. The file was limited almost entirely to society page clippings. There seemed to be little else to the man's life. He was about thirty, had inherited too much money and not enough brains to know what to do with it. He'd fallen in with the pseudo-Bohemian scene and all the would-be avant garde artists and second-rate literary parasites who recognized a grade A sucker when they saw one. The parties Sline threw in his penthouse quickly became legendary, though they were shunned by the serious artists, poets and writers, who simply sneered and went back to work. Fortunately for his self-esteem, presuming he had any, Sline didn't know the difference. So his guests postured and talked nonsense and ate his food and drank his liquor and smoked his marijuana and everyone seemed perfectly happy. The clippings in the file were all pretty much interchangeable, except for one. It was dated only a couple of months ago and announced Sline's engagement. It was only an inch or so of column space and the picture wasn't much, just Sline and some horse-faced woman with a blank expression who looked easily ten years older than him. I recognized her name; she was heiress to some *nouveau riche* millionaire who'd made his fortune in plastic spatulas. I would've liked to have seen what their kids would've looked like. I couldn't find any overt connection between Sline and Noorvik, worse luck.

The DA's folder, on the other hand, was a good two or three inches thick, but I already knew pretty much all I would probably ever care to know about the man. I just wanted to get a fresh handle on the bozo I browsed through the clippings, picking up whatever details struck my eye. Even at that, the man left a bad taste. He had come up from nowhere, fresh out of law school and straight into the seamier strata of city politics, where honesty and fair play got you nowhere fast, but the kind of games King seemed to have a natural talent for not only got you places in a hurry, they could make you very rich in the process. By the time he was forty, King Noorvik had power and money and the city pretty much in his back pocket. There were few people in City Hall who he didn't have something on, and nearly as many in the state legislature. He had greased the ways from his office to the mayor's and once he'd started the machinery going, there was going to be precious little anyone could do to stop him from going on to the governor's mansion.

Then I found a clipping that raised both eyebrows.

Well, well, well . . . Noorvik didn't come out of nowhere after all. He came up from Florida. Jesus. I'd completely forgotten that he'd gone to law school and met his wife there. Florida, Florida, Florida. What in the hell kept bringing Florida into this?

Someone once said that you can judge a person by the quality of their enemies, in which case I should have felt some personal satisfaction in having achieved the animosity of King Noorvik. An enemy like him would make me pretty high-class stuff. But so far as I was personally concerned it only bore upon the spectacular nature of my demise, which event I was pretty sure would be high on the DA's agenda should my name ever again be brought to his attention.

While I would be seriously surprised to learn that Noorvik had ever given me a thought until recently, if he had even been aware of my existence, I certainly wasted no love on him. He had been instrumental in blacking my father's name, seeing that a departmental scandal was placed squarely on his shoulders . . . an act made all the more cowardly since my father was in a hospital bed dying at the time, having taken a belly full of slugs in the line of duty. He was never able to answer the allegations made against his character since he died without ever regaining consciousness. No one ever said so, but I knew Noorvik's hand was behind my dad's assassination—and assassination it was, too, since my father valued his good name even above his life.

So far as the kid, Bill, was concerned, there was less to learn. My impression was that he was far from being a chip off the old blockhead. That is, he seemed like a reasonably decent human being, if one overlooked him leaving Cleo in the lurch. His only ambition seemed to be architecture, to which end he attended classes at Pratt and the Art Students' League. He had no interest whatsoever in politics, dirty or otherwise, and kept himself as distant as possible from his father's machinations. In fact, I got the distinct impression that father and son didn't like each other very much, which sentiment certainly stood the kid in good favor with me. Bill appeared to be moderately popular at school, being neither the best-liked kid nor the most disliked. He dated some girls, no one regular and no one seriously, was considered moderately desireable but wasn't exactly the first name on every debutante's dance card, either. Just an okay kid. There was no mention of any connection with Sline, but it wasn't a stretch to figure he must've run across the guy sometime at either

Pratt or the ASL. Since Max had modeled at the League, it was entirely possible that she was the connection between Bill and Sline—which would certainly go somewhere, though I'm not sure how far, toward explaining why both she and the boy were at Sline's place the night he was croaked.

When I got back to my place, Maggie told me that Chip had called. He'd left a number, so I rang him back.

"What's up, hack?" I asked when he answered.

"I have got something for you on our little friend Ruben."

"Oh, really? Nothing good, I hope."

"Good or not, it is certainly most interesting."

"Yeah? Well, shoot it to me."

"The Forts lived in a little town called Plankton Key, on an island of the same name, one of those little coral jobs that dribble off the chin of Florida?"

"Yeah, I know what you're talking about. Like in *Key Largo*."

"Right. Just like that, I guess. Well, about two years ago Ruben was picked up for assault and battery."

"Really? What a surprise."

"That is not the best part by any means."

"Mm?"

"The man whose eye he blacked was one Jackson Sline."

Well, well! That *was* a surprise, indeed, indeed.

"What in the world was Jackson Sline doing in a backwater dump like Plankton Key? I thought the only way anyone could drag him more than two miles from Broadway would be to chloroform him first."

"You are most correct, there is not much that could have torn him away from the city. In fact, only one thing could have. Guess what that would be?"

"I don't know, but could it's initials be King Noorvik?"

"Bingo. Noorvik has got a big motor yacht, the *Flying Fish*, he keeps down in Miami. Noorvik runs it down to the Keys at least twice a year to fish for marlin, swordfish, sharks—though thinking of him going after sharks seems just a little too ironic, you think? Anyway, he always took guests, people he was trying to impress and the toadies who hung around licking his boots. Guess which catagory Sline was in?"

"I'm sure he kept King's boots spotless. Well, it's our first real connection between Cleo—or at least her family—and Sline. And maybe even Noorvik, maybe. I'm not sure what to make of it all, though. So Ruben blacked Sline's eye? Who wouldn't want to? I still don't see why Ruben would want to kill him two years later. There had to've been something between them."

"There might have been something at that."

"Yeah? Like what?"

"Like Cleo. Ruben beat the hell out of Sline because Sline had tried to rape Cleo."

Two years ago Cleo would have been about seventeen. A nice kid. Very pretty, too, even beautiful, judging by the snapshots I'd found. Tall, slender, with long black hair and big dark eyes like those refugee kids you see in the newsreels. Naïve and trusting. And a dead ringer for Maxine Polketta. What did Sline think when he saw her? I don't know why he was on the Key, not yet anyway. Who knows? Maybe Plankton was the nearest post office or the only phone or telegraph link to New York, it had to be something like that. It didn't make any difference at the moment. What mattered was that Sline was on a pier overlooking the Bay of Florida and admiring the sunset or whatever when he noticed a girl running up the beach toward him. I can imagine him watching her with increasing disbelief as he slowly realizes it's a girl he thought he left back in New York.

"Max!" he must have shouted. "Hey! Maxie!"

I can see Cleo coming to a skidding halt. She'd adopted the name of her dream-self years before, but no one outside her family had ever used it, or even knew about it. Hearing a stranger call her Maxie must have stopped her cold. Who was this man who seemed to know her as Max? She would've come up to him warily, curiously.

"My God, Max! Why didn't you tell me you were coming down? How'd you get here? You must've flown, but why didn't you say anything?"

Cleo wouldn't have known what was going on. Maybe she recognized him from her dream-life, her life as Max . . . if so, seeing him there in the flesh on Plankton Key must have been monumentally shocking, she would have been shaken to her core. Am I dreaming? she would have asked herself. Already she was having difficulty distinguishing between reality and her reveries and when she was in their grip, she *was* Maxine Polketta. She must have been wondering, Am I awake or am I asleep? Who am I now? Maxine or Cleo?

"Come on with me," Sline would have said, taking her arm, "we need to talk."

I don't know yet what passed between them, what they said or did, I'm just guessing at all of this, but when Ruben, out looking for his sister an hour later, heard her whimpering behind a palmetto grove, he found Sline crouched over Cleo's half-naked body, his face pressed to her breasts, his hands groping her . . . Well, as reluctant as I am to give Ruben any credit I have to admit he did the right thing. He beat the living shit out of Jackson Sline.

The ruckus—first Cleo's screams and moments later Sline's—attracted people and someone called the police and Ruben was arrested, which was lucky for Sline because I'm pretty sure Ruben was out to kill him that day. Sline refused to press charges, though, and cleared out of Plankton Key as fast as he could. The sheriff urged Cleo to file a complaint against Sline for rape, since everyone in town liked Cleo Fort and were outraged at what had happened to her, especially by some city slicker from New York. Or nearly happened, since the doctor said she'd not been violated, thank God, just roughed around some and scared simple. Cleo for her part refused to discuss the matter, let alone file a complaint, and before long the whole thing blew over and—so far as anyone suspected—was forgotten.

Apparently they were dead wrong about that.

Chapter Twelve

"Here's what I think," I told Maggie and Chip. We were having dinner at my place. I'd sprung for the pizza and Chip had brought the beer. "I don't know yet what the link is between Maxine and Cleo, but there's no question there is one. Each girl had dreams about the other's life, although apparently Cleo's were by far the more vivid of the two, to the point where she sometimes had difficulty distinguishing her real life from her dream life. Because of this link, whatever it is, Cleo is dying. I think this is because *Maxine* is somewhere sick or dying and whatever's happening to her is also happening to Cleo. If we can't find Max in time, well . . ."

"We lose both of them," said Maggie.

"But where *is* Maxine?" asked Chip. "Why has she disappeared? I can see her running from a potential murder rap, or accessory to murder at the very least, but she has abandoned her child. I can not see her doing that."

"That's what I don't understand, too," said Maggie. "For all her faults, and no one ever accused Maxie of being an angel, she was devoted to Jackie. She worshiped the kid. She would've gotten word to me at least, if nothing else, if she were able to."

"Then we can only assume she's unable to," I said, "and that she's unable to because she's sick or hurt. But even so, surely she'd find *some* way to get a message to you. Like you just said, Max was no angel for sure, but she wouldn't just walk away from Jackie. If all that's true, then, I can see only one conclusion: she hasn't gotten word to Maggie because she *can't*."

"Can't?"

"Can't. I think she's being held somewhere. I think she's a prisoner."

"Are you not being a little melodramatic, Slim?" put in Chip. "What would be the point of someone kidnaping her?"

"I don't know yet. It just seems like the only logical explanation. Maybe King feels that he's got such an open and shut case already going against Cleo, why muddy the waters by bringing in a new defendant? Or maybe Max's got something on King. That's entirely possible, you know, given her intimate contact with Sline."

"Speaking of logical, by the way, that was a pretty stupid stunt you pulled at the morgue this morning."

"What?"

"'What?' Getting more than your pretty ribs kicked in is what. You think Noorvik is going to let you off with a warning if he finds that you are still poking around in his business?"

"So how's he going to find out?"

"How did he find out the last time? He is the DA, he knows everyone, he has got everyone in his pocket. He is going to find out he did not scare you and the next time you hear from his boys you just might disappear forever permanently."

"Yeah? Well, what if his son *is* a murderer and he's not only covered it up and hid the kid out somewhere but tried to make a scapegoat out of some poor, sick kid who never did anyone any harm? Let *that* get out and he can kiss the mayor's office goodbye, that's for sure. He may think he's got the city in his pocket now, but when the dust settles he'll be lucky if he can find anyone who'll even admit to remembering his name."

"You are playing a very damned dangerous game, Velda, and I most sincerely wish you would drop out of it."

"What d'you expect me to do? Never mind Sline and the Noorviks, am I supposed to let that poor kid waste away in jail? She trusts me, Chip."

"If I know anything about you at all, and I do, God knows, I know it is never worth the energy arguing when you have got your mind, such as it is, set on doing something. Go ahead, walk in front of the oncoming truck. I warned you not to step off the curb. Now it is your look-out."

"Will you still help me?"

"Sure, did I ever say I would not?"

"You're such a pal. Push me in front of a truck any old day, huh?"

"It would be my pleasure, too. Maggie," he said, turning toward her, "what is the dope on the kid, on Jackie?"

"She's Max's little girl."

"I know that much. Max and Sline, right?"

"Yeah."

"Did Sline know that Max had a baby?"

"Oh yeah, sure, and he wasn't very happy about it, either."

"Really?" I said. This was news to me.

"I don't know any of the details, but I'm pretty sure Sline tried to pay her off, get her out of the country."

"Why? What'd he care?"

"Well, he was planning to get married this Spring, to that horsefaced heiress. Maybe he figured having Maxie show up at the wedding with a kid in tow would be a little embarrassing, all things considered."

"I suppose so. Where was Max living all this time? She wasn't with Sline, I take it?"

"No, no she wasn't. She had a room down on Wooster Street, but she was never there much. It was just a convenient address. I saw it once, just a room with a bed and sink, that was about all."

"You remember the address?"

"Sure. Two-seventeen, between Spring and Bloome. I forget the apartment number. It was on the fourth or fifth floor, I think."

The conversation shifted to inanities after that—no, worse than inanities. The transition was subtle, but after about half an hour I realized that I'd settled back in my chair nursing a beer while Chip and Maggie, wholly oblivious to my non-participation, were engaged in an animated mutual cross examination. Jesus Christ, he's flirting with her right here in my own living room, the lousy bastard. He was just too, too fascinated by Maggie's colorful life and she absorbed with breathless awe his self-description as a cross between H.L. Mencken and Walter Winchell. Jesus Christ almighty, it was disgusting. Well, what was I getting into such a swivet about, anyway? I had no hold on Chip and God knows he'd made it clear enough he neither had nor wanted one on me. Who did? At thirty I'd tried damned hard to convince myself that the answer was no one, and that there would likely be no one. I'm no dog, God knows—I wish I were, it'd sure make things a lot easier, but men liked Maggies and I'm not a Maggie and there you are.

The hell with it all.

It took no more persuasion than a five-dollar bill to get the landlady of two-seventeen Wooster Street to let me into 6C, Maxine Polketta's room. I'd told her I was Max's sister and she never blinked an eye, the fact that I was lying and that she knew it being an unspoken agreement between us.

The room was exactly what I'd expected from Maggie's description, except maybe worse. It was no more than ten by ten, unwallpapered since Dewey took Manila, the only light a single fly-specked bulb under a tin shade hanging from the center of the ceiling. When I flipped the wall switch the light just served to make the room dingier. There was an iron-framed bed, which I noticed was neatly made, a wooden chair with one slat missing from its back, a dresser with its veneer peeling off in thin, brittle curls, and a sink, its bowl stained a bright poisonous-looking green. Except for a cracked mirror over the sink and a colorless circular braided rug that covered about half the wooden floor, that was pretty much all there was to it. I went through the motions of tossing down the room, but I didn't really have my heart in it. There was nothing of Max Polketta there. It was only a hollow shell.

I sat on the edge of the bed, chin in hands, wondering what to do and not coming up with very much. I don't know what I'd been hoping for—it wasn't as though I'd expected to find a map with a big X on it marked "Max's secret hideout". But this was even more impersonal than the Fort's apartment had been. It had all the individuality of a shoe box. It was obviously just what Maggie said it was: an address of convenience, someplace for Max to get her mail, a place where she could find a bed when she needed one . . . or needed one to herself, I thought a little meanly. Well, hell, why not think meanly of Max? Somehow—no matter how unfair it was—I couldn't help but feel that this was all her fault. It was as though a single person had been split in two at birth, split into good and evil twins, and a decent, sweet, bright young girl was being made to suffer through all the pain and guilt and shame of her doppelganger, if doppelganger is the word I want. Dr. Jacqueline and Miss Hyde.

I sighed and stood up. When I did, the bed rocked slightly as though one leg were too short. I hadn't noticed it when I'd sat down. When I looked I saw that the rug was under one leg at the foot of the bed and flopped up against the other one. I don't know if I was thinking anything. I was just looking at the turned-up edge of rug, my thoughts still on Maxine, when something clicked. *Why* was one leg on top of the rug and the other leg not? Because someone had pulled the rug from under that leg, which you'd have to do in order to turn the rug over.

I went to the far side of the rug, took hold of the edge and rolled it half over on itself. There, pinned to the underside, was a white envelope. *Holy cow*! I sat back down on the bed and turned the envelope over in my hands a couple of times, mainly just to give myself a chance to catch my breath. There was nothing written on it. It was just a plain, cheap envelope like you'd get at any five and dime. It wasn't even sealed, the flap was just tucked under. It had been pinned to the rug with one of those big safety pins you use on diapers. One of Jackie's, I supposed. I opened the envelope. Inside was a heavy sheet of paper, folded into thirds like a letter. I took it out and unfolded it.

Well, well, well.

It was a marriage certificate.

Dated just two years earlier, it attested to the marriage of Maxine Polketta and Jackson Polberg Sline III in the City and County of New York. No wonder Sline was a little nervous about his engagement to the spatula heiress. He was about to become a bigamist.

This was all well and good—and certainly surprising enough—but how did it bear upon Sline's murder? If anything, *he* had more reason to get rid of *her* than *vice versa*. He certainly wouldn't be able to marry the spatula queen if he were already married to someone else. To get his grubby paws on Spatula's money, he'd either need a divorce from Max or her permanent disappearance. If anything, *Max* was the one who ought to have been murdered if anyone was going to be. Had she been threatening him with blackmail? Extorting money from him in exchange for her silence? A quick, quiet Mexican divorce and a tidy little nest egg and he'd never hear from her again? Could be, but that was even less reason for her to have killed him. She'd be killing off the golden goose. Maybe someone *did* bump her off and that's why no one can find her. No—that makes no sense. Why kill her *after* Sline was murdered? What would be the point of that? I'd hardly think anyone'd want to avenge Sline's death. It's more likely that the murderer'd be thrown a party.

I'm in the wrong business. I hate mysteries.

There was nothing else in the room so I tucked the certificate and its envelope in my bag, replaced the rug and left, my brain all atwitter.

I wanted to talk to someone who'd known Sline intimately, someone to whom he may have confided his relationship with Max. I wasn't too sure who to turn to. I didn't think he'd had any close friends, not real friends I mean, only that collection of toadies and sycophants who had disappeared as soon as they'd realized their source for free eats, booze and dope was no longer among the living, no more willing to hang around then a gang of vultures lingers over a carcass once it's picked clean. I was pretty sure King Noorvik knew plenty about Sline's private life, but I was just as sure he wouldn't be in any mood to chat with me about it.

I stopped in a deli down the street from Max's room for some coffee and between cups I had an Idea. I called Finlayson from a pay phone in the back.

"I know Cleo's dreams have stopped," I told him, "because they have her on some kind of dope, right?"

"That's right. She's been sleeping peacefully."

"If she stopped taking the medication, the dreams would start again?"

"I'm sure they would. Why?"

"Just something I was wondering about. Have you seen her lately?"

"I was at the infirmary this morning."

"How's she look?"

"Terrible, Velda, just terrible. It's like something is eating her alive. I don't know how much longer she can hold out. I think she'd be dead already if she didn't have such a powerful will to live. But you know, Velda—"

"What?"

"Well, that will is Cleo's and I don't know how much of Cleo there is left."

That missing six months in Max's life bothered me considerably. Maggie had no idea where she'd gone. There were probably only two people who knew the answer, other than Max herself of course. One was Sline, I'd be willing to bet, and the other was Cleo, who had been living Max's life at the same time Max was. I'd been over Cleo's diary half a dozen times and it just wasn't any help. Aside from the fact that she kept it only sporadically, recording only those visions that had most impressed her, the descriptions were tantalizingly vague—they were, well, dreamlike. She didn't know the people she met, she didn't know the places she found herself in. She had to describe things the best she could, using images and ideas that were familiar to her.

It had started snowing again. Huge soft flakes like feathers drifted into the streets, like a pillow factory had exploded somewhere nearby. It was one of those snows you just know is going to go on all night. Tomorrow the streets and parked cars and ashcans and mailboxes would look as though they were covered in whipped cream and for a few hours at least, until the plows came through and the traffic and the pedestrians turned the snow into grey slush, the city would look beautiful and serene and clean. Fooling no one, of course.

Maggie had put Jackie to bed and sat with me by the window to watch the snow fall into Pith Street. I'd made martinis in the old milk bottle I use for a shaker and we used them as an excuse to not say very much for quite a while. When I'd finished my first drink, I set the glass onto the window sill and brought out the thick manila file folder that had been laying on the floor beside me.

"What's that?" Maggie asked.

"It's the *Graphic's* morgue file on King Noorvik."

"Oh, really? How'd you get hold of that?"

"We probably shouldn't go into that, if you get my drift—"

"I gotcha."

"I was wondering if you'd mind helping me go through it?"

"Sure. What're you looking for?"

"I don't know exactly," I answered, handing her half the clippings. "Whatever strikes you as, I don't know, odd, I guess. Anything that might suggest a connection with Max or Sline or anyone else involved in this mess. I just think there's gotta be more to his interest in this than his son's involvement, I don't know why. A hunch I suppose?"

"Well, it's something to do anyway."

I refilled our jelly glasses and we got to work. The clippings were more or less arranged chronologically, though obviously no one had made any great effort to keep them that way. Still, the files went back pretty much to the beginning of Noorvik's political career. As a young prosecutor, he'd been responsible for some high-profile cases. He'd quickly become an eager beaver assistant DA and finally, just two years ago, DA. There was little in the clippings about his shady dealings and questionable connections, just a few hints in the early years. By this fact alone—the decline in critical stories—I could gauge the increase in his power and influence. The paper was obviously taking no chances. But there was plenty that could be read between the lines, especially if you read them with the inside knowledge I'd picked up from Chip and my cop friends. Still, while I was aware of all this in a vaguely piecemeal kind of way, the impact of seeing it all presented *en masse* there on my lap made a big impression on me. It was dead clear that Noorvik was the most dangerous man in the city, much more so than any of the hoods and mobsters whose names immediately come to mind when the subject of crime, organized or otherwise, comes up.

"Look at this," Maggie said, then, "Sorry," as I'd jumped at the sound of her voice. I'd almost forgotten she was there. Thank God I hadn't spilled my drink, I can't afford to buy more gin.

"What?"

"Take a look."

I took the clipping from her. It was a single yellowed column. The white paper tag attached to it bore a date nearly twenty years old. It wasn't much more than the announcement of a divorce. City assistant prosecutor King Noorvik had separated from Olivia Noorvik née Poffle, his wife of three years, citing infidelity as cause. The Noorviks had recently had a child together, William Noorvik King, whom the court had placed in the father's custody, Mrs. Noorvik being deemed as unfit for reasons that were only vaguely suggested—but the hint was strongly made that there was more to her unfitness than mere promiscuity. Mrs. Noorvik had not contested the divorce nor was she available for comment, having immediately left the city for parts unknown along with her presumed lover.

"Well, this isn't exactly *un*interesting, but—"

"Yeah, but look what someone had paper clipped to it." I noticed her hand shaking as she passed over another, even smaller slip of newsprint.

It was only a quarter inch of column, from a different paper than the *Graphic*. It had a looped brown stain on it from the paper clip that had held it to the first clipping. Someone had scribbled a date on it of about seven months after the Noorvik divorce. It simply said that one Olivia Polketta had given birth at home to two infants, both girls, one of which had been stillborn. She had been attended by Mrs. Lily Paughner, a licensed midwife, and an unnamed neighbor.

After reading that far, I looked up at Maggie, a questioning frown on my face.

"Keep reading," she said.

There was only one more line. "Mrs. Polketta expressed her intention of returning to New York, where Mr. Polketta has been offered a position with the Port Authority."

Return to New York? I looked at the tag that identified the source of the clipping. It had come from the Plankton Key *Observer-Herald*.

"Wait a minute," I said. "Are you thinking the same thing I am? That Maxine Polketta is the daughter of King Noorvik's ex-wife?"

"Someone at the *Graphic* certainly thought so, connecting up the two items that way. Who else could she be?"

"Did you know that Max had been born in Florida?"

"No. Her mother never said anything to me about it. So far as I ever knew, they'd both been born and raised in the city. I don't think Max herself ever thought otherwise. Mrs. Fort didn't like to talk much about Max's father."

"Yeah. Max's father. You noticed the date on the Florida paper? It's only seven months after the divorce. Just who *was* Maxine's father, Maggie? Max Polketta—or King Noorvik?"

"I don't know."

"I wonder why she dared come back to the city, and why, when she did, she chose to live in poverty when she could have been supported by Noorvik?"

"I don't know that either. Maybe she was scared? God knows she had good reason to be afraid of Noorvik. I can only imagine the threat she might have been living under. Then again, she was never really right in the head all the time I knew her. Maybe she just—I don't know—didn't really know what she was doing, somehow?"

If Noorvik knew that his ex-wife had moved back to the city . . . I thought about a man who'd not only let his wife live and die in abject poverty, but his daughter besides, even if he thought she weren't his blood child. And what if he not only allowed it, but forced her to do it?

"I don't know what it means," I said, "but it can't just be a coincidence that both Max and Cleo were born in the same podunk Florida town. But even that doesn't explain their connection and the fact that they're practically twins, unless there's something really weird in the water down there."

"They might have been born in the same town at about the same time," put in Chip, "but that does not change the fact that they had different mothers and fathers. That stillborn child might have been a twin sister for all you know, but she was born dead. You can not get around that. And do not forget that Mrs. Polketta told you that she could not bear any more kids after that."

"I know, I know. Mrs. Fort swears up and down that Cleo and Ruben are the only children she's ever had. It all beats me." Then something clicked, something that'd been ringing a bell in the back of mind for the past five minutes, and as it dawned on me what it meant, a chill ran down my back. "Let me see that clipping again, the one from the Florida paper."

It was dated August four. That meant Maxine had been born on the third—and so had Cleopatra Fort. I showed the date to Maggie and explained the significance. "They weren't born *about* the same time, they were born at *exactly* the same time. There's still no connection between them, but it's gone beyond coincidence that their birthdates and places both match. That's too much to ask."

"I wish I had some idea that would help." She suddenly sat bolt upright in her chair. "*Who's that?*"

I glanced out the window in the direction she was looking. Below the window, a hulking figure was lumbering up the front steps of the building, silhouetted by the streetlight and blurred by the swirling snow.

"Oh. That's Ruben Fort. Cleo's brother. He works in Jersey and usually gets home around this time. I don't blame you for being startled, he's not a pretty sight."

"I know. I've seen him before."

"Oh?"

"Yeah. It was just a few days before Sline's murder. Max and I were walking down the street when this big guy stopped us. I'd completely forgotten about it until this very moment. I hadn't thought it about it at all since it happened, but seeing him down there reminded me. He passed us and then suddenly turned and grabbed Max by her arm. 'My God!' he said. 'What're you doing here? What're you doing with someone like *this*? Get on home right now!' Neither of us knew who in the world he was and he frightened us, he was so big and angry. We ran into the nearest shop, but he followed us in, still shouting for Max to come home with him. The manager of the store, who knew us, called the police. When they came, he tried to tell them that Max was really his sister, but it was our word against his. Max showed them her driver's license and the manager backed her up as well. The guy really got angry then, so the cops arrested him and took him away. Max and I were frightened and didn't go to the station the next morning to press charges. We were afraid of what the big guy might do to us if we got him arrested. I know we should've, but if you'd seen him you'd understand."

"I have seen him and I assure you I do understand. He's much too big for as few brains as he's got. He'd scare me, too. He *does* scare me."

"Yeah, and you're half again bigger than me. Well, anyway, they must've let him go because a day or two later Max said she noticed him following her. He never bothered her again, though, not like the first time."

"Did Max ever take any dope?"

"I think so. Yes. I never cared for the stuff and Max knew that. I tried not to notice, tried, to be honest I guess, to at least pretend that I didn't know. But the last week I saw her was when I couldn't ignore it any longer. I think she'd been using dope since getting back from the reformatory, but like I said before, I didn't see as her often then as I had before. I think she'd been careful, keeping me from knowing, but after she started being followed she made no secret about it."

"I was just wondering about the syringe the police found. Cleo'd dreamed about using it."

"I'm sure Sline supplied Max with whatever she needed—I have no doubt at all but that he's the bastard who got her hooked in the first place."

Maggie had long since gone to bed, but I was still up, sucking on my fifth martini, thinking, thinking, thinking. I had Cleo's diary on my lap and kept flipping through the pages, first one way, then the other. Why had Max disappeared for six months? Why did she come back on the day Sline had died? Where had she come back *from*? I flipped back and forth, back and forth, not even reading the words any more. Then I stopped, realizing that the sound of the pages had half-hypnotized me. I took a sip of my drink and looked at the page my finger held. It was the first entry I'd read when I'd found the diary. *Last night I dreamed I was in the desert walking through the Sands with bright, colored lights flashing all around me like*

Fireworks." Something seemed vaguely odd about that and I couldn't quite put my finger on it. *Walking through the Sands.* That was it. Why had she capitalized "Sands"? Was it just a teenager's slip—after all, she had used inappropriate capitals elsewhere—or was it something else? Desert—sands. But she hadn't been walking though sand, she'd been walking through *the* Sands. The Sands.

Los Vegas.

I called Chip.

"Do you have any idea what time it is, Slim?"

"No, why? Did you hock your watch again?"

"Come on, baby—it is one o'clock in the morning. I have had a long day. I would ask if you were calling just to be pleasant if I thought it was within your powers to do so, so you must want something. You always want something."

"A little of both this time. I have something for you, and I want you to do something."

"Well, well, Slim! That is more like it! Let me get the place straightened up a bit before you come over. And do not forget your toothbrush as I do not have a spare."

"You just said you were wide awake, so you can quit dreaming. Look, I'm serious. I've got two things for you. First, Maxine was married to Sline."

"*Married*? When?"

I told him about finding the marriage certificate. He tried not to sound impressed but of course he was.

"That might go some considerable way toward explaining why Max vanished," he admitted.

"Yup. Sline was getting her out of town, is what I figure."

"What is the other thing?"

"I know where Sline got her out of town to."

"Oh, yeah?"

"At least I think I do. He sent her to Los Vegas. I think Sline probably paid her to go there to get a quick divorce. I think she stayed at the Sands Hotel. If not there, then someplace else in the city. Do you think you could find out where she was? Maybe if I can get a handle on what she was doing there I can figure out why she came back."

"Can this not wait until morning?"

"No. Look at me, I'm up and working on this case, bright-eyed and bushy-tailed."

"We will leave your bushy tail out of this for the moment if you do not mind. All right, all right. Let me make a couple of calls. It is what, ten o'clock yesterday evening out there. I know not who is going to be around. I will call you back as soon as I find out anything."

"If she registered somewhere, it might have been under Sline's name. Check both."

"Yes yes yes. Give me some credit. I will call you later."

"I'll be waiting." I blew a kiss into the phone just to be snide and hung up.

As it turned out I was sound asleep in my chair when Chip called back a couple of hours later. I fumbled the phone off the hook.

"Mm?"

"Ha! You were asleep!"

"Me? No! Not at all! Of course not!"

"Yes you were, you lousy rat! Got me up chasing around in the middle of the night and then you tuck yourself back in your cozy little beddy-bye. I know you need all the beauty sleep you can get . . ."

"Ha ha. You're a riot. So? Did you waste the last two hours or did you actually accomplish something?"

"Just you wait and hear what I accomplished my little chickpea. You were right about Max being in Los Vegas."

"See?"

"Shut up and listen. She arrived in Los Vegas six or seven months ago in the company of a gentleman named Probisci."

"Pro what? Who's that?"

"Probisci. P-R-O-B-I-S-C-I. Eduardo Porbisci. You would know the name if you ever read the papers."

"I do too read the papers. I read the *Graphic*."

"I meant something besides the funnies. Probisci is Jackson Sline's lawyer. Would you be really surprised to learn that he was partner in the same firm as our pal Flan?"

"Nope."

"He was also campaign manager for King Noorvik's mayoral bid. And I emphasize the past tense."

"Why? King fire him?"

"I'm sure Probisci would have preferred that. Nope. He died in Los Vegas."

"Died?"

"D-I-E-D. Deceased. Passed away. Gone to the other side. Or, rather, was apparently sent on his way prematurely by none other than our mysterious little friend, Maxine Sline, née Polketta."

"Wait a minute. Are you saying she *killed* this Probisci?"

"Sure looks like it. Hotel maid—at the Sands if you must know—found the body, little hole square in the middle of the forehead, the rest of his head scattered all over the white shag carpet which I suppose completely ruined it."

"Max is the presumed killer?"

"Who else? Los Vegas cops and the state patrol have been scouring Nevada for her. Seems that Probisci lied his head off when they registered so no one knew where the hell they had really come from."

"When did this happen?"

"Just a few weeks ago. To save your pretty little head all the trouble of making the calculation, Probisci was whacked just a week before Sline was murdered. Plenty of time for Maxine to have gotten back here."

"Jesus. But what'd this Probisci have to do with anything? If Max'd gone to Nevada for a divorce, why didn't she get one? I was assuming Sline'd simply paid her off to clear the way for his marriage to Miss Spatula. Why didn't she take the money and the kid and hit the road?"

"Evidently there was a little more to it than that."

"Evidently. Look, we both need to get some sleep. Let's meet at Joe's for breakfast. I'll buy—" with what? "—and bat my big blue eyes at you."

"Do that and I will just bat them right back to you. Okay, it is a date. What time?"

"Six."

"Six? It is three in the a.m. now!"

"G'night dear." I hung up.

Chapter Thirteen

"I THINK I'VE GOT IT," I TOLD CHIP AS OUR COFFEE WAS BEING POURED. Chip just glowered at me. He looked as though he'd been up all night and I told him so, suggesting that it wasn't healthy for a man his age to get so little sleep. It didn't look good, professionally, for him to be running around with bloodshot eyes and an unmown face. People might draw the wrong conclusions. He said something very unkind and Joe glanced at me. I shook my head. No, I didn't need the bum thrown out on his ear. Not yet at any rate.

"What have you got?" Chip growled and out of sheer meanness ordered the most expensive breakfast on the menu.

"I think I have a good idea why Max went to Los Vegas with whatisname—"

"Probisci. Remember? I spelled it for you."

"Probisci, then. Why she went to Los Vegas with *Probisci*, why she didn't get a divorce and, maybe, why she came back to New York."

"All right, Shirley Holmes. Let's hear your great big theory."

"Well, I figure she didn't *go* to Los Vegas, she was *taken* to Los Vegas."

"You mean kidnapped? That does not sound very plausible. For one thing, no one is kidnapped *to* the Sands Hotel.."

"Well, no, not kidnapped exactly, but coerced. She was forced to go. Sline didn't give her any choice."

"How so?"

"She didn't have the kid with her, right? Jackie?"

"Nope, not so far as I know."

"Well, that's it, then. Sline had taken the kid. Maxine, whatever other faults she may have, is utterly devoted to the little girl. She'll do anything for the brat and when Sline took Jackie and told Max that she'd never see her again unless she gave him an uncontested divorce, what else would she have done?"

"What the hell would Sline do with a kid? I would imagine that would be the last thing in the world he would want."

"I figure it this way. By law Max'd be due half of everything Sline had if they divorced, but Sline had an ace. If they divorced openly, she might get half his estate, but she'd also lose the kid. There's no way the courts would have given *her* custody, not with her background and record, which you can be sure Sline'd spread far and wide. And don't forget, Sline had the best legal advice in the city at his finger tips. Where would Max get an attorney? Not that any court would think that Sline'd be any great shakes as a father, God forbid, but he at least had a home and an income and by the time things would have gotten around to child custody, he would've been married to Miss Spatula. The courts would've given him the kid without batting an eye and he would no doubt have promptly found an entirely new home for her, maybe even put her up for adoption, which really would have killed Max. So he took the girl away from her and told Max that she couldn't have her back until she'd given him a divorce on the terms he wanted, which were, of course, that she get the kid and absolutely nothing else whatsoever. Not a single solitary nickel."

"But what about Probisci? What do you suppose that was all about?"

"I'll be glad to tell you. I think the idea was that once the divorce was granted and everything was hunky dory for Sline, Max would have just quietly disappeared."

"You think he was going to have Probisci kill her?"

"Yup. Why not? So long as she was around, there'd always be a chance she'd spill the beans to the new Mrs. Sline—just out of spite if for no other reason—and if that happened he could just kiss those spatula millions goodbye. So Maxie beat him to the draw as it were. Did you happen to find out if she'd filed for an uncontested divorce while she was there?"

"She did."

"See?"

"That is quite a theory you have, uh, theorized."

"I just overflow with smarts, do I not?"

"You are overflowing all right but I am afraid if I say with what that big goon behind the counter over there will throw me through the window."

"I have no doubt about that at all. Joe likes me, unlike some people. He'd gladly throw you through a window just to see me smile. Don't you think that's sweet?"

"She's a nice girl, bub," Joe snarled over his shoulder.

"I like you, too, Slim, you just drive me nuts, is all. You always did."

"That's what all my men say."

"Yeah. Well, look, I will not say that your theory does not have any merit. It at least has the virtue of explaining some things even if it has got holes in it big enough for your chum Joe here to walk through."

"It'll do until something better comes along. At least it gives us a motive for Max, why she disappeared last year and why she came storming back to New York looking for blood."

"I'll grant you that. What now?"

"I'm going to ask Dr. Finlayson to request that Cleo be taken off her medication."

"What? What for?"

"The medication's been suppressing her dreams. She's not had one since she was moved to the infirmary."

"But what would the point be?"

"Isn't it obvious? Somehow she and Maxine are sharing their lives with one another. Cleo dreams she's Max and sometimes Max dreamed she was Cleo. I have no idea why, but when Cleo dreams she's Max, she knows exactly what Max is doing right at that very same moment, like—like watching a live broadcast on television.

That's why she had the dream about the murder at the same time it was happening. If Finlayson takes her off her medication, Cleo may dream again and if she does, she may be to describe where Max is. Then all we have to do is go there, get Max and Cleo's in the clear."

"You make it sound so simple. But you think Max is dying. What happens to Cleo if Max dies while, while they are *linked*, I guess you would say? What if Max is *already* dead?"

"I hate to think. But Finlayson thinks Cleo's dying anyway. Even though she's not actually dreaming about Max, the link is still there, working, somehow. Whatever it is that's happening to Max is happening to Cleo, too. It's certain she's going to die if we don't try this and she might not die if we do. We might be able to save Max and if we can save her, we might also save Cleo."

"You are as nuts as she is and I would give a lot to be able to come up with a better idea, but I can not. It is going to take a lot to sell Finlayson on it, let alone the authorities. And God help you if Noorvik gets even so much as a hint about what you are trying to do."

Finlayson was pretty doubtful about my suggestion, but couldn't think of anything better to suggest. The girl was dying, there was no question about that, and no one had any idea why, let alone what they could do about it. The doctor at the infirmary was a good man, Finlayson said, and was doing everything he could for Cleo, but it wasn't amounting to much. She was slipping further away every day.

"The medication has stopped her dreams," I said, "but it obviously hasn't broken her connection, whatever it is, with Max. Let her dream again, just for one night. I think it's a chance worth taking, don't you? The only alternative is to sit here and watch her fade away like a ghost. How can we make her worse off than she already is?"

"It's up to Doctor Albertson. All I can do is make the suggestion. The final decision is his."

"Will you do that, please? As soon as you can?"

"I'll call him right now."

"Give me a ring as soon as you hear what he'll do, will you?"

"I'll let you know immediately."

I had some time to kill so I decided to have another chat with Mrs.

Fort. I hadn't seen much of her since the incident with Maggie at the infirmary. She had kept to herself, never leaving the apartment except for her visits to Cleo. I wanted to report to her, give her what news I had, but she had no phone so I'd been slipping notes under her door. There hadn't been much *to* report, so I just tried to make them sound as encouraging as I could. She never replied to any of them.

I went upstairs and knocked at her door. There was no answer, so I knocked again. This time I heard some rustling on the other side. Finally, the bolt unlatched and the door opened half an inch, revealing a rheumy-looking eye peering from beneath the chain.

"Mrs. Fort?"

"Miss Bellinghausen."

"May I come in? I'd like to talk with you for a few minutes if it wouldn't be inconvenient."

"No—no, that would be all right." She unhooked the chain and swung the door open. "Come in, please."

Mrs. Fort looked just godawful and I wondered if whatever Cleo was dying of might not be running in the family. She looked at least a decade older than the last time I'd seen her and she had been no spring chicken then.

"Would care for some coffee or tea?"

"Yes, please, thanks."

While she fussed in the kitchen, I looked around. The place hadn't changed in the week since I'd broken into it. It still had the same impersonal, hollow look, like a bus station at two in the morning.

"Have you seen Cleo lately?" I asked.

"Yes, but it's awful hard to bear, seeing her like that. It's, it's wearing me down something awful."

"You should take it easy. You won't do Cleo any good by getting sick yourself."

"I know. I have to keep my strength up for her sake. I don't know what I'd do if it weren't for Ruben. It's been a tower of strength."

"I'm sure. He's seems very protective."

"Oh, yes—yes, ever since Mr. Fort passed away, Ruben's taken care of the family. He's worked very hard, too, harder than he ought to. I know he doesn't like the work he does, but there's nothing else he can do. He works such long hours and comes home so tired he can hardly move. Would you care to sit in the parlor?"

By "parlor" I guessed she meant the front room. I took the cup she offered me and settled into the old armchair near the window while Mrs. Fort sat bolt upright in one of the wooden chairs by the table. She looked like one of those Depression era Farm Security Administration photos of an Okie .

"Ruben just dotes on his sister," she said as she stirred sugar into her tea, the spoon tinkling against side of the cheap mug. "Did you know that he actually helped Mr. Fort with Cleo's birth? He was just a wee lad, only five years old. Can you imagine such a thing? His father said Ruben never turned a hair."

"Has Ruben ever mentioned knowing anyone named Sline or Noorvik?"

"Sline was that man who got killed wasn't he? No—no, he's never mentioned the name so far as I know."

"And Noorvik? Cleo was apparently friends with a Bill Noorvik."

"No. I knew Cleo had found a boy she liked a lot, but she hadn't gone out with him or anything, not really. She's a good girl. She wouldn't have seen him without telling me first. I think maybe they had lunch together sometimes and walked in the parks. But she never went out at night. She said his name was Bill, so I guess it was the same boy you're talking about."

"She never said anything about him?"

"No, no—not really. Just that she was glad to have found a friend in the city so soon."

"Cleo was born in Plankton Key, wasn't she?"

"Yes. Lived there her whole life until we came north to see the doctors. She was very happy there."

"Did you know a Lily Paughner?"

"Lily? Sure, everyone knew Lily. She was a midwife, a good one, helped birth half the children on the Key, much to Dr. Coggins' annoyance, I can tell you! He he! She and him used to fight like cats and dogs."

"But she wasn't there when Cleo was born?"

"No—I don't know why. Mr. Fort went for her, of course, first thing, but she was already busy—someone else, I think, needed her that same night, too. Mr. Fort and Ruben had to help me all by themselves, Lord bless 'em."

"Did you know a family by the name of Polketta? They would have lived there only a short time—maybe just a few weeks?"

"Polketta? I'm not sure. I don't . . . yes, I think so. The name sounds sorta familiar. It was an awful long time ago. I may have heard it but I'm sure I never knew nobody by that name. There was a couple what moved in at the end of our lane, years and years ago, they had a foreign-sounding name like that—Italian or Polish, something like that. It could have been Polketta, I guess. All them spic names they all sound alike, you know. They didn't stay long enough to get to know no one. Moved in one month and were gone the next. I ain't got no idea where they came from or where they went. I doubt if I nor anyone else ever said a word to them."

"Do you think they might have come from New York?"

"I just ain't got no idea. I'm sorry. Is it important?"

"I don't know. Maybe. Cleo was born at home, you say?"

"Oh, both of my children, Ruben and Cleo, were born at home. We had a midwife—Lily Paughner, of course. She was a wonderful woman—helped me with Ruben. Would have helped with Cleo, too, if she hadn't had to have been somewhere else."

"Do you know where else she was, Mrs. Fort? Who the other mother was?"

"No—no. I'm afraid not."

"You've only had the two children?"

"Yes. You see, something went wrong inside me when I had Ruben. I didn't think I'd never have no more children. Mr. Fort and I tried and tried, but I had two stillbirths. I took 'em mighty hard. That's a real hard thing, you know, Miss Bellinghausen? A stillborn baby?"

"I can imagine it is, Mrs. Fort. You must have been very happy to have had such a beautiful little girl as Cleo."

"Oh, yes! She's my darling, my angel. The sweetest little girl any mother could ever have wished for."

"I can see why. I was very impressed with her from the first time I met her. She seems very bright, very alive."

"That's very nice of you to say so. I know that Ruben is—well, is a little slow. But he's really a wonderful boy and works himself to the bone to take care of his mother and sister, but I know he's not never going to make much more of himself than he is now. But Cleo—Cleo's a bright girl, just like you say. Always did real good in school, talks about going to college now. She was right excited about coming to New York, because of the schools and libraries and museums and all. She just loves that sort of thing. She was scared of leaving home, of course, that's only natural—the city frightened her. But she was excited, too, and I think she'll probably stay here . . . that is, I mean if—"

"She's going to be all right, Mrs. Fort. My friends and I are doing everything we can to help her."

"I know, and I'm right most grateful. I sorry I ain't thanked you properly—you've been so very kind—it's just that I've been so awful tired, and everything is so hard to talk about . . . I—"

"Don't worry about it. I've only got a couple more questions, if you don't mind—I'd just like to know what Cleo's life was like at home. What was she like as a kid?"

"Cleo was always a right special child. She did wonderful good at school—I always wished Plankton had a better school, Cleo was always so frustrated. She was always way ahead of the other students, always wanting to know more about every subject. She was always reading, reading, reading. The school liberry was the only one we got and it had only a few shelves a books. The bookmobile come down from the mainland ever couple months and there was a subscription liberry on the mainland and Cleo worked at all sorts of odd jobs to make enough money to get books from it. She read everything she could get her hands on, it didn't seem to matter much what the subject was."

"Did her father support her interests?"

"Oh, Edwin just worshipped little Cleo, and Cleo thought that the sun and moon and stars went round him. They were more like best friends than father and daughter. When he passed away, when Cleo was only six, I thought her poor little heart would just bust in two. I don't think she's ever gotten over losing her poor daddy."

"It must have made things hard for you, too."

"Oh, it did, it did. It was awful hard to make ends meet. Edwin never did make much money at the sponge packing plant, but we paid our bills and had plenty to eat, even if it wasn't fancy, and the children had clean clothes and decent shoes. When Edwin passed away, I had to take in borders to make ends meet. Ruben was old enough to get work and once Cleo was old enough, bless her heart, she took jobs after school to help out. It was special hard for her, too."

"Why was that?"

"Well—well, it was her dreams. They'd started just after her daddy died. She made the turrble mistake of telling the other children at school 'bout the other little girl she sometimes was and they teased her something awful about it. It wasn't long before everyone knew 'bout her and them dreams and as she got older, people started treating her as though—I don't know, as though there was something *wrong* with her. Isn't that the most awful thing? She never hurt nary a soul in her life, no one could have been sweeter nor more generous nor more gentle. But them little kids would just all the time follow her round shouting 'Cleo is crazy! Cleo's a screwball!' and the older kids would just snigger behind her back and make turrble jokes. It drove Ruben just plumb crazy to hear such things. He just adores his sister, you know, and is awful protective of her—"

"I know exactly how she must have felt." Just try being a skinny six foot tall high school girl sometime.

"—and would get into just the most turrble fights with the other youngsters. One time, not long before we moved, Ruben beat a man who'd bothered Cleo and was put in jail for it. The man didn't press charges, thank the Lord. Even when she got older, got into her teens, Cleo had no real friends. It was turrble bad, at an age when other kids're out having fun with each other, having boyfriends and all, to always be left behind."

"Do you remember the man's name, the one Ruben beat up?"

"No . . . I don't think I do. It were a while ago." I let her answer go at that—there'd be no point in suggesting a link between her family and Sline. She had enough on her mind.

"Cleo didn't have any boy friends, then? Back in Florida, I mean?"

"No. And can you imagine such a thing? A girl as sweet, as

beautiful as Cleo? I think the boys were interested, but they was afraid. Not of her, no one could ever be afraid of Cleo, but of what their parents would say and what their friends would say if they went out with someone crazy. I know this hurt Cleo something awful, just broke her poor little heart, though she tried to never show it. I could tell, though—a mother can tell these things you know. She was awful lonely, awful unhappy."

"Did anyone ever see her have these dreams?"

"Oh, no! Never! Never! Only me and her brother and Dr. Coggins."

"Dr. Coggins was your family doctor?"

"Yes. A wonderful man, a wonderful doctor. He just loved Cleo to death. But he was just a old country doctor—he could patch people up, set a broken leg, deliver a baby—and oh! how he hated Mrs. Paughner, the midwife!—all the things that usually happen to people, but Cleo was beyond him. He knew there was something wrong, but he didn't know just what it could be. It was his idea we take Cleo to a doctor in the city."

"But why New York? That's a hell of a long way from Plankton Key, Florida. Why not, oh, I don't know, Miami or, or Atlanta? Someplace like that, closer to home?"

"It was partly Ruben and partly Dr. Coggins. There was a man the doctor had gone to school with, someone he was sure could help Cleo, and this man was in New York. And Ruben, he heard about a job he could have if he wanted it, from a friend of his who worked in the same place and wrote to Ruben and told him about it. It was for real good money, too, more than Ruben had ever made before.

"I think Cleo was anxious to leave Plankton, too. I don't think she cared much where we went, so long as it was somewhere no one had ever heard about her dreams. But this was later, we didn't move until Cleo was nineteen."

"Sorry. I didn't mean for you to get ahead of your story."

"That's all right. I just want you to understand."

"Please, go on then."

"When Cleo was sixteen, she got a job in the general store, in charge of the fancy-goods section—ribbons and notions and cloth, things for sewing and suchlike. She'd been making lace to sell and had sold a passel to the tourists who passed through Plankton, on their way to Key West. I don't know how she learned to do it, but she'd become wonderful good at it, her fingers being so nimble and delicate an' all. She told me once that she'd dreamed how to do it, but I think she must have learned how from one of her liberry books. She took some samples to show Mr. Fimble and he let her bring some in to sell at the store. He was right kind and let her keep everything she made from selling her lace."

I remembered, with an uncanny shiver, how Max's mother had taught her and Maggie how to make lace and the similarity of the two handkerchiefs. Had Mrs. Polketta at the same time been teaching an invisible child two thousand miles away?

"This doctor here in New York—what did he have to say about Cleo?"

"We ain't seen him yet. It took all we had just to get here and get settled. Besides, Cleo's dreams had all but gone away, the bad ones, I mean, until that one you saw. I reckon I figgered maybe moving away had fixed them and maybe we didn't need no doctor after all. I reckon I was wrong, weren't I, Miss Bellinghausen?"

I thanked Mrs. Fort for her time and told her that she needed to be careful about her own health. It'd do Cleo no good if her mother got sick, too.

I went back down to my place and with some time to kill yet I thought it might be gainfully spent following up an idea that had been slowly percolating through my brain. Mrs. Polketta was supposed to have had twins on the same night Cleo had been born. One of them was allegedly stillborn. But whose word did I have for that? I didn't know what I was getting at, exactly, just fishing for any long shot, I guess—but I knew if I didn't follow up the idea it'd drive me crazy the rest of the day. I suppose I was thinking that some sort of weird swapping had gone on, some kind of mistaken identity thing like in *The Prince and the Pauper* or something like that. A mixup at the maternity ward, I don't know. Didn't such things ever happen for real?

I knew Chip'd hang up if I asked him to make another long-distance call for me, so I swallowed hard, picked up the phone, dialled O and asked for the long distance operator. It took a few minutes to get a call through to Dr. Coggins but I finally got a connection. He sounded like Andy Devine. I told him who I was and what I was doing and asked if he remembered the birth of Cleo Fort.

"Well, I remember when she was born, Miss Bellinghausen, but I can't say that I remember her birth since I wasn't there."

"No?"

"Nope. Mrs. Fort was attended by a local busybody named Lily Paughner—"

"She's a midwife, I take it?"

"She likes to think she is, at any rate. Half the people 'round here'd rather have her attend a birth than me," he said and sounded pretty bitter about it, too.

"She ever have any—accidents? I mean, ever lose someone their baby?"

"No-o-o, at least not so's anyone would have admitted to. Stillbirths, of course, an' miscarriages, but I never learned about 'em 'til it was too late to figure out what went wrong."

"Do you remember someone named Polketta? Mrs. Max Polketta? She only lived down there a short while, maybe just a few weeks. She had twins around the same time Cleo was born . . ."

"Polketta, Polketta . . . Somethin' rings a bell 'bout that name. Seems t' me I recall somethin' about 'em. Why?"

"Well, Dr. Coggins, I was just wondering—I'd heard that one of her twins was stillborn. Is that true? I mean, did anyone keep any record of something like that?" I gave him the date. "Could you tell me if anyone knows if the baby really died?"

"Where'd you say y'all callin' from?"

"I'm calling from New York, Doctor."

"Ah see . . . well, I'll tell you what. You hold on there for a minute. Ah'll get th' record book an' see just what it says. Hold on now, that was quite some time ago an' Ah got to find it."

"I'll hold," I said, thinking that the phone company had no idea of the fraud I was committing, using their long distance lines this way and having not a clue as to how I was going to pay my bill at the end of the month.

It seemed to take Coggins forever before he finally returned to the phone.

"Y'all still there, Miss Bellinghausen?"

"Did you find what you were looking for, Doctor?"

"Surely did. Nineteen years ago that was. Lemme see . . ." I could hear pages rustling. ". . . here it is. Yes ma'am. Ah went out to th' Polketta place th' mornin' after th' birth. A pair a baby girls. One healthy as could be, one stillborn. Made out one birth certificate an' one death certificate an' filed 'em with th' county. That's about all Ah got here, Miss. If you need copies of th' certificates, y'all'll have t' call th' county seat."

"You saw the two babies?"

"Yes, ma'am, Ah surely did. Wouldn't've made out th' certificates otherwise. 'Gainst th' law."

I thanked the doctor and hung up. So much for hunches.

I called Sally, who chastised me for tying up my line forever because Finlayson had tried to call a couple of times. She thought he sounded pretty anxious so I thanked her, hung up and dialled his number.

"It's not good, Velda," he said. "Noorvik's not allowing any change in Miss Fort's medication."

"How can he do that?"

"He can do what he wants. Not only is he forbidding anyone from changing her medication, he's going to get a court order forbidding any further interviews with her by anyone other than her appointed attorney."

"Oh, right! 'Her attorney'! Flan's just Noorvik's stooge. They're going to railroad Cleo, they're going to send her up for something she didn't do, all to keep Noorvik's punk son out of the picture."

"I don't see what we can do about it, Velda."

"Neither do I, but not knowing what I was doing never stopped me before."

"As I know all too well."

"Look, how's Cleo right now? Have you seen her yet today?"

"No, but I talked to her doctor. She's in good spirits. Weak, of course, but lucid. Why?"

"I'm going over to the infirmary right now. Noorvik's not going to have had time yet to have built his wall around her. I'm going to try to talk to Cleo, it might be my last chance."

"Be careful, Velda. Remember what happened when Noorvik was just mildly annoyed with you. This could make him very angry indeed."

"Fuck Noorvik."

"*Velda*!"

There was no problem getting in to see Cleo. Word about Noorvik's sanction hadn't yet filtered down from the DA's office, though I expected the boom to fall at any moment. I probably had only minutes with her and I had to make them all count.

Cleo had been moved back to the main ward, among a dozen other patients. I pulled a chair up to her bedside and said, "Hi Cleo. How're you doing?"

"Hi, Velda. Okay, I guess. I—I don't feel all that bad, you know, just awful weak, like there's a tap open somewhere and, and all my energy's just draining out of me."

"I'm doing everything I can to help you, you know that?"

"Sure, Velda. I know that."

"You had nothing to do with the murder of that man, you've never done anything wrong in your life. I don't think you could. Maybe I can prove that and, with any luck, maybe your dreams will stop, too. The only life you'll have to live from then on is your own."

"That'd be wonderful."

"All right, then. You're not having your dreams now, are you?"

"No. Not for a long time now. Not since I started taking my medicine."

"That's good. But I was wondering, Cleo—is there anything? I mean, there must still be some sort of connection between you and—your other self. Otherwise, you see, you wouldn't be sick. It's not *you* that's sick, you understand? It's the other girl. You know that?"

"Yes, I think so. I feel—strange about that, you know? I mean, she's not just *part* of me, like a, a sister or something. For most of my life she's *been* me—my, my *other* me. Max, I mean. It's not like she and I are two different people. In my dreams I *am* Max. Thinking of her not being there anymore, it's, it's like thinking about not having one of my legs or something. I, I don't know how to explain it, Velda."

"You don't have to. Look—I know you haven't had any dreams about Max for more than a week, but I was wondering . . . is there anything else? Something you can tell me now? Can you describe how you *feel*?"

She closed her eyes. Without their deep, obsidian glitter her pale face looked hollow and lifeless. "I haven't been dreaming, you know," she whispered, her eyes still shut. "I can't dream. I don't see anything any longer. I close my eyes and all I see is blackness. At night, when I fall asleep, it's like dying. But . . . I . . . I smell things, Velda. Right now. While I was just now talking to you, when I was looking at you, all I could smell was that awful hospital smell. But now, with my eyes closed—it—it smells like home."

"Home?"

"Yes. I can smell the—the sea. You could always smell the sea at home, no matter where you were on Plankton Key. But there are—bad smells, too, Velda."

"Bad smells?"

"Yes. Like—like something rotting and—and—"

"Go on, Cleo."

"It smells like—like I'd—I'd peed myself. No, worse, it smells—I don't know how to say it, Velda, it's not at all nice. It—it smells like someone did the other thing. You know—number two? Once I found a possum that'd crawled under our porch and died. This is what it smelled like."

"That's okay, Cleo. I understand. Is there anything else, Cleo?"

"I can—feel—" her hands moved up and down the sheet that covered her "—I can feel something—hard, hard and rough and cold. Like iron. It's, it's rough and cold and, and *curved*—like, like I'm in the bottom of a big bowl—"

"Or maybe in the bottom of a boat?"

"I guess—I don't know. Maybe."

"Is that all?"

"Yes . . . no . . . I can, I can hear something too." Her head turned as though she were listening to something. It was uncanny—I nearly turned to see what she had heard. "I can . . . I can hear a ship's bell and, and birds."

"Birds?"

"Gulls, I guess. You know how they sound. I can—"

"Get this woman out of here."

That last came from over my shoulder. I turned and saw Flan, flanked by two cops, their hands on the butts of their revolvers, looking very uncomfortable and red-faced.

"She has no right to be in here, officers. The District Attorney has issued strict orders that no one—*no one*, understand?—is to be allowed anywhere near this girl other than myself and her doctors . . . and those doctors do *not* include this Dr. Finlayson. If he *is* a doctor."

"Look, Flan," I said, rising. "You can't keep Cleo from seeing who she wants to. She's been indicted, but she's not been convicted of anything yet. She has her rights."

"She has whatever rights Mr. Noorvik and I say she has. Officers, you will escort this woman from the building. If she so much as sticks a toe in here again, arrest her. Use as much force as is necessary. Use more if you like."

The cops each took a step toward me and I held up my hands. "All right, Flan. I'm going. Just don't look too smug yet, this isn't over by a long shot."

"It is if you know what's good for you, which I seriously doubt you do. How are your ribs feeling by the way. Not still sore, I hope?"

"You ain't seen sore yet, shyster."

Chapter Fourteen

I FIGURED I KNEW WHERE MAX WAS AND MAYBE EVEN BILL, TOO. Noorvik had shipped both of them down to Florida. It took about three minutes to discover that the DA's yacht, the *Flying Fish*, had left New York the day after the killing, so it was no big deduction to figure where it was headed. But why had Noorvik kidnapped his own son, if you *could* kidnap your own kid, that is? And as far as Max was concerned, why didn't he just have one of his goons ice her and discretely drop her in the East River? It seemed to me that he was making things unnecessarily difficult for himself. It didn't make a whole lot of sense but so long as it made more sense than any other idea I'd had I was going to cling to it. Who knows, I might not get another one.

I went to my bank and withdrew the balance of my savings, such as it was. The teller had the decency not to laugh at the amount as she counted it out. I then walked down to the end of the block to the travel agency, where I learned that only way to get to Plankton Key (which no one in the agency had ever heard of—they had to find it on a state map before they'd believe it really existed), or any of the other Keys for that matter, was to either take a train or fly into Miami and then rent a car or take a bus. I opted for flying, because time was literally a matter of life and death I was sure, and a bus ticket, because my money had just run out.

I went back to my place and packed a bag. I wasn't sure what to take, having never been further south than Atlantic City before. The travel agency told me that it was going to be pretty tropical, even at this time of the year, especially down in the Keys, so I dug out the cardboard box from under my bed where I store all my summer things. I had it half in mind to try to pass for a tourist if I could and chose things accordingly. I then called Chip and told him that I was on my way to La Guardia—reluctantly, because I knew what his reaction was going to be. And I was right, too.

"Are you out of your mind?"

"If anyone knows the answer to that, you ought to."

"I certainly do not know what you hope to prove."

"I wish I had time to argue with you, but my plane leaves in an hour and I gotta get to the airport. I just wanted to make sure you keep an eye on Cleo. If anything happens to her, I want Noorvik to go down for it."

"I will watch out for her, Velda, do not worry about that. You just watch out for yourself. Like I am always telling you, Noorvik is not going to fool around any more so far as you are concerned."

"I'll be careful," I told him, which pretty much brings things up to the point where I was getting the crap beat out of me by a hick cop in the middle of some godforsaken podunk island.

The cop's gun is pointed squarely at the bridge of my nose, in case you've forgotten where we left off. I like my nose and am going to miss it when it's blown through the back of my head. I'm probably going to miss the back of my head, too.

"I don't know what Noorvik's paying you," I say and the way the big thug's eyes squint for a split second I know I've hit the mark, "I can offer you more."

"Yeah? What y'all got he ain't?"

"Well, this, for instance," I reply, shrugging off what remained of my halter. The cop gulps audibly, but the gun doesn't waver. I unbutton my shorts and draw the zipper down. Slipping my fingers under the waistband, I give them a little shove and let my shorts and underpants drop to my ankles. Stepping out of them takes me two feet closer to the goon. Who'd ever've figured my experience at

Slotsky's would eventually save my life? Just goes to show you never know about these things. The little black circle at the end of his gun is less than a yard away now. It looks the size of the Holland Tunnel.

I put my hands on my hips, run my tongue around my lips and say, "Tell me King Noorvik can offer you *this*."

The cop's jaw drops with an audible click and I can read what's going through what passes for his brain like it's in words of one syllable, which it probably is. It doesn't augur well for me, of course, since it's pretty obvious he's figuring to get the best of both worlds: my still-warm body *and* Noorvik's reward for icing me.

"Yeah, he surely can't do that," he says—inadvertantly confirming my suspicions about who was pulling the strings down here—and just as the full import of the sexual fantasy hits him the gun drops an inch, which I'm about to make the biggest mistake in his life. I still have the belt in my right fist and it whips out like a striking cobra, wrapping once around the revolver. I jerk it from his grasp—taking the first joint of his trigger finger with it—while at the same moment lashing out with my foot, catching him square in his crotch. Tobacco-colored spit flies from his mouth and I follow up with another kick, this time to the pit of his flaccid belly. My foot sinks in past the ankle and the air goes out of him like a busted balloon. I snatch the gun on the first bounce and crack him over the head as he doubles over toward me. He goes to his knees with a grunt so I keep pounding on his head until he finally drops face first onto the ground. I grab his hair and lift his head out of the pool of water it'd fallen into. The eyes are half-open slits with only the whites visible. Bloody spit drools from his mouth and more blood is trickling from his ears. He looks like a raccoon that's been on the road a few hours too long. He's still breathing, more's the pity, and I let his head fall back into the puddle, where he immediately starts blowing pink bubbles. Maybe he'll drown, which'd be fine by me. I sure can't imagine an alligator being desperate enough to eat him.

"That'll teach you to hit a lady," I tell him as I pick up what's left of my clothes. Damn. I don't have enough nice things to have them torn up like this. Shoot, I don't have enough things nice or otherwise. And I'd just gotten the shorts last summer, too, for God's sake, and now look at them. I make myself as decent as I can and make my way back to the car. Fortunately, I'd tossed a beach robe in the back seat and wrap myself up in that. With my big straw hat I again look just like a tourist, more or less.

I stop at the first house I come to and ask for directions.

"Shore don' know wutcher doin' away out here, ma'am" said the elderly black man who'd answered the door. "Ef yo' be lookin' fo th' beach, ain't nothin' enda dis shere ol' road. Don' go nowhere, nohow."

Well, that's fine by me. Maybe it'll be a while before anyone finds the deputy. I'm not particularly worried about him. He'll not be likely to brag about having his balls kicked into his throat by a woman—he'll be more likely to go after me personally or have me picked up on some trumped-up charge, but by then I'll be long gone and the hell with him.

I ask the old man if he knows where the Paughner place is.

"I sho'ly do, ma'am. Ev'body know where Miz Lily Paughner live."

He tells me and as I'd figured, the Paughner place is on the opposite side of the island from where I'd been sent. I'm disgusted at what a sucker I've been. I thank him, climb back in my car and head for the other end of the road. It takes only five minutes.

The Paughner house is one of a cluster of half a dozen pastel-painted cinderblock cottages and twenty-year-old house trailers in the midst of a grove of those ridiculous-looking palm trees. I go up to number thirty-two, the one I was told belonged to Mrs. Paughner. I knock at the screen door. Shading my eyes from the glare of the sun I can see a sparsely-furnished room—mostly cane furniture and sea-shell ornaments.

"Jes' a moment!" someone calls from the back of the house. I rock back and forth on the balls of my feet, looking around at the neighboring houses. They look like marshmallows out there in the sun. The only shade comes from the palm trees and that's not much. The glare from the barren sandy soil is blinding. I just can't figure why anyone'd want to live down here. I hear a noise from inside the house and turn to look. A chubby little old woman has just come into the room, evidently from the kitchen since she's got an apron on and is wiping her paw-like hands on a towel. "Somethin' I c'n help you with, Miss?"

"I hope so. Are you Mrs. Paughner? Mrs. Lily Paughner? The midwife?"

"I usta be. I mean, I'm still Lily Paugnher, but I ain't been a midwife fer a goodly many years now. But then, y'all don't look like y'all's got much call for a midwife, neither."

"I'm mighty glad to hear that. Could I talk to you for just a few minutes?"

"Surely. Come 'round to th' back, though. It's a lot cooler under th' trees than in th' house. I'll fetch us some lemonade."

I walk around the house and find a little grove of low-slung palms shading the sandy back yard. She's right, it is cooler, thank God. There's some ratty-looking lawn furniture, the kind made of aluminum tubing and plastic webbing. I hear a screen door slam behind me, turn and see Mrs. Paughner waddling toward me, carrying a couple of plastic glasses and a pitcher of lemonade.

"Have a seat, honey," she says. "It's powerful too hot to stand."

So I sit on one of the wobbly lawn chairs, hoping it'll hold me, and take a good look at Lily Paughner as she pours out a couple of glasses of lemonade. I figure she's probably about eighty, her age betrayed only by the soft lacework of fine wrinkles that cover every inch of her pudgy face. She's only about five feet tall so I'm glad I'm sitting. My eyes are level with hers and she's still standing.

"Been t' th' beach, honey?" she asks and I say, no, I'd come to the island especially to see her.

"Me? Whatever for? No one comes t' see me anymore." And I knew that she had just lied to me. It was easy to tell—she was one of those people to whom lying doesn't come easily, probably hadn't told a lie since she was a little girl, which would be sometime around 1875. So she tells her lie to a perfect stranger and then fumbles around with the pitcher and spoons and napkins and whatnot, trying to cover up her humiliation.

"Did you know the Fort family?"

"I—I s'pose so. Everyone knows—knew th' Forts."

"Knew?"

"Well, they moved away a few months ago, up north someplace."

"Did you know them personally, Mrs. Paughner?"

"I—s'pose—I might've, I s'pose."

"Did you know their daughter, Cleo? Cleopatra Fort?"

"Well, I guess everyone did."

"Did *you*?"

"Well, yes, I s'pose I did."

"What are you afraid of, Mrs. Paughner?"

"Afraid?"

"You're terrified. I'm not going to do you any harm—you've nothing to fear from me. I'm only here to help the Forts. Cleo's in trouble, Mrs. Paughner. She's very ill."

"Cleo's sick?"

"She may die, Mrs. Paughner."

"Oh dear oh dear—"

That had to gotten her. Anyone could tell just by looking at her that Lily Paughner was just overflowing with maternal instincts. After all, she looked like Mrs. Santa Claus for God's sake. Touch her on that nerve and you had her good, I figured.

"What—what can I do to help, Miss—?"

"Bellinghausen. Velda Bellinghausen. Cleo's a friend of mine, Mrs. Paughner. Back in New York, where she's living now."

"New York? Oh my goodness! Whatever's she doin' in a place like that?"

"She's dying unless I can help her."

"Dying? But I don't understand—what can I do?"

"Has anyone threatened you, Mrs. Paughner?"

"Threatened?"

"Did anyone tell you not to talk about the Forts? Or to not talk to me?"

"Well, no—not exactly. Deppity Mackanaw come round yesterday—you don't know th' deppity—"

"We've met."

"Well, then mebbe you know he's a bad 'un. Everbody on th' island's scared t' death of 'im. Deppity Mackanaw, he come 'round an' tol' me that I wasn't nohow t' talk t' nobody 'bout th' Forts if anyone was t' come 'round askin' 'bout them."

"Did he say why?"

"No—no, just that I wasn't t' answer no questions nohow. You say you met th' depitty so you know how—"

"Intimidating he is? Yeah, I know. He's real scary. But I need some information, Mrs. Paughner—"

"Please, call me Lily. Everyone else does. 'Mrs. Paughner' makes me sound so old."

"Lily, then. And please call me Velda. Like I said, I need some information but I don't even know for sure what I want to ask. Anything you can tell me about Cleo might help her. Anything at all."

"All right—if it'll help Cleo. I midwifed th' deppity's birth, th' good Lord forgive me, an' known him since he was pukin' an' soilin' his diapers. He might think he do, but he don't scare me none not at all. After all, I'm eighty-six years old—what's he goin' t'do t' me?"

"You were Mrs. Fort's midwife?"

"Yessiree. That must've been, what? Twenny years ago now."

"Nearly."

"Poor Mrs. Fort, she was just terrified that night. You know she'd had two miscarriages before Cleo was born? She just hated losin' them babies somethin' awful an' I think she'd've gone clean mad if she'd lost Cleo too. I know Mr. Fort sure thought so."

"Where'd the Forts live, Lily?"

"Right over there, last house on th' loop, jus' where th' dunes start."

I look in the direction she gestures and can just see the house, about a thousand feet away. It's identical to the others, but strange at the same time, kind of weird. I guess it comes from knowing it'd been Cleo's home for most of her life.

"Did you know a family named Polketta?"

I couldn't have gotten a better reaction from the old woman if I'd thrown a rattlesnake in her lap. She gasps and leaps to her feet so suddenly she spills her drink down the front of her apron. The glass bounces off the sandy soil and lays there at her feet. She's gone as pale as a sheet of twenty-pound typing bond and I'm afraid that maybe I've just given her a heart attack.

"Lily—"

"Y'all have t' leave. I'm sorry. Y'all must. I—I can't—I mustn't—"

"You can't what, Lily? What can't you do?"

"I can't answer y'all questions. I mustn't. Y'all better go."

"Lily . . . a girl's life depends on you, maybe the lives of two girls. If you don't talk to me, I won't be able to help them. Cleo'll die, Lily. I won't be able to help her."

"No—I—"

"No one's going to hurt you, Lily, I promise. Cleo's going to *die* unless you help me. Please, for her sake. Don't let her die, Lily."

She collapses into her chair as bonelessly as a marionette that'd just had its strings cut. She puts her face in her hands for a long moment, sighs, and then looks up at me. I feel awful bullying an old lady like this, but what the hell. I'm not exactly overwhelming with sympathy after the morning I've had.

"Y'all's right, Velda, I better tell y'all—everything. God help me, but I should've told someone sooner . . . but for Cleo. I kept th' secret for Cleo's sake an' now for Cleo's sake I have t' tell it. God forgive me."

"That's right, Lily—for Cleo's sake."

"I knew th' Polkettas all right, Mr. and Mrs. They'd come t' Plankton Key only a short time 'fore Cleo was born. They come from up east somewhere, no one knew where exactly. They stayed t' themselves, never talked t' no one. They were city folk, you could tell that easy, an' Mr. Polketta's ways were—well, pretty rough, an' Mrs. Polketta was too pretty, had too many nice clothes for anyone from round here. She looked much too elegant for someone like Mr. Polketta, who was just an awful roughneck. I don't think no one really b'lieved they was married. Most folk figured they was on th' wrong side o' th' law somehow an' were laying low on th' island. It'd happened before, bein' so close t' Miami an' all. But so long as they didn't bother no one, no one was goin' to ask any questions neither. Besides, Mrs. Polketta was, well, not quite right it seemed. Like she was funny in th' head, you know? Acted like she hardly knew where she was half th' time. People just kinda stayed clear of her an' her man too. Well, Mrs. Polketta was pregnant when she come to th' island an' she went into labor th' same night as Mrs. Fort. She was all alone. Her husband, if he was her husband, no one really believed he was—*I* surely didn't—was in town gettin' drunk like he did ever' night. Left her there all alone, can you imagine! Anyway, I was with Mrs. Fort when I got a call from Mrs. Polketta.

I weren't surprised she knew where I was since I'd told Ruby, th' operator at th' exchange, that I'd be tendin' t' Mrs. Fort all night. Mrs. Polketta told me she was in awful pain an' was all by herself th' poor thing. She lived only a couple houses up th' road from where I was so I told Mrs. Fort that she was goin' t' be all right for th' time bein' an' I was just goin' to look in on her neighbor an' that I'd be right back. I give her somethin' to calm her down some an' that helped a whole lot. Whatever I may have thought 'bout Mrs. Polketta she *was* a human bein' after all an' I couldn't rightly let her suffer if I could do somethin' 'bout it. Mrs. Fort had Mr. Fort there with her, you understand, an' li'l Ruben too, an' he knew everythin' there needed t' be done just in case, so she was perfectly safe.

"I hurried over t' Mrs. Polketta's an' found her t' be in just terrible pain. Oh, it was just awful th' way that poor woman suffered. She was goin' into labor right then an' there an' there was nothin' I could do but stay there an' help her. I heard someone come into th' house an' I thought it was her husband but it turned out t' be Mr. Fort."

"Mr. Fort?"

"Yes'm. He had a little bundle with him, but I didn't pay no mind to it with me bein' so busy with Mrs. Polketta and all. Mr. Fort ast me if I needed any help an' as I knew he knew his way 'round a birthin' I told him I'd be right glad of an extra hand. A few minutes later, Mrs. Polketta gave birth to a pair o' girls. Li'l twin girls."

"Twins?"

"Yes an' right then Mr. Fort grabs me by th' arm an' drags me into th' next room. He shoves th' little bundle he'd brought with him into my arms an' says, 'This is th' other girl, Lily. That woman in there, she had one one live baby an' one stillborn.' It took me a second t' realize that he was talkin' 'bout th' woman in th' next room. 'No, Ed,' I said. 'Y'all's wrong. She jus' had a pair a healthy twin girls.' It was then he leaned over an' looked me in th' face with a look like I ain't never seen on a human bein' before. It was somethin' awful an' just scared me t' death. He held up that little bundle he had and said, 'This *here* is one a her babies. That other one you got there is my Cleo's.' I told him I didn't understand but I know I really did. 'Cleo's passed out,' he said. 'Her strength just went from her. Give me one a them babies there an' take this one.

No one'll ever know th' diff'rence.' I tol' him I couldn't do any such a thing, that it would be an awful thing to do, a terrible sin, takin' a mother's baby from her. But he said, 'Cleo'll *die* if she knows she lost another baby, die or go mad. You know that, Lily, and that'd be a greater sin, t' let somethin' like that happen. Give me that baby. Take this one.' I tol' him again that it was goin' against God's will t' do such a thing an' he said that Mrs. Polketta weren't no fit mother nohow, anyone with half an eye could tell that she were simple and God alone knew what she was up north, what she'd done up there, probably a fast an' loose woman, jus' look at her now an' y'all can see that yourself, just look at the way she dresses. And then he said, 'If you don't do this, Lily, I'll tell th' sheriff what you been givin' Cleo t' make her sleep, what only th' doctor's s'posed to give out'."

"What'd you do, Lily?"

"God help me, but I traded them poor little babies. I let Mr. Fort take one of Mrs. Polketta's twins an' leave his little stillborn daughter. I only took one li'l baby into that room an' told that poor woman that her other baby'd died. She just looked at me like I'd told her it was rainin' outdoors and I could see that some a what Mr. Fort'd told me was right. When th' doctor come 'round th' nex' day I showed him th' body of that other baby an' he wrote a death certificate for it. Oh, what'd I do, Velda? What'd I do?"

She was crying and I never know what to do around people who are hysterical. I patted her on the back and handed her a dry napkin and said the only thing that seemed to make any sense.

"You didn't do anything wrong, Lily. Mrs. Polketta went back to New York and lived a terrible life in awful poverty. I think something'd happened to her mind—maybe from something her first husband had done to her—she was married before, you know—maybe something Mr. Polketta had done, I don't know. Her little girl had an awful rough time growing up. She did some pretty bad things. She may even have killed a man. But the baby you gave to Mrs. Fort has had a wonderful life, Lily, in a fine home with people who love her very much. If everything turns out all right, she plans to go to school, to college. What you did saved her, Lily, from what happened to her sister."

"Oh, I hope y'all's right, I hope y'all's right. It's been a turrible secret I've kept all these years, but with th' Polkettas gone an' Cleo round all th' time an' watchin' her grow up it was easy t' forget what happened."

"Everything's going to be all right, Lily, don't you worry about it any longer. You did the right thing back then, and now, too, talking to me."

"Will it really help little Cleo."

"I sure hope so."

"Will you let me know how Cleo is? Will you tell her Miss Lily sends her love?"

"I promise."

Well, well, I thought as I climb back into the car. Well, well. Maxine Polketta. Cleopatra Fort. *Twins*. There it was then. *Twins* for God's sake. Twins who were like the same person. I'd heard about such things—who hasn't? Twins separated at birth who twenty, thirty years later discover they'd married women with the same names, had the same jobs, had dogs named Rover, hung the toilet paper roll up the same way, had the same number of kids, had the same model car. I never heard of twins having the kind of rapport that blurred the lives of Max and Cleo, blurred their very individuality, but I suppose it's not impossible. No—it *is* possible—I've seen it for myself.

I drive back to the motel, expecting to be stopped at any moment but the town is as dead as I'd left it that morning, with no one paying me any more attention than they had before. Once in the room, I lock the door, shower and change clothes. Jesus, I thought, looking at my battered body in the mirror, I look like an old banana. I repair as much damage as I can—fortunately, most of my scrapes and bruises don't show, or don't so long as I keep to slacks, a long-sleeved shirt and my big hat.

I return the car to the old man at the hardware store and thank him for its use.

"Weren't gone very long—guess y'all saw all a Plankton Key there is t' see, huh?"

"All I cared to see, that's for sure."

"Goin' t' b'leavin' us now, Miss?"

"Not quite yet. I've got just a little more business to take care of first. I was wondering, you know what's that good-looking boat parked out by that little island?"

"That's Mr. Noorvik's yacht, the *Flyin' Fish.* Comes down here couple a times a year. Never seen 'im this early in th' season before."

"Anyone from the yacht been on shore?"

"Nope, but that's nothin' unusual. Don't hardly never see anyone from th' *Flyin' Fish* 'round here. Ain't t' say, though, that no one from Plankton don't go to th' *Flyin' Fish.*"

"Someone like Deputy Mackanaw, maybe?"

"Mebbe. Been out t' th' yacht couple times I know of."

"What about the sheriff?"

"The sheriff? Naw. He's a good feller, been sheriff around here's long's anyone can remember. He ain't th' least bit impressed by Noorvik an' his crowd."

"You know where I can rent a boat around here?"

"Surely do, ma'am. Got a nice little twelve-foot johnboat you c'n have f'r th' whole day f'r five bucks. Got a new motor, practic'ly. Take y'all t' th' *Flyin' Fish* an' back at any rate easy as ridin' a bicycle."

Little did he know that I'd never owned a bike.

"You figure I'm going to visit the yacht?"

"Yup."

"Can I use the boat right away?"

"Sure ya can. I had it out just yestiddy, so there's still plenty o' gas. She's tied up at th' dock at th' end of the street, th' red johnboat at th' third finger pier. Jus' go ahead an' take 'er, no one'll ask any questions."

I thank the old man and turn to leave when he says, "Ma'am. I surely do hope you'll be careful."

"With your boat?"

"With y'all self."

I thank the old man and step back out into the blinding glare of the sun. My pupils are still in the process of shrinking to pinpoints when someone behind me says, "Scuse me, ma'am."

I turn and for a moment I'm sure my heart has come to a complete stop, because all I can see is the khaki jacket with the big tin star pinned to its breast. And all I can think is that it's Depitty Mackanaw come to shoot me down in the street like the goldurned Yankee bitch I am. But the face in the shadow of the round-brimmed campaign hat's sure not the ugly mug I'd made even uglier a couple of hours earlier. It's no beauty, either, but the expression is blandly cautious—not exactly hostile, but not about to tell me anything either.

"Yes?"

"How're y'all enjoyin' your visit t' Plankton Key, ma'am?"

"Just fine, officer, just fine. I'll be recommending it to all my friends with great enthusiasm."

"Well, that's right nice o' you, ma'am. Right nice. I see y'all's headed for our fine marina. Mind if I stroll along with y'all?"

"Not at all, officer," I lied.

We mosey down the blistering sidewalk, the sheriff talking in that slow drawl that didn't have a hint of unfriendliness or guile, and me wondering what in the hell he was up to.

"Can't say we get many visitors t' our fine little island, mostly in too big a hurry t'get t' Key West an' all. I guess we're just too close t' th' mainland t' be interestin'. Usually we just get folks who want t'stop for a coke or gas. Plankton Key, I gotta be honest an' admit it, ain't too much more'n a big pile o'coral. Ain't got any o' th' nice beaches th' other keys got."

"It seems all right to me."

"Nope, don't get many visitors, leastways no one who comes here on purpose. For sure no purty ladies like you, ma'am, all by their selves."

"Well, I'll tell you, officer, I just kinda felt like getting away from it all. You know what I mean?"

"I surely do, ma'am, I surely do. This'd be th' place t'do that, it surely would. Plankton Key's 'bout as close t' nowhere as you can get." He laughs a little at this slur on the good work of the Plankton Key Chamber of Commerce and walks beside me in silence for half a minute.

"Folks been treatin' you all right, ma'am?"

"Pardon?"

"Folks been treatin' you all right? Like I said, we don't get too many tourists, leastways not many who want t' see much o' our little island. Sometimes they get a little spooked, seein' strangers 'round where they ain't used t'seein' 'em."

"No complaints, sheriff. Everyone's been just swell."

"That's jus' fine, Miss Bellinghausen. Glad t' hear it."

I take two steps before I realize he's just used my name. That's certainly interesting.

"You've been checking up on me, haven't you, Sheriff? That's not a nice thing to do."

"Nothin' personal, ma'am. Jus' curious. Like I tol' you, don't get too many people aroun' here as innerested in th' goin's on o' Plankton Key as y'all been. Jus' found myself wonderin' why."

"Nothing else piqued your curiosity?"

"Well—now y'all mention it, I'd say, yes, there was. Seemed t' be some folks aroun' here who been mighty innerested in *you*."

"Me? Goodness gracious why?"

The sheriff had been strolling alongside me for half a block or so and hadn't yet looked in my direction. Now he stops and turns to look me full in the face. I still can't read his expression, what little I can see of it in the shadow of his hat. Just the glint of a pair of eyes like a couple of well-oiled ball bearings.

"Well, ma'am, y'all's certainly a looker, if you'll forgive me for bein' so personal, but I don't think th' folks I'm talkin' 'bout were partic'lar innerested in askin' y'all t' th' Friday night Rotary dance. Y'all gettin' my drift?"

"I'm pretty sure I am."

"That's good." He turns away from me and starts walking again. Neither of say anything for half a dozen paces. Then, without looking at me, the sheriff asks, "Y'all ain't run across my depitty yet, Miss Bellinghausen? Big fella name Mackanaw?"

"Why do you ask, sheriff? Have you misplaced him?"

"Naw. He's jus' not th' fella t' overlook a pretty new face in town, if y'all know what I mean. Don't want t' speak too poorly o' my own depitty, y'all unnerstand, but, well, it's no big secret, neither, that Depitty Mackanaw's a pretty hard-boiled egg. Not much I c'n do 'bout 'im, seein' he's Joe Spelunder's boy an' all, th' feller what owns th' big tourist camp out on Dawn Key, but I do what I can t' keep 'im in line, if you see what I mean."

"I think I do."

"Ain't seen th' depitty at all you say . . . Well, if y'all do, watch out for yourself. Like I say, he's kind of a mean boy but I'd hate t' have anythin' happen to 'im—nothin' too bad at any rate. Sometimes he jus' brings things on himself, you know what I mean?"

"I'm sure he must be a trial to you."

"All part o' th' job, I s'pose. Y'all from New York, you say?"

"I didn't, but I imagine you know exactly where I'm from."

"Deed I do. Y'all got some friends down here, I b'lieve."

"I don't think so."

"Well, now, a coupla big city fellers was askin' 'bout y'all, jes' this mornin' in fact."

"Asking about me?"

"Well, askin' Depitty Mackanaw anyhow."

"Tell me, sheriff. You know a fellow named Noorvik?"

"Sure. Who don't? Comes down here ever' summer like clockwork."

"That's his boat out there now, isn't it?"

"Yes'm, it surely is. Coupla months early this year he is. Guess he ain't so reg'lar's I thought."

"Anyone seen him?"

"Ain't no one seen no one, 'cept those boys what was askin' 'bout th' pretty lady who jus' come in from New York."

"You know who they were?"

"Nope. Didn't talk to 'im myself like I said. They talked t' th' depitty. I take it y'all's plannin' t' take yourself a boatride? Well, y'all take care, hear?"

"I'll do my very best, sheriff."

I turn to go, thinking that this has had to have been the damnedest conversation I've had in quite some time, when I hear the sheriff's quiet voice behind me. "An' Miss Bellinghausen . . . I'd surely take care o' them awful-lookin' bruises on that there purty face o' yours."

I find the the old man's boat with no problem, a rectangular, flat-bottomed thing that looks more like a raft than anything else. I gingerly clamber down into it, which doesn't rock around half so much as I thought it would—it's certainly much more stable at any rate than the rowboats I'm used to renting in Central Park. My confidence grows—then I realize I've not untied the lines that moor the boat to the dock. This takes a little more scrambling around, but finally I'm free and the boat is still floating, amazingly enough, with me still in it. I'll get the hang of this yet. The motor's no big deal, being no different than a lawn mower engine in any important detail. I'm a little wobbly getting started but before long I'm cutting a straight line for the yacht without the slightest idea what I'm going to do when I get there.

As I near the *Flying Fish* I wonder just how much money New York DAs get paid. Not enough, I bet, to afford ocean liners like this one. I take the .45 out of my bag, check to make sure there's a cartridge in the chamber, flick the safety off and put it on the seat next to my right thigh, where it won't be easily seen by anyone on the yacht.

There's no sign of life at all as I approach. I get a creepy feeling, pulling up to that big white boat—it seems dead, lifeless and gleaming in the sunlight like a bleached skull. There's a gangway or whatever it's called—a retractable stairway thing—hanging from ropes on the side and I shut the motor off and drift up to it. While the nose of the johnboat bumps against the hull I manage to get it tied to the little platform at the foot of the stairs. Shoving my gun into the waistband of my slacks, I clamber clumsily out of my little craft. I've got the uncanny sensation that a bead's been drawn on the back of my head, but the big boat still seems lifeless.

I reach the deck and take a quick look around. There's no sign of life and the creepy feeling of being on a deathship is becoming overwhelming. And I don't much like boats to start with. I take about two steps toward the front when someone behind me says, "Get your hands up." I jump, but it's as much with relief as with surprise. There are a lot of things I would have prefered hearing, of course, but just the sound of a human voice at all was welcome. I raise my hands.

"Turn around."

I do. What I see in front of me is a tall young man, about nineteen or twenty, who I will bet my last dime, if I have one, is the famous Bill Noorvik. He's a dead ringer for his dad and, architect or not, he's built like a linebacker. He holds a revolver on me. It's shaky but never wavers very far from the middle of my chest.

"Who're you?" he demands.

"My name's Bellinghausen. Velda Bellinghausen. I'm a detective. I've been looking for you, Bill."

"Oh yeah?"

"Yeah." I step forward, snatch the gun with my left hand and slap him across the face with my right. Maybe I shouldn't have done that, but I was getting damn sick and tired of people with attitudes. Besides, the dope had never taken off the safety. I step back a few paces, reaching into the small of my back for my own gun.

"What'd you do that for?"

He's got his fists all balled up, ready to fight, but can't take his eyes off my nickel-plated automatic. I admit, it's an awful pretty gun. And about five times bigger than the one he'd pulled on me. I snap the safety off his revolver and hold both guns on him. This seems to cow him even further.

"Because you're an idiot, Bill. I'm here partly to help you but mostly to help a girl named Cleo—the girl you know as Max."

"Max? You know her?"

"I do and I know she's going to die—if she's not dead already—if I can't get you back to New York like right now."

"I don't get it."

"I'll bet you don't. Why are you down here, anyway?"

"I—I'm not really sure. My dad told me that there'd be trouble if I stayed in New York—that a man had been killed—"

"Jackson Sline."

"Yeah. That he'd been killed and because I'd been seen leaving Sline's place at about the time he'd been murdered there'd be all kinds of questions asked. Dad was afraid it would hurt his bid for mayor if there was a scandal. This is an election year coming up, you know. He said he could fix it all up, but I had to get out of town for a while. I didn't think there'd be any harm in it . . . after all, I was innocent. I didn't know anything about the murder or who did it."

"Well, that was real big of you, Bill. Did you know that you left your girlfriend Maxie holding the bag? She's in jail, indicted for the murder of Jackson Sline. She'll go to trial in a few weeks, if she lives long enough."

"Yeah? So what? I learned what kind of girl she *really* is—

she'd strung me along the whole time with that sweetness and light act of hers. If she's tied up with Sline's murder, well, that's her lookout."

"Listen, stupid, I don't have the slightest idea what you think you're talking about but I'll tell you right now that the girl you know as Max is the real thing. She's a good kid and needs your help bad. The Max that knew Sline isn't the Max you know."

"I don't get it."

"Look, I'll explain it all as soon as I can, but the most important thing to do right now is to get you back to New York. Is there anyone else on board?"

"No, not really. There's a steward and the cook and an engineer. Everyone else was given leave just after we arrived."

"We?"

"Yeah, me and the bodyguards Dad sent along."

"Bodyguards my ass. They were your keepers, Bill. Where're they now?"

"The went ashore about an hour, hour and a half ago, in a big hurry."

"I bet. Look here, Bill—those men were sent along to keep you here until the Sline case blows over—maybe even until after the election. Your dad's set Maxie up as the scapegoat for Sline's murder, to keep your name out of it."

"I—I know Dad isn't—well, I wish I could say I thought you're wrong about him, but I know him too well. We've never gotten along, you know—I—I've tried to distance myself from him as much as possible. He's been involved in some shady deals, I know, but I never thought he'd do something like this. Geez—pinning a murder on Maxie!"

"Well he did. Hasn't there been anyone else on board, though? Anyone besides you and the crew and the goons?"

"No."

"Are you absolutely sure? No one's talked about a girl being around?"

"A girl? No—I've been over every inch of the *Flying Fish* in the last week and a half and there's no one else on board but me and the people I told you about. You're the first girl I've seen in weeks."

Damn.

"Here they come now."

"Who?"

"Two of the men Dad sent down here with me."

"*Two* of them? How many are there?"

"Three, but one of them, a little fellow named Lister, is in the hospital. Says he got himself concussed by a car."

I look toward Plankton Key and see a big motor launch heading for us with two dark figures aboard.

"Who are they?"

"The big one on the left's Gus Abramson, the other's Johnny Gee. I'm pretty sure both've got guns."

"I'll guarantee it. Look, you make yourself scarce, Bill. I'll take care of this."

"But—"

"Listen, stupid—the only thing that matters right now is saving Max's life, which I don't think I can do if you get yourself shot. Now shut up and find someplace safe for about fifteen minutes."

The launch bumps against the hull and I hurry toward the front of the boat and get behind one of those ventilator things that look like big tubas sticking out of the deck. I peek around just as the first goon steps onto the deck. It's the big guy and he has a gun in his fat paw. He steps aside as the smaller man joins him. The first guy, the big one, is wearing a seersucker suit with a bright yellow shirt and a straw hat. The other's wearing a purple Hawaiian shirt with big orange flowers printed on it and Bermuda shorts. Both of them look just awful.

"Hey, Velda!" the skinny guy calls and I recognize his voice immediately—it's the creep who'd ordered my ribs kicked in. I grit my teeth until I can hear the enamel chipping. "Come on out, Velda, no one's going to hurt you."

Yeah, sure. What's he think, that he'd knocked my brains out in that alley? I lean out just a wee bit and take a bead on the big goon, the one who'd tap danced on my ribcage. I squeeze the trigger easy and send a slug zinging toward the center of his chest. The man's too lucky, though, and he turned just as I'd fired. I see the lapel of his jacket whip as the bullet snatches at it. His chum isn't so lucky, though, and catches the slug square in the throat. He's flung back by the impact like he'd been hit by a truck, splashing the superstructure with the blood that's fountaining from his ruined neck. It looks impossibly red on all that gleaming white paint. Before I really notice that, though, I've squeezed off two more shots, but Gus is fast on his feet for such a big man, more's the pity. He ducks behind the far end of the deckhouse, getting off at least one shot at me as he does. The slug goes completely through the sheet metal of the ventilator, which startles me no end I can tell you. I make a dive for the shelter of the other end of the same deckhouse. Between the deckhouse, which is about the size of Joe's diner, and the bow of the yacht there's not much but a big open triangular space. Nothing much there but a couple of deck chairs and the framework for an awning. There's no time for fooling around—I'm sure Gus isn't wasting any and he's got the advantage of knowing the layout of the yacht.

Three sides of the front half of the deckhouse are glass, kind of like a greenhouse, so I'm hunkered over afraid to stand up and no less reluctant to stick my head around either corner to see which way the gunman's coming, so I decide to split the difference. Big lugs like him never think anyone can do something they can't so sticking my gun in my waistband alongside Bill's revolver, I swallow hard, and in one quick movement stand up, jump and grab the edge of the deckhouse roof. A second later I've hoisted myself up over the railing. I'll tell you what—it can be a pain being as tall as I am but sometimes it really comes in handy.

The roof's about fifteen feet wide, broken only by two rows of skylights and a couple of those tuba-shaped ventilators. On my left is the top of the stairs I'd been standing beside while talking to Bill. I'm not too hot on the idea of going to the edge to see if I can spot Gus but the question becomes moot when I hear the scuff of a shoe on one of the metallic rungs. Evidently Gus's had more or less the same idea I did, figuring he could plug me from the roof no matter where I was on deck. He's just thirty seconds too late. I flatten myself as quietly as I can, my gun held in both hands, elbows braced against the roof. Gus's big head bobs up above the level of the roof and for a split second we're eye to eye, not six feet apart. He doesn't even have time to look surprised, which is kind of a shame, before I drill a hole right through the middle of his forehead. He topples over backward, his head passing through the pink cloud that had once been the back of his skull, and tumbles to the deck like a two-hundred-and-twenty-five-pound sack of potatoes. King is going to be really pissed off at the mess I've made of his pretty white boat and ain't that just too bad. I scramble to my feet and down the same stairs, leaping over the still-twitching body that lay at its foot. He's dead all right. His body just hasn't quite caught up to the idea that it hasn't got much of a head left anymore. That'll teach him to kick a helpless woman.

"Bill! It's me, Velda! Everything's all right."

A door opens in the deckhouse and the boy peers out, his face as pale as Cleo's.

"What happened?" he asks, then sees first, because the body's practically at his feet, the nearly decapitated corpse of the late Johnny Gee, then the even more gruesome remains of Gus sprawled at the bottom of the stairs with the contents of his head spilled all over the deck. "Jesus, Velda."

"Shut up and listen. I think the sheriff's given me the benefit of the doubt about my business here, but those shots will've been heard from one end of Plankton Key to the other and someone's going to want to check them out."

"Hold on—"

I follow as he ducks into the deckhouse, where I hear the buzzing that must've alerted him. Inside, there's a big wheel and what I assume are duplicate controls for those in the wheelhouse above. Bill goes over to a radio mounted in the wall. It's this that's been doing the buzzing. Now I hear a tinny voice coming from a little speaker. Someone's saying, "Plankton Key callin' *Flyin' Fish*, Plankton Key callin' *Flyin' Fish*, y'all read me *Flyin' Fish*?"

Bill switches off the speaker, picks a headset off a hook and says, "Plankton Key, this is *Flying Fish* . . . yes . . . yes . . . This is Bill Noorvik, sheriff . . . yes . . . no, no problem. Sorry if we bothered anyone, sheriff, a couple of the crew were taking potshots at sharks . . . yes . . . no . . . no. Yes, Miss Bellinghausen's here. We're just having something to drink . . . no . . . Everything's fine. I'll be sure to let you know. Thank you, sheriff, I appreciate your concern. I'll be sure to tell my dad. Same to you, sir, and thanks again."

He hangs up the headset and turns toward me.

"Well, that's that, Velda."

"You just think so. Can that launch get us to Key Largo?"

"Sure, why?"

We go back out onto the deck, where a couple of men in clean white uniforms are doing their damnedest not to get too close to the blood splattered all over the deck. None of them look as though they miss Gus or Johnny very much. They look more annoyed about the mess they have to clean up.

"What are these boys going to do about this?"

"Exactly what they have to do." Evidently the acorn hadn't rolled quite so far from the oak tree as I'd thought. "In fifteen minutes there won't be a sign of so much as a nosebleed."

"We need to get back to New York as quickly as we can, by tomorrow noon if possible. I can't go back to Plankton Key, but we can catch the Miami bus in Key Largo. There's a New York plane at six tomorrow morning."

"The launch is a ChrisCraft Cobra. We can reach Key Largo in an hour, well before dark."

"Then get together whatever you want to take, we've got to be out of here in ten minutes."

I wait until Plankton Key is over the horizon before I start to tell Bill what'd happened since the night of Sline's killing. He's shocked at what his father's been trying to do, but not very surprised, evidently knowing his father pretty well. He's more upset about Maxie, who he evidently has more of a crush on than I'd thought. He had no idea that she'd been tapped for Sline's killing and was even more astonished to learn that she had a twin sister.

"Max and Cleo aren't just twins," I tell him. "They're your half sisters."

This shuts him up for a while since, admittedly, it's not the sort of thing you want to hear about the person you're madly in love with.

"She could be more than just my half sister, couldn't she? She could be my sister for real?"

"I honestly don't know."

"Jesus."

"Whether your father was also Cleo's father or not, *her* mother was *your* mother. Noorvik let her die and never raised a finger to help her. He went out of his way, even, to make sure that Max—your sister—that Max's life was hell. Fortunately for Cleo, he never even knew she existed."

"Jesus, Velda. I always knew Dad was—well, not a really good man. We've never got along, I guess that's why. But I always thought it was all just shady deals—I never dreamed he could do things like this."

"Yeah, well, he's a real pip, your dad is. What happened the night Sline was killed, Bill? What were you doing there?"

"Someone'd told me they'd seen them together, Sline and Max. I wouldn't believe it at first. I just couldn't see Max hanging around with a crowd like that. But I also knew she didn't know her way around town, either, and was awfully sweet and naïve. If she had fallen in with Sline, I knew what kind of rat he was and knew the sort of thing he would have in mind for her. Dad's never approved of any of the girls I've been interested in and I figured he'd put Sline up to it—Sline's been in Dad's back pocket for as long as I can remember. But Max's a sweet, trusting kid, you see—like a breath of fresh air, nothing at all like any of the girls I've known before, the kind who were only interested in me because of my dad and his connections or his money. Maxie was just, well, innocent's the best word I can think of even if it sounds pretty corny."

"No, I've met her—it's not corny at all."

"You know what I mean, then. So I couldn't figure for the life of me what my dad'd have against her. I can see now what it must've been. Sline thought she was the girl he'd tried to rape down here and told Dad it was Max—I mean, the other Max, the one Dad knew was his daughter. Must've given Dad a real jolt to find out I was seeing her. Anyway, all I knew was that Max—Cleo, I mean—was the sweetest girl I'd ever met, so you can understand that the idea of someone like Sline getting his hooks on her really gave me the willies. So I went to talk to him, to tell him to lay off her. I was pretty sure he would since he was terrified of Dad."

Bill said he met Sline at a bar about three blocks away from the apartment building. Jackson just laughed in the boy's face when he heard what he wanted. "You don't know what kind of a girl your precious little Maxie is, do you?"

"I think I do. Too good for you, at any rate."

"If you think that then she's even better than I thought she was. That girl's black as sin, I tell you."

Bill would've strangled Sline on the spot if the bozo hadn't tossed a photo onto the table between them. Bill glanced at it and paled. It was his Maxie all right, there was no mistaking that face, but for the rest . . .

"Where'd you get this?"

"Get it? You can buy that photo yourself and a dozen more just like it, better even, under the counter at every cigar stand in the city."

"I don't believe it!"

Sline looked at his watch and said, "Come back to my place with me now and I'll show you proof even you won't be able to deny."

Bill followed Sline the few blocks to his building. It was after midnight, around one o'clock, and snow had been falling for some time. The super greeted them as they entered the lobby. They took the elevator to the penthouse floor. The apartment was dark.

"Come on in here," Sline said, crossing the room. He opened a door and gestured for Bill to step up beside him. Beyond was a bedroom. The only light was from the fireplace, which cast a lurid, flickering light into the room, like a faltering neon sign. "Take a look at what your girlfriend's really like, if you think you can take it."

Bill looked and saw, sprawled unconsciously across the bed, half naked with her thin, cheap dress unbuttoned from neck to waist, his beloved Maxie. Feeling his gorge rising, he turned away. Sline followed him into the living room.

"See enough? Cheap little slut, ain't she? Satisfied now?"

Bill didn't answer. He went to the hall and rang for the elevator. Sline came to his side and repeated his question. "I said, you seen enough now?"

"I ought to kill you.".

"Don't take it so hard, boy. Women'll be women and it's not too soon for you to learn that."

The elevator doors slid open at that point and as Bill stepped into the cage, he turned and said again: "I ought to break your filthy neck."

Sline's only reply was to laugh in his face as the doors closed.

"I was in a fury, I admit," Bill's telling me as the Chris Craft bounces across the waves like a skipped stone and me holding on for dear life—damn, but I hate boats. "I could think of nothing but beating that leering face to a pulp. I tore out of the elevator like a raging bull. I nearly ran over the man who'd been waiting for the car, a big bruiser who I thought was going to punch me for nearly knocking him down. He gave me as ugly a look as I've ever seen, but all he said was, "Sline up there?' 'Yes he is," I said, 'damn his rotten soul,' and ran from the building. That was the last time I saw either of them, Sline or Maxie."

"You know now that she wasn't the girl you'd been seeing? That wasn't Cleo up there?"

"I know it now that you've told me, but even then I couldn't really believe that the girl on Sline's bed was the same one I'd seen just a few days before. By the time I got home, all of my anger was directed at Sline—I'd already forgiven Max, had invented a thousand plausible reasons for her to have been in his apartment. I wanted to find her, apologize to her for ever doubting her, but one of my father's men was pounding on my door at dawn and . . . well, here I am."

"And here you are."

What particularly interests me about Bill's story is the man he'd nearly run down, the one who'd asked about Sline. No one had mentioned him before. That means there was one other person who'd gone up to the penthouse that night. If Bill's been telling me the truth and he left Sline still alive, then there's no doubt in my mind that this guy was probably the murderer. And I have a damned good idea who it is, too.

CHAPTER Fifteen

BILL AND I TAKE A CAB DIRECTLY FROM LA GUARDIA TO THE INFIRMARY. Flan's there and when he sees me coming starts to fluff up like a pissed-off cat, but then sees Bill Noorvik and doesn't know what to do, other than huff and splutter and wave his scrawny arms around. I disregard him.

"Cleo—look who's here."

I think we've arrived at the last possible minute, seeing the wan, colorless figure on the bed. Cleo looks like a ghost. There's little left of her face but her thick black hair and enormous eyes and it's a struggle for her, I can see, to focus on the boy standing next to me. The sight must be even more shocking to Bill, I can feel him stiffen beside me and hear the sound of a single sharply-drawn gasp.

"Bill? *Bill*? Oh, is it really *you*, Bill?"

That little cry and that wan smile is all it takes. The boy throws himself onto the bed beside the girl and scoops her into his arms.

"Maxie!"

Just like in the movies. I watch their reunion with emotions that are very mixed: sympathy with an unhealthy dollop of envy stirred in. It's been too long since anyone'd felt about me the way Bill does about Cleo, too long since anyone's held me in their arms or kissed me passionately or caressed me . . . and I become all too aware of how little I can look forward to the future being particularly different in that regard. I turn away from the couple on the hospital bed with lips compressed to hold back tears that are more from pity for myself than happiness for them.

But if you don't particularly care about my problems, if you're wondering instead about what Bill and Cleo are doing—well, you'll just have to use your own imagination and if that's not good enough, tough.

Flan draws me aside and hisses, "What the hell's this all about, Bellinghausen? What's your game?", but I'm in no mood for this kind of crap.

"Get your paw off my arm, shyster, before I break your sticky fingers. I'm leaving anyway, so kindly get the hell out of my way you motherless little sycophant."

I go down to the lobby to call Chip but before I get to the bottom of the stairs I come face to face with probably the last person I want to see. He nearly passes by me without so much as a glance in my direction when he suddenly freezes, turns and says, "*Bellinghausen*!" I feign surprise.

"Mr. *Noorvik*! I'm sorry . . . I didn't recognize you out from under your rock."

This makes him go all red, which amuses me no end. I can see that he has no sense of humor whatsoever. It was the first time I'd ever seen the man in the flesh, let alone practically nose to nose. He was tall, handsome and dapper, with glossy slicked-back hair and a little Clark Gable moustache.

"I know you think you're funny, Bellinghausen. We'll see how loud you laugh when I pull your license."

"Ha ha. On your way up to see your son and daughter?" He froze when he heard that.

"I beg your pardon?"

"Well, your son and his sister or or your son and his half-sister—I'm not too sure yet how all the relationships work out. Unless I'm confusing Bill with some other son you have kidnapped somewhere? And Cleo with some other daughter you've tried to send to the chair?"

"You're pushing your luck, Bellinghausen."

"My friends call me Velda, but you can call me *Miss* Bellinghausen if you like. I don't mind. And we'll see whose luck is running out, Mr. District Attorney. Well, I don't want to be rude, but I got some phone calls to make as I'm pretty sure you can figure out for yourself. You might have the local papers scared silly, but I think the ones in Albany couldn't care less about your feelings. Say hi to Gus and Johnny when you see them in hell."

I leave Noorvik standing there puffing like a steam engine. Maybe with any luck he'll have a stroke. I go on down to the pay phones in the lobby and give Chip a ring. I give him just enough information to drive him nuts.

"You have got Bill Noorvik there with Cleo?"

"Yup. And the DA should be up there with them by now, too."

"Jesus, is that safe?"

"Sure. The place is full of people and, besides, Bill knows the whole story now anyway."

"No sign of Max Polketta, though?"

"Not a hair. I'd thought for sure Max would've been tucked away with Bill, but no soap. He says he was alone down there and I believe him. I have no idea where she is."

"Damn . . . sisters, huh?"

"Bill's half sisters for sure and just maybe King's own daughters. I've got the whole story for you, witnesses and all."

"This is just too good. Noorvik will not be able to run for dogcatcher in the Yukon after this. When I get this to the wire services—"

"Look, hotshot, before you start rehearsing your Pulitzer acceptance speech, meet me at my place first. I think I'll have even more news for you. And bring a couple a cops with you, a couple of tough ones, the bigger the better, ones you know you can trust. And while you're at it, make sure you get some people you know up here, too—I don't know what Noorvik's going to do about all this but the more witnesses around Cleo the better I'll feel about it."

"Will do."

"See you in half an hour."

I hang up and get out of there. I still have on the slacks and blouse I'd been wearing in Florida. The only reason I haven't frozen to death yet is because of a peajacket and watch cap Bill'd found for me before we left the yacht, but the coat isn't much given how short it is and how little I'm wearing underneath, but my canvas sneakers are soaked and my feet are growing numb. I have exactly one dollar left to my name and I consider it well spent on a cab to Pith Street.

By the time I've taken a scalding hot shower and changed clothes, Chip shows up at my door with a pair of husky-looking cops I recognize as being a couple of square shooters. Big cops like this always look to me like aliens from some other planet, one with a lot stronger gravity. I recognize them as a couple of the boys who stood behind my dad during the hard times—which is why they're still walking beats instead of wearing suits and sitting behind desks. I grin at them and say, "Hi boys, good to see you."

They grin back like a pair of schoolboys and say, "Howya doin' Velda?"

"Jesus, Velda," says Chip, "you look like someone has gone over you with a ball-peen hammer."

"You look swell yourself, handsome. Come on in, I'm just making up some coffee."

"I thought there was some big hurry?"

"Not really. What time is it?"

"Nearly five. What is up, if I may inquire?"

"Have a seat, boys, and make yourselves comfortable, I've got a story to tell you first."

It's about seven when, after all the questions and interruptions, I finally finish bringing Chip up to date.

"You had yourself quite a time down there in Florida, did you not?"

"I did indeed," I answer, going to my front window and looking down into the street.

"What do you think is going to happen about that cop, that deputy you beat up?"

"I don't think anything's going to happen. If I ever hear from him I'll just hit him with an attempted rape charge and he knows that. He might've tried to frame something on me while I was down there, but I think he's just going to forget the whole thing. I don't think the sheriff'll let him get away with much on my score."

"It is going to be harder—"

"Hold it. Here he comes."

"Here who comes?"

"You boys," I say to the cops, "get yourselves ready. This fellow's a tough customer and I don't know what he's going to do."

"Who is it?"

"The man who killed Jackson Sline."

I turn off the room lights and open the door an inch. I can hear heavy footsteps coming up the stairs. In a moment, a huge shadow looms over my landing and makes the turn to take the next flight. As soon as it passes my door I step out on the landing behind the figure and say, "Good evening, Mr. Fort. Care to step into my place for a moment?"

Ruben Fort stares for a moment, sees the cops standing to either side of me, shrugs his massive shoulders and makes his way past me into my apartment. I turn one of the floorlamps on and shut the door.

"I guess you can figure out why my friends are here?"

"Yeah."

"You killed Sline, didn't you?"

"Yeah, I sure did!"

"Would you like to have a seat? Take your coat off and make yourself comfortable. I got plenty of hot coffee."

"Sure, thanks," he says, sloughing off his heavy coat and falling onto my sofa, which has never before in its life suffered such abuse. Chip drags a chair over in front of Ruben and the two cops flank him, arms crossed.

"What happened that night, Ruben?" he asks as I come back from the kitchen with a mug for Fort.

"You boys all right?"

"Sure, ma'am, we're fine."

"You need anything in that coffee, Ruben?"

"No, thanks, ma'am, it's fine."

"You okay, Chip?

"I am very fine, Velda, thanks. All right, Ruben. What happened?"

"I never much liked guys hangin' 'round Cleo all th' time like they did," he said, hanging his head and shuffling his feet around like an abashed schoolkid. He'd beaten up more than one boy back on Plankton Key, he told us, because he didn't like the way they looked at his sister or because they'd said something he didn't consider sufficiently respectful. After the family had moved to New York, he'd been surprised as hell one day to see his sister out on the streets at midnight, walking with another girl whose looks he hadn't liked at all. "You could tell she was cheap. I knew Cleo shouldn't be hangin' 'round people like that, cheap little hussies like that." So he'd chastised her and when she refused to recognise him he raised a ruckus that got him arrested. The next day, when he confronted her about the incident, Cleo had flatly refused to acknowledge that it'd ever happened, so he became suspicious about where she was going during the day, what she was doing and who she was seeing. There wasn't much he could do about this curiosity, given his job and all, but he did what he could. You can imagine his astonishment when he saw his sister, just a few days later, walking arm in arm with the very man he'd once beaten nearly to a pulp for assaulting her.

Fortunately for Ruben, it didn't take too much intelligence to discover who the man was or where he lived. He started staking out the apartment building whenever he could get time away from his job. Finally, one night, Jackson Sline's last night on earth, Ruben saw his sister come down the street and enter the building. She'd been wearing clothes he'd never seen before, cheap stuff that showed too much leg to suit him, but there was no mistaking who it was—he not only recognized her face but the almost imperceptible limp caused by her odd foot. He never noticed it was the wrong one.

He waited until he saw the lights go on in the penthouse. When they went off, he nearly went mad, but still held his hand. He was glad he did, because not long afterward he saw Sline enter the building in the company of a young man he didn't recognize. He hadn't realized that Sline wasn't already up in his place. He waited about ten minutes but the lights in the penthouse never went on again. Unable to control himself any longer, he entered the building just as the young man was leaving. Ruben asked him if Sline was still upstairs and was told that he was.

He took the elevator up and when he tried Sline's door, it was unlocked. He let himself into the dark apartment. The only light was what streamed from the half opened door of what he later learned was the bedroom. He made his way across the room as quietly as he could and pushed the door open. Sline had his back to him and hadn't heard his approach because he was engrossed in cursing the girl he had gripped by the arms. He was shaking her, calling her awful names, slapping her face. She was half awake, her glazed eyes wide with uncomprehending horror and panic. When Ruben saw his sister once again in Jackson Sline's arms, her dress practically torn from her slim, naked body, hearing Sline say those terrible words to her, when he heard her whimper in pain and fear, he lost all control.

"I hardly remember what I did then," he says, twisting his cap in his hands like a chastened altarboy. "I hit him, I know that. I just don't remember stopping. I guess I didn't."

The girl had thrown herself at him, begging him to stop, but the big brute was lost in an animal rage. When he'd finished pounding the lifeless corpse of Jackson Sline into the carpet, he fell onto the hapless girl. He grasped her hair in his fist and pulled her from where she'd thrown herself onto the dead man, he kicked and slapped her and threw her into a corner of the room, where she lay half senseless.

As suddenly as it had come, the rage was gone. He looked down at his huge hands, all bone and gristle, at the bloody body at his feet and, finally, at the pitiful figure slumped in the corner. *He* had done that, he realized, *he'd* done that to the girl he'd sworn to protect! Overcome with grief, he went to her and picked her up as gently as he could and placed her on the bed. He was brushing her hair from her eyes when he suddenly stood bolt upright, the shock of his discovery being more than his simple brain could comprehend at one blow. He shook his huge head and looked again.

The girl on the bed wasn't his sister. It wasn't Cleo. She looked a lot like her, but it was someone different. Her hair was short, and her eyes . . .

By then the magnitude of what he'd done had begun to sink in.

He'd just killed a man with his bare hands—for the wrong woman. He'd been following the wrong woman all along. He'd not slept nor ate for worrying about the wrong woman. He thought maybe he'd gone mad.

He fled the scene of his horrible crime and rushed back to the apartment on Pith Street. There she was, in her bed, with her mother and some strange women he'd never seen before. Could it be the same girl after all? Could she have somehow beaten him home? No . . . that was impossible. For one thing, there wasn't a mark on her—he knew he'd left the girl in Sline's apartments with bruises that were as much from his own hand as Sline's—and her hair was long again.

"They told me Cleo had had another one of her dreams, one of her spells. Now she's dreaming she's dying. Well, let her. Better for her that she does die. She deserves to die. I've fought for her all my life, I've killed a man for her and—and for what? So she could become—what she was?"

"For what?" I repeat. "Because she's your sister, Ruben."

"No," he says, looking up at me with just the same expression he must have seen a thousand times at the stockyards, on the faces of the countless cattle who'd also looked up at him in the same way just before he let his hammer fall between their eyes. "No, she ain't. She's the woman I love."

"The problem," I tell Chip after the cops hauled a disturbingly subdued Ruben away, "is that we still don't know where Maxine is. And without Maxine we might—probably will—lose Cleo anyway."

"Looks that way. You got anything to eat around here?"

"Take a look in the icebox and take your chance with whatever you can find."

"Thanks. I have not had anything since a couple a sinkers at four this morning."

"The cops aren't going to be interested in Max anymore, or Cleo, either, for that matter. They got Sline's confessed killer and that's the end of it so far as they're concerned. She's in the clear and so is Bill, for that matter."

I slouch sideways in the overstuffed chair by the window, letting my legs dangle over the arm. My back is to the kitchen and my mind wanders while Chip rustles about among the shelves.

"I think my big mistake's been in making the whole thing too complicated."

"Yeah, that always was one of your big problems. Is this ham?"

"If you can't tell I wouldn't touch it. Could be most anything by now. In the meantime, I'll ignore your wisecrack. Look, what I mean is—I jumped to all sorts of conclusions, assuming right off the bat that Noorvik must've had something to do with Max's disappearance."

"A natural enough thing to think."

"Probably—but I really didn't have a thing to base it on. I took everything Cleo said and twisted it to fit my preconceptions, when all I really had to do was take her at her word."

"What do you mean?" he says, flopping into the chair beside me, a bottle of beer in one hand—my last one, I realize—and some sort of sandwich in the other. I hoped to God it wasn't the ham.

"What I mean is—Well, look. Cleo said that after she—Maxine, that is—witnessed Sline's murder, she ran off into the night, barefoot and coatless. She'd been beaten half to death, first by Sline and then by Ruben, who so far as she was concerned was some overmuscled nut who had some sort of weird fixation on her. She'd just seen a man beaten to a pulp right in front of her and, to make matters worse, he was the only person, so far as she knew, who knew where her kid was. If he'd hidden Jackie somewhere, she'd never found out now. She was probably half nuts herself by then. Cleo told how she ran through some alleys and dark streets until she got to the river, and how she thought about ending it all right there."

"Do you suppose she did? Commit suicide, I mean?"

"I don't know—no, I really don't think so. I don't think she would've given up on Jackie so easily. She really wanted the kid back. She sure wouldn't have done anything as drastic as killing herself without at least trying to find where the kid was."

"All right, what then?"

"I think maybe Maxine Polketta is still exactly where she told us she went."

It takes some considerable doing, but I finally talk Chip into going with me. He protests that he has to get back to the *Graphic* to get the Fort story written up in time for the evening edition, but I know he's just reluctant to go back out into the cold, the big sissy. On the other hand, I know he'll do just about anything I ask him to and allow him his token, face-saving excuses. While still on a roll, I talk him into springing for a cab to Sline's place. When we get out, it's snowing again, which gives Chip another reason to start complaining again.

"Look, hack," I tell him as he's paying the driver, "if we can find Max it'll tie up everything, lock, stock and barrel. Otherwise, there'll always be this big question mark. And what about Jackie? Max is her mother, after all. Besides, what's going to happen to Cleo if we don't find her? Nothing's changed so far as she's concerned."

"All right, all right," he says as the cab pulls away and he pulls the collar of his trenchcoat up around his neck. "Now what, Sherlock?"

"We head west, toward the waterfront."

There's no real compelling reason to choose one direction over another, I suppose. But if Cleo's dream really meant anything, then Max went to the river the night of the murder. The water's only half a dozen blocks from the apartment house, in a straight line. The account I'd overheard that night in Cleo's bedroom hadn't taken more than fifteen or twenty minutes, between the time she described the killing to when she said she was at the docks. If time in the dream was the same as the real world, she couldn't have wandered too far off a straight line.

It's cold as hell and the narrow streets are funneling the bitter wind coming off the river. The sleet stings like buckshot. My old cloth coat isn't worth a damn in weather like this and I all have for my head is a wool scarf. I wish I'd worn Bill's watch cap, too. I forgot my gloves, like an idiot, and my hands are balled into tight fists deep into my pockets. It's so cold my teeth hurt. Beside me, Chip is muttering through his chattering teeth.

"You are just about broke, are you not?" he asks, suddenly, apropos of nothing.

"What business is it of yours?"

"I know you have been living off your savings for most of the past year."

"Yeah? Well you can kiss my fine white ass, too."

"That is not the threat you think it is."

"My money—or the lack of it—is no concern of yours."

"Jesus, Velda, I am freezing. Where the hell do you think you are going?"

"If you're just going to keep on whining, why don't you go home, for God's sake?"

"I am not whining, I am freezing."

"Good. Maybe your mouth will freeze shut."

"Come on, Velda, I do not get it. What is the deal? I know you have not had a case in months and before that what did you get? Lousy divorce jobs. Jesus, I thought you left Slotsky's because you were sick and tired of sleaze."

"You're right, Chip."

"What?"

"You don't get it."

When we get to the river, the gusting sleet is an opaque grey curtain into which the lead-grey water disappears not a hundred yards out. We cross the West Side Highway at about Perry Street and start walking south. Most of the piers are gated off with no way to get to the water, but before we go two blocks I find what I thought I'd remembered: an abandoned wharf sticking out from the shore like a rotten tongue.

With Chip grumbling beside me, I go out onto the planks as far as I dare.

"Jesus, Velda, you are going to get yourself killed for sure."

"This is where Max came, Chip, I'm sure of it."

"Yeah? What, are you psychic now, too? There are a dozen piers up and down the river."

"She had to've come here, there's nowhere else—there just wasn't time."

"Well, so what? So she came here—it does not mean she stayed."

"I think she did, Chip."

Turning to look back toward the city from twenty feet out on the pier, I see that the river bank under the docks is built up by huge blocks of cut stone, pierced at irregular intervals by the openings of pipes and culverts of all sizes. Where the wharf meets the shore, a half dozen rickety-looking stairs lead down to the water's edge.

"If she croaked herself," Chip says, "you will never find her. And if she did not, she could be anywhere in the city by now—or anywhere in the country, for that matter."

"She didn't kill herself. I'm sure of that. She wouldn't, when it really came down to it, no matter how bad she felt at the time. We can't forget Jackie."

"Then what the hell are we doing out here, for Christ's sake?"

I ignore him and head back for shore, Chip beside me thanking God that I've finally gotten some sense into my head, a notion of which he is quickly disabused when he sees me turn for the first of the stairways I'd spotted.

"For Pete's sake, Velda, what are you going down there for? Let the cops search for the body if that is what you are looking for. There is no way in hell you will ever find it—and what would you do if you did?"

The base of the stone wall has a slope of broken rocks piled up against it—rip-rap I think it's called, put there to keep the bank from eroding, I suppose. It's tough going, since the rocks are as big as shoeboxes, sharp-edged and covered with a skin of ice. The river's choppy and the wind is blowing a fine spray of salty water that seems to shoot through me like needles. I stumble a couple of times, nearly pitching myself headlong into the ice-crusted river, or, worse, braining myself on one of the rocks. The worst I do is skin my knee. After a couple of angry protests, Chip gives up and clambers down to join me, picking his way gingerly over the slippery rip-rap.

"Are you out of your mind, Velda? You are going to cripple yourself down here and if you think I am going to carry you out of here, you have another think coming."

"Have I ever expected anything from you, Chip?"

"What is that crack supposed to mean?"

"Forget it."

"Hell no I will not forget it! What do you mean, 'never expected anything from me'? It is all you do is sponge off me, every chance you get. I never hear from you unless you want something from me."

"I said forget it. Say, what's that?"

"What is what?"

Directly under the wharf, a big concrete culvert protrudes a couple of feet out of the stone wall, about five feet above where we're standing and about two feet beneath the wooden planks above. The opening is maybe two yards wide. A thin trickle of water drooling from its lip has formed a long, thick icicle connecting the pipe with the slope below. It's not easy making my way to the culvert—its lower edge is well above the rip-rap and there's not much in the way of hand or footholds in the stone wall, which is not only nearly vertical, is coated with a thin rime of ice. Still, by clinging to the rim and standing precariously on tiptoe I can just get my chin over the edge.

Maxine is slumped against the inside curve of the pipe. It's the first time I've ever seen her, other than in the photos, and I'm overwhelmed by how beautiful she is, even in death. And even in death, especially in death, the resemblance to Cleo is disturbing. She's lying on her back, her knees together and slightly drawn up, her hands crossed one over the other on her stomach, like someone taking a few moments off to relax. Her face is half turned toward me, her eyes open, her mouth parted just enough that I can see the tip of her tongue. The skin of her face and hands and feet are as white as the snow around me. It's been nearly two weeks since the murder yet she looks as though she's going to speak to me at any moment. I wonder what she'd say.

Chip comes up beside me and I let him take my arm. I don't look at him as I lay my head on his shoulder. I want to say, We all have our dream lives, don't we, Chip? I've tried to live my dream of being something other than what I probably am, whatever that may be, in the hope that if I try hard enough and wish hard enough one day the dream will become the real world and all the rest of my life will become a half-remembered dream. But I don't say anything at all.

"She has been there the whole time, Velda. The whole time. It means that Cleo is going to be all right. She may have shared in Maxine's death, but however strong their connection was, it did not drag her over *that* boundary. It had its limits."

Maybe it had it's limits, but I didn't like to think about Cleo's last dream about Maxine Polketta, the dream where she'd told me what Max was *feeling*, what she was seeing and smelling and hearing. That'd been just a couple of days ago—when Max'd already been dead for—how long?

Yes, Maxine had been there the whole time, from the night of Sline's murder. She'd probably gone to the river in a fit of despair. She must have changed her mind about killing herself, but was it then too late? Was she too cold, too tired, to make it back? How long had she lain there, waiting for death to overtake her? A few hours? A day? It couldn't have been very long, at any rate, not in this weather. In what awful despair she must have died. What dark hopelessness. But then, perhaps she'd died dreaming of her other life, of going to school, of a devoted mother, of good friends, of a man who loved her.

Jesus, I sure hope so.

On the following pages is a special preview of the nextadventure of Velda Bellinghausen . . . from *The Thirteen Labors of Velda.*

THREE NEIGHBORLY WOMEN

IT'D BEEN PREYING ON ME SOMEWHAT THAT JUST ABOUT EVERY ONE of my cases had originated within a block of my apartment. So I gave up beer for a week, scraped together a few bucks and took out an ad in the paper. So where did my next case come from? Apartment 1A.

Doesn't that just figure?

Worse yet, it was three o'clock in the morning when I was awakened from a sound sleep by someone shrieking "Murder! Murder!" Served me right for leaving my window open, but it was the middle of August for God's sake.

Whoever it was wouldn't shut up, so I threw on my kimono and went out to the hall to see what the hell was going on. Most of my neighbors were already there. None of them looked any happier than I was at being awakened in the middle of the night.

"What's going on, Miss Bellinghausen?" asked Mr. Arkady, the book dealer who lives in the apartment directly across from my own.

How was I supposed to know? "I have no idea," I replied, heading down the stairs, since that's where all the yelling was coming from. I live on the third floor of the Zenobia Arms and by the time I got to the ground floor I had a half dozen people following me.

The door to 1A was open. I knew the tenants were Alonzo Porff and his wife, Ethelreda. She ran a little day care nursery a few blocks away and he, so far as I knew, had no regular employment. Word had it he made his living as a card player and was supposed to be pretty good at it, too. Beyond this, there really wasn't too much I knew about them except that they had four little kids. It was Ethelreda who was running around in circles in the hallway outside her place, screaming her silly head off.

I stepped in front of her and took her by her shoulders. I had to shake her a couple of times, hard, to get her to shut up.

"What the hell?" I asked.

"What th—Oh, it's you, Miss Bellinghausen."

"What in the world's going on?"

"Oh—oh—oh! It's Lonnie, my husband! Someone's killed him!"

"Where is he?"

She pointed into the apartment. I handed her over to the Sapersteins and went in. I found Lonnie in bed. He wasn't murdered, though. Not yet at any rate, though he was pretty close to it. The bed was soaked in blood that leaked from holes in his head, face and chest. He was unconscious and breathing heavily. I called the cops from the phone in the kitchen. I told them to bring an ambulance, which, given the looks of the guy, was a pretty optimistic suggestion.

I went back out to the hall, where the Sapersteins, a nice old couple, had managed to get Ethelreda calmed down. They were sitting at the foot of the staircase, with everyone else in the place either hovering on the steps above or in the hallway outside the apartment. The Clarence sisters had brought some brandy and were getting the woman to sip a little of it.

"What happened, Velda?" asked Mr. Myagkov, the violinist.

"Someone's shot her husband."

"Shot? You mean—*murdered?*"

"Not murdered yet. He's still alive, more or less. I called the cops and an ambulance should be here in a few minutes."

"Is he—is he—?" asked Mrs. Porff.

"No—he's still alive—but barely. Can you tell me what happened?"

"I—someone knocked at our door. It was three o'clock in the morning and I couldn't understand who it could be. I tried to wake Lonnie, but he'd gotten in late and was sound asleep. I couldn't get him to wake up, so I went to the door myself. It was a tall, well-dressed, thickset man wearing glasses. I'd never seen him before in my life. He asked if he could speak to Lonnie. He was very well dressed and seemed so polite that I let him in, telling him that I'd go get my husband. But as soon as he got in, he pushed me into a chair and went straight back to the bedroom. It was like he'd been there before and knew just where to go. I—I was frightened to death but I didn't know what I could do to stop him. I was still in the chair when I heard—heard shots."

"How many did you hear?"

"Four, I'm sure."

"Did you see him leave?"

"No—no, now that you mention it. I—I've been too upset to think about it. He didn't come back out through the living room. He must have gone out the back window, I guess."

That would've been easy enough. Their bedroom window would look out over the alley and was probably no more than a half dozen feet above the pavement.

The wail of sirens interrupted us at that moment, as the police and ambulance finally arrived. That pretty much seemed to be that, so I went back to bed.

The next morning, being a Saturday, meant that most of my fellow inmates were at home and, naturally enough, were all atwitter about the excitement the previous night. I finally stumbled from my place about eleven, putting on shorts, a halter and sandals and grabbing a Blue Ribbon from my fridge on the way past. I took this out front, where I liked to lounge on the broad, sloping stone railing on hot, sunny days. It didn't take more than four minutes before I was being interrogated about the incident. The truth was that I learned a lot more from my neighbors than they learned from me since most of them had hung around long after I'd gone back upstairs.

"Didn't you hear anything?" I asked Mrs. Skittleberg, who lived directly over the Porff's apartment.

"Not a thing. It was as big a surprise to me as anyone else."

"Hear the latest?" said Audrey Mott, coming up the sidewalk with that brisk trot of someone who has news they're just itching to tell the world. "Lonnie Porff is dead. Died about half an hour ago. Ain't that something?"

"Jesus," I said. "He ever regain consciousness?"

"Nope. And I bet I know what you were going to ask, too. If he said anything about the guy who shot him. Well, he never said a word."

"How'd you find all this out?"

"Aw, that was easy. My boyfriend's a custodian at the hospital. He heard the whole thing."

"Anyone tell Mrs. Porff yet?"

"Yeah, I guess so. She was there the whole time."

"Jesus."

"Cops got any idea who might've done it?"

"Beats me. You're the detective."

So they say. But there wasn't anything to detect so far as I could see. The man was a professional gambler, so there were probably a dozen disgruntled players who might have wanted to even the score for a big loss. So there you are.

I spent the rest of the day doing what I usually do when I don't have much to do. I lounged around on the steps for another hour or so then strolled over to Joe's for lunch. It was a broiling August afternoon and hardly anyone came in the place so Joe stood me to a couple of Blue Ribbons, bless his hairy heart, even if it was just to keep me around for the company. I do improve the place, though, I have to admit.

Since I was halfway there already, I decided to stroll over to the precinct station and see what I could find out about Porff's murder. I did and could have saved myself the sweat for all I learned.

Lonnie'd been shot four times with a .22 caliber weapon. One bullet had entered near his right ear, passing through the brain. That's the one that finished him. Two others had gone into the upper part of his cheek and the fourth had hit his chest. Three slugs had been found in his body. The fourth had gone clear through him and had been found in the bedding. There'd been powder burns around all four wounds, which meant they'd been fired at point blank range.

"Twenty-two's kind of a funny weapon, isn't it?" I asked Lieutenant Holmes, and don't think he's not had his share of ribbing about that name because he has.

"Yeah, for a professional. But it could've been something picked up on the spur of the moment, or something someone who didn't know nothing about guns carried for protection just because it was small. Who knows?"

"Got anyone in mind?"

"Are you kidding? The guy was a cheap cardshark. There are probably a thousand might've had enough grudge to kill him. Could've been someone he'd welshed on, could've been someone who owed him money and didn't want to pay. Could've been a hundred other reasons."

"You don't sound very enthusiastic."

"Enthusiastic, hell. I got a man on it, don't worry about that, but I can tell you this precinct's got better things to do than hunt down every person who knocks off every cheap, petty crook. Between you and me, Velda, I think they do us a favor."

Personally, I was inclined to agree.

When I got back to the Zenobia I went straight to my apartment and took a shower. After I'd sluiced off a sticky layer of salt and sweat, I got dressed and went back downstairs, confident that I'd no longer offend.

I was surprised to see Mrs. Porff sitting on the front steps, with a couple of other women. Normally, I've never been crazy about hanging around sharing gossip. That sort of thing usually bores me simple. But I figured maybe I could pick up something. It kind of annoyed me the way the Lieutenant was brushing off the killing of Ethelreda's husband. I mean, he might've been a rat, but he still had a wife and kids and all. The Porffs had only lived in the place for four or five months and I really didn't know too much about them. Other than what was passed on to me by my neighbors, that is, who knew pretty much all there was to know about the Porffs within a week of their moving in. Being a detective living in the Zenobia is practically redundant.

"I'm sorry to hear about your husband," I told her.

"Thank you. He was a good man, really. I know everyone thinks he was just a cheap gambler, but he was really good at what he did. He wasn't no cheat like the cops been saying."

"He work somewhere around here?"

"Yeah. There's a club over on Chester, the Kit Kat Klub, he worked at a lot, but not for the last couple-three weeks."

"Good thing you've got a job then, huh?"

"Yeah. I manage the Jolly Teddy Bear Nursery School. It helps—*helped* us get by when Lonnie was out of work." She dabbed at her eyes with a hanky and then blew her nose into it.

"Look here—if you like, I could take a look into things. Sometimes the police overlook a lot, especially when, well, ah—sometimes they take too broad a view."

"That's very kind of you, Miss Bellinghausen—"

"Velda, please."

"Velda. That's very kind of you, but I have every confidence in the police. I think it'd be best to leave things in their hands."

I thought that was very complimentary to the police but it sure wasn't an opinion *I* shared. It was a little weird, too, I thought, for a grieving widow to not take advantage of every offer to help find her husband's murderer. But then, I've never been a grieving widow, so what did I know? She obviously wasn't thinking straight, so I thought I'd take a look around on my own. If I discovered anything helpful, well, I'd be gracious when accepting her gratitude and not remind her of how she snubbed me.

About eight o'clock, just after it started getting dark, I changed out of my shorts and halter and into my black capris and red scoopnecked top (in which I think I look just swell) and strolled over to the Kit Kat Klub to see what I could see.

I'd been there a couple of times in the past with Chip and the bouncer at the door recognized me right off.

"Hey, Miss Velda! Long time no see!"

"Howya doin', Ralph?"

"Okay, I guess. Gettin' useta da dizzy spells helps a lot."

"Well, you oughta get an electric razor, just to be on the safe side, you know what I mean?"

"I guess dat's a purty good idea, Miss Velda."

"Who runs this joint, Ralph?"

"Mr. Chillicothe does. Ya wanna see 'im?"

"Maybe Like to get a drink first, though. Okay if I go in?"

"Sure thing! You're okay here anytime!"

He held the door open for me and I went in. The place was as I'd remembered it: a wee tad too high-class for the neighborhood, too cheesy for anywhere else. A lot of chrome and stainless steel and glass and bakelite and indirect lighting and not a hell of a lot of customers. Most of the people in my neighborhood go to a bar to get some drinking done—not be extras in a Busby Berkley musical.

I said Hi to Jerry, the bartender.

"Say, Velda! Long time no see! Howya been doin'?"

"Fair to middling. Let me have a martini, will you?"

"Sure—and it's on me for old time's sake." I'd been hopiing like anything he'd say that. "Heard you took up a new line of work."

"Yeah. I took a correspondence course and got my PI ticket."

"No kiddin'? You're a private dick? Jesus, that's sure a hell of a change of pace from Slotsky's ain't it?"

"You said it. Say, Jerry, you know a fella named Porff? Lorenzo Porff?"

"You on a case, Velda? Gee, that's really swell! Just like in the movies, huh? Yeah, I know Porff. Ain't seen him in a coupla weeks, though, maybe a month. Cop's been crackin' down on gambling and Mr. Chillicothe thought it'd be best to cool it on the back room, if you know what I mean. If you're lookin' for Porff, I wouldn't have the slightest idea where to find him."

"I know where he's at, Jerry. He's stretched out on a slab in the morgue."

"Aww, Jesus! He's croaked, huh? That's pretty rotten. What happened?"

"Got a fatal case of lead poisoning the other night, while he was sleeping in bed."

"Jesus, that's awful. I guess I shouldn't be surprised, though."

"Yeah? Why's that?"

"He was good, real good, always took home a decent profit. Could've done it just about every time, too, playin' square. The problem he had was that he was too greedy. He wanted to win every time."

"You mean he cheated?"

"When he thought he was inna slump he used a deck a marked cards. I always told him someone'd catch on one day and fix him and I guess someone did."

I talked to the woman who was filling in at the Jolly Teddy Bear—a nice old lady with a hearing aid who was really impressed by my badge—and she gave me a list of the nursery's clients: a dozen women who regularly left their children in its care. Fortunately, all of them lived within a three-block radius of each other. It was tedious talking to all of them, but at least it didn't require a lot of hiking. They were all working wives whose lives were pretty much interchangeable. There wasn't a whole lot to distinguish one from another. Another thing they were unanimous about was their lack of information about either Lonnie or Ethelreda. One of them, though, an attractive woman named Clestell Gay, distinguished herself from the others by indignantly expressing her opinion that Mrs. Porff would've been much better off if her husband had a legitimate job instead of hanging around night clubs playing cards even if he did occassionally pretend to help his wife out at the nursery. "And you can't tell me," she finished, "he wasn't fooling around with those awful women who frequent places like that. He even went to *burlesque* houses and you know the sort of cheap floozies you find there!"

"Uh, well, yeah. You think he was having an affair?"

"I'm not saying he was and I'm not saying he wasn't, but it wouldn't surprise me in the least."

Well, I now knew at least two reasons for knocking off Porff. It might've been someone who lost a bundle to him or it might've been a disgruntled husband or boyfriend.

The next morning, as I came back from my coffee and donuts at Joe's, I found Mrs. Porff and a couple of her usual cronies out on the front steps, pretty much as I'd left them the day before. They'd been chatting but quieted when I said good morning.

"Say, Mrs. Porff, I was just wondering. Did you have any other visitors the night your husband was—died?"

"No, why?"

"Well, now, Ethel," interjected one of the women. She was the Saperstein's niece, who lived with them across the hall from the Porffs. "Clestell Gay was by to see you, don't you remember? I saw her coming out of your place when I got back from the button factory, must've been just about midnight."

"Oh, I'd forgotten all about that. She just stopped by for a few minutes."

"Kind of late for a visit, wasn't it?" I asked.

"Oh, no, not really," put in the other woman. Her name was Hilda Sklar. I didn't know too much about her other than that she was a stenographer for a broker and lived by herself in the apartment adjoining the Porff's. "Clestell was staying over with me that night. Her husband was out of town for a few days and she didn't want to stay with the baby alone in her place. She just had a question about the nursery she wanted to ask Ethel and ran next door for a minute."

"You live next door to the Porffs. Didn't you hear anything?"

"No, not at all, and I'm sure Clestell didn't either. She told me she'd been sound asleep when poor Ethel's cries woke her up. It was just awful."

I learned from Ethelreda that the police had asked her to come by the station for a few minutes later that morning to take care of some paperwork regarding the disposition of her husband's body, after which she planned to spend a few hours at the nursery to give the old lady some time off. I thought that would be a perfect opportunity to poke around in the Porff apartment.

Getting in was no more difficult than it was getting into any of the apartments in the Zenobia (how I know that is another story). The place smelled funny. That awful sour milk smell of little kids was mixed with the coppery-sweet odor of blood. It was a mess, too, which was okay since I didn't have to be particularly careful with things. I could hardly make the place look any worse.

I spent about an hour but didn't turn up too much. There were a couple of suggestive things, though. I found a half dozen deck of cards and a pair of black plastic-rimmed glasses in the top drawer of the bedroom dresser. When I looked at the back of the cards though the glasses, the names of the cards stood out like little neon signs. Well, well, Lonnie was a cheat, all right. I already knew that, though. What puzzled me was how openly he kept his paraphernalia. Surely Ethelreda couldn't have overlooked it. Did she know he was a cheat in spite of what she told me? A desk drawer in the living room produced fistfuls of unpaid bills—the Porffs were evidently heavily in debt—and an insurance policy. This last was pretty interesting since it was on Lonnie's life and had been made out fairly recently. But it was for only twenty-five hundred dollars, which hardly seemed worth killing someone for.

I went back up to my place, stripped to my skivvies and fixed myself a pimiento loaf sandwich and a beer. I slouched in the big chair in the living room, put my feet on the window sill and pondered in the breeze from my electric fan.

The whole thing was getting to be naggingly funny, but for the life of me I couldn't put my finger on what was wrong. I didn't like Mrs. Porff very much, but maybe it was because she was tall and pretty, though I'd rather think I wasn't that petty. She seemed a cold fish to me, aloof and distant, which didn't exactly make her very appealing. I would've thought anyone'd be a little more broken up by having their husband's head half blown off in their bed, but then it's hard to predict how people will react to things like that. Some just don't express their emotions openly, no matter how they may actually feel. For all I know, she was weeping and wailing and beating her chest somewhere deep inside. But then, she certainly didn't have any good reason to regret her husband's passing, either. He wasn't supporting the family and when he did make any money it was from cheating at cards in cheap nightclubs. And for all I knew he was messing around with other women on the side. Lonnie was no prize, that was for sure.

Was Lonnie, I wondered, worth more dead than alive—even if it was just twenty-five hundred dollars? Had Ethelreda been willing to kill her husband for such a measly amount of money? Maybe it seemed a lot to a woman with a pile of bills and four little kids. Well, there *were* a lot things about her story that just didn't seem to ring true. I mean, what kind of woman would open her door to a stranger at three o'clock in the morning, even if her husband was in the next room? What kind of woman would just sit in a chair with her face buried in her hands while a killer drilled four bullets into her husband's head? Jesus, even if she hated the man, it's hard to imagine her just sitting there like that. And there was that gun. A .22 sure seemed more like a woman's weapon than a man's (though, of course, I prefer my dad's nickel-plated .45 automatic myself, but I'm different).

I must've been getting really suspicious, because I was even beginning to think Ethelreda's friends, Clestell and Hilda, were fishy, too. Gay, for one, seemed to protest a wee bit too much about Lonnie's indiscretions. I added jilted lover to my list of motives and went to the fridge and got another beer.

The next morning, I walked the few blocks over to where Clestell Gay worked as a waitress in a pretty nice restaurant. She seemed surprised and not a little displeased to see me, though she put on a big smile when I sat in a booth near her. Only her mouth was smiling, though. Her eyes held an entirely different expression.

Clestell was a large, blonde woman, several years older than either Ethelreda or Hilda, but still good-looking in a kind of coarse, obvious way. She would have been a few months from retirement at Slotsky's.

She handed me a menu and while I pretended to glance over it, she asked me if I'd heard anything from the police yet.

"Well, yes, I have as a matter of fact."

"Yeah?"

"Yeah. That's why I came by today. I think you might be in trouble."

"Trouble? Why should I be in trouble?"

"Well, they seem to think you did it—that you killed Lonnie."

"What? That's ridiculous! I didn't shoot him, I only bought the—"

I raised an eyebrow.

"I didn't shoot him."

"I'll have a cheeseburger with fries. And black coffee."

Sometimes I'm not nearly as bright as I like to think I am.

I thought I'd go over to see Chip, my pal at the *Graphic*, to see if maybe my suspicions about the Porff murder might be sufficiently interesting to get me a dinner invitation. I went home to change into something more interesting than my old sundress. I picked out something I knew Chip would like (he goes nuts when I wear red and while there wasn't much to it, what there was of it was red) and laid it out across my bed. I took a quick shower and was still towelling myself off as I went back into the bedroom. Well, I wish I could make this sound as interesting as those mystery writers who talk about plunging into swirling black abysses and whatnot, but there was just a kind of hollow *plonk* and the next two things I knew were that I had a splitting headache and was tied to a bedframe.

It took me a few seconds to get my eyes pointed in the same direction, which effort at least distracted me from the throb in the back of my skull. What I saw wasn't the least bit edifying. First of all, it wasn't my bedroom. It wasn't anyone's bedroom, near as I could tell. The room was empty, with the exception of the metal bedframe I was tied to. The layout was exactly the same as my room, so it hardly took me—even with my rattled brain—more than two seconds to figure out that it was apartment 4A, which had been unoccupied since the Bolasses family had moved out two weeks earlier. All they'd left behind, apparently, was this cheesy frame and a thin mattress. I didn't blame them: it was cheap crap anyway.

It was still light out, so unless I'd been unconscious for twenty-four hours, which seemed unlikely, only a short time had passed since I'd been cold-cocked downstairs. I was laying flat on my back with my arms and legs spread-eagled. I was too tall, stretched out that way, to fit on the bed, so my elbows were tied to the cornerposts and my wrists just above them with what looked like lengths of clothesline. My legs went past the corners, so the rope went around my calves, just above my ankles. It was hard to get my head up to see anything from that position, not the least reason being that it hurt like hell to do so. The knots weren't tight, which I was glad of since it relieved me of worrying about my hands and feet falling off. They were tight enough, though, and I didn't think I could wriggle free. I was naked, too, which was kind of annoying. At least it was August, so that was something.

Discover what happened to Velda and how she solved the case of the Three Neighborly Women in The Thirteen Labors of Velda, *an anthology of thrilling stories featuring Velda Bellinghausen, girl detective.*